THE SILVERSKIN LEGACY
Onaj's Horn

About the Author

Jo Whittemore has been captivated by fantasy since she was a child, dressing up as a fairy for Halloween (which also happens to be her birthday). She currently lives in Austin, Texas with her husband Roger, but longs to return to her California roots.

To Write to the Author

If you wish to contact the author or would like more information about this book, please write to the author in care of Llewellyn Worldwide and we will forward your request. Both the author and publisher appreciate hearing from you and learning of your enjoyment of this book and how it has helped you. Llewellyn Worldwide cannot guarantee that every letter written to the author can be answered, but all will be forwarded. Please write to:

Jo Whittemore
℅ Llewellyn Worldwide
2143 Wooddale Drive, Dept. 0-7387-1125-X
Woodbury, Minnesota 55125-2989, U.S.A.

Please enclose a self-addressed stamped envelope for reply, or $1.00 to cover costs. If outside U.S.A., enclose international postal reply coupon.

Many of Llewellyn's authors have websites with additional information and resources. For more information, please visit our website at http://www.llewellyn.com.

THE SILVERSKIN LEGACY

Onaj's Horn
Jo Whittemore

Llewellyn Publications
Woodbury, Minnesota

First Edition
First Printing, 2007

Book format by Steffani Chambers
Cover design by Gavin Dayton Duffy
Cover illustration by Marc Sasso
Editing by Rhiannon Ross
Interior art by Gavin Dayton Duffy
Llewellyn is a registered trademark of Llewellyn Worldwide, Ltd.

The Cataloging-in-Publication Data for *Onaj's Horn* is on file at the Library of Congress.
ISBN-13: 978-0-7387-1125-6
ISBN-10: 0-7387-1125-X

Llewellyn Worldwide does not participate in, endorse, or have any authority or responsibility concerning private business transactions between our authors and the public.

All mail addressed to the author is forwarded but the publisher cannot, unless specifically instructed by the author, give out an address or phone number.

Any Internet references contained in this work are current at publication time, but the publisher cannot guarantee that a specific location will continue to be maintained. Please refer to the publisher's website for links to authors' websites and other sources.

Llewellyn Publications
A Division of Llewellyn Worldwide, Ltd.
2143 Wooddale Drive, Dept. 0-7387-1125-X
Woodbury, Minnesota 55125-2989, U.S.A.
www.llewellyn.com

Printed in the United States of America

Carnival

The city of Pontsford was awash with the sights and sounds of Carnival, its annual harvest festival. Gypsy girls slapped tambourines to their palms as they danced around a faun twittering a swift melody on his panpipes. Peddlers shouted above the din of the festivalgoers, hawking exotic merchandise or cheap impersonations of the same. Outside every tavern, inn, and restaurant, various young boys rang various gigantic handbells to announce the availability of an evening meal. Fireworks exploded in orange and green starbursts even higher in the night sky than the city that already floated among the clouds.

And Ainsley Minks and Megan Haney drank it all in.

It wasn't that neither of the fifteen-year-olds had ever been to a fair. They had just never been to one in an entirely different world where magic was part of the everyday. In fact, being in a foreign world was a new experience for them, altogether.

A few weeks earlier, Ainsley and Megan had been on Earth, facing the end of the school year and the beginning of their summer break. They had been spying on their elderly next-door neighbor, Bornias, who had turned out to be a wizard returning to his home world. Unfortunately, when he left Earth, so had Ainsley and Megan. Even more bad news came when they realized their only way home lay in a magical staff of the elements, the Staff of Lexiam, which had been stolen.

They had been able to recover the staff, but before they could return home, Ainsley had been stricken with a magical illness that revealed his ties to the foreign world through his father. Together, Ainsley and Megan had given the dragon that had infected Ainsley her freedom, and she in turn, had returned Ainsley to normal, with the exception of the dragon's wings he'd acquired while ill. He'd become rather fond of them but knew he would have to give them up once he returned to Earth. Somehow, he didn't think people back home would understand.

In their present surroundings, however, a blonde, blue-eyed young man with wings didn't get so much as a second glance. The crowds in Pontsford were far more interested in picking their way through the busy streets to get to whichever merchant or attraction held their fancy. The situation was not made easier by the fact that the wily Ponzipoo who had designed the city had every building covered with mirrors just for Carnival. The resulting effect magnified the crowd and provided late-night entertainment when the drunks would attempt to pick fights with their own reflections.

Ainsley caught his own image in the mirrored door of a closed shop and spread his wings menacingly for effect. An exasperated sigh came from behind him, accompanied by the reflection of a dark-eyed brunette girl.

"Ainsley, stop ogling yourself!" chided Megan. "We need to move faster if we're going to keep up with everyone."

He turned away from the mirror to where Megan's finger pointed out the backs of several of their friends disappearing into the mass of people.

"Damn. We're too late," said Megan, rising onto her tiptoes though she knew it was a futile effort. Even if she could become taller than everyone else, there would be no quick way through the crowd.

Ainsley flexed his back muscles and levitated a dozen feet into the air. "Don't worry. I see them. They've stopped to wait for us." He waved to Bornias before dropping back down beside Megan. "Are you ready to bum rush the crowd?"

Megan leaned towards him. "What?" she yelled, pointing to her ear.

Ainsley rolled his eyes. He'd forgotten about the clots of beeswax Megan had jammed in her ears to drown out the voices of passersby. He wondered if she saw the Pearl of Truth lodged in her chest as a burden yet. When the fairy had originally given it to her, the pearl had proven quite useful, even stopping a ball of fire aimed at Megan's heart. Now, because the Pearl of Truth was a part of her, Megan's pain was visible any time she witnessed deception.

Rather than force her to suffer more to hear him, Ainsley grabbed her beneath the arms and hoisted her into the sky.

"I see them!" she shouted, pointing to the building entrance where Ainsley had already spotted their friends. "Let's go!"

She immediately regretted saying this, for even though Ainsley was becoming more adept each day at using his wings, he still hadn't mastered carrying more weight than his own. She cringed and drew her legs to her chest as they dipped low in front of a startled couple.

"Sorry!" she called over her shoulder, thankful she couldn't hear their replies.

The building toward which they headed was a tavern shaped like an ale barrel with "The Swig and Sleep" painted across its mirrored surface in huge yellow letters. The keystone of the barrel had been fashioned into a large window where several patrons had poked out their heads to watch the crowd below. At The Swig and Sleep, however, there was no young boy ringing a bell to indicate a hot meal within the reflective walls.

Megan was actually glad for this. Since their arrival in Pontsford the previous evening, she and Ainsley had eaten their way through several food vendor's booths on the ground below the city. Their original goal had been a gaming arena hidden within the center of the palatable paradise, but pastries dusted with sugar had called to Ainsley, and Megan had fared no better, waddling into the city that evening after gorging on roasted vegetables and crisp-skinned sausages.

As they neared the building, Ainsley swooped again, but this time it was to land. "Thank you for flying Air Ainsley," he said, lowering Megan, and then himself, to the ground.

Megan leaned close. "What?" she shouted.

Ainsley made a dismissive gesture. "Never mind. I was just being funny."

Megan started to nod, but then her forehead wrinkled. "What?" she shouted again.

Beside them, Bornias chuckled, his gray beard and round belly jiggling. Neither Ainsley nor Megan could have ever imagined him an important figure, but up until a few weeks prior, Bornias had been ruler of the kingdom of Raklund in southern Arylon. His family line, the Silverskins, were keepers of the Staff of Lexiam, and that honor had now been passed along to his grandson, Rayne, one of the other people who had been awaiting Ainsley and Megan's arrival.

Rayne couldn't have been but a few years older than they, a handsome boy whose dark hair had recently been shaven after a bad bout of mind control. He earned admiring glances from the women who passed, though not as many as his right-hand man, Frieden Tybor.

Frieden governed the Protectors of the Staff of Lexiam and had become Ainsley and Megan's surrogate uncle since their arrival in Arylon. But Ainsley had a feeling neither Frieden's paternal disposition nor his political power had anything to do with the women adjusting their bosoms to almost spill out of their bodices.

If he was interested, Frieden didn't show it, merely nodding to the women, his jade-colored eyes focused on their faces. Ainsley watched their chests became mottled pink with embarrassment. Megan noticed this, too, and smothered a grin, glad that Frieden didn't share Ainsley's wolfish ways.

"Let's go inside!" she shouted, pointing to her ears again.

They had been lucky to come across a beekeeper from the Elven city of Hylark the previous evening. For harvesting the sweetest honey, the man had a won an all-expenses paid trip to Carnival, as well as a complimentary booth to display his wares. Granted, the beekeeper had the excellent advantage of living within the petals of the giant hylark flower, but when he had allowed Ainsley and Megan a taste of the award-winning honey, they had to admit it was nothing short of marvelous.

Though he had been puzzled that someone Megan's age would have a need for beeswax, his primary customers being candlemakers, he had pinched off a small glob for her at no charge. She had tried to avoid putting it in, but the boasting vendors coupled with the young men and women telling white lies to impress one another had Megan jamming the beeswax in her ears.

As they stepped into The Swig and Sleep, Megan exhaled a happy sigh and popped out her earplugs. Every patron of the tavern was silent, their attention focused on a stage against the far wall, illuminated by snow lights. Occupying the stage were two men, one holding a mandolin and the other a flute, and a woman. Before the woman, a table had been arranged with a row of delicate crystal goblets set atop it, each filled to a different level with water. A small bowl of water had been placed between her and the goblets, and it was into this she dipped a spindly finger.

She ran her finger around the rim of the goblet, and it rang with a sweet note. While she continued to circle the goblet's rim, she dipped a finger of her other hand in water and reached to another goblet, coaxing a different note from its lip. Her first hand reached for another goblet and extracted a new note while her other hand followed suit with another goblet. This continued until she was playing a melody with the crystal vessels. The mandolin player accompanied with a gentle strum of his instrument, and the flautist chimed in on his flute. The song they played was slow and graceful, like a waltz. When it ended, the room was silent for a moment until the audience burst into applause.

"That was amazing!" yelled Megan, though this time her voice mixed with the noise from the crowd.

"I thought you might enjoy that!" Bornias shouted back. "Now, let's join Lady Maudred in our quarters."

He led the way toward the stage, and Ainsley and Megan glanced at one another. Neither was particularly shy, but they were none too thrilled about having an audience while they slept.

"Don't worry." Rayne appeared between them and ushered them after Bornias. "My grandfather knows where he's going."

Much to the relief of Ainsley and Megan, they didn't ascend the stage steps to bunk down for the night. Instead, they slipped through a backstage curtain where two soldiers waited. They nodded to Bornias and stepped to either side of a barred door.

Megan fished her earplugs out of her pocket and prepared herself for the din of the street masses, but she didn't end up needing them. The barred door led not to the busy streets of Pontsford but to a massive, musty storage room that was empty except for a regal-looking older woman who was busy drawing circles on the stone floor in chalk.

"Uh, Gran, what are you doing?" asked Ainsley as his grandmother, Lady Maudred, lowered herself to the floor and lay down in one of the circles.

"I'm making our sleeping chambers for the night," she said, stretching her arms out on either side. "Ah. Just the right size."

"Don't forget that Rayne and I are taller than you," said Frieden. "Maybe we should make our own circles."

Lady Maudred sat up and tucked away the wisps of hair that had escaped her normally immaculate coif. "Suit yourself." She held the chalk out to Frieden, who took it and helped her to her feet. She turned to Ainsley, Megan, and Bornias. "Step into your circles, won't you, and get on your knees?"

They did as they were told, and Lady Maudred walked to the edge of Bornias' circle. "Shelter up!" she trilled.

Ainsley and Megan watched a translucent dome rise from the chalk circle to encase Bornias.

"You're making sheltered domes for us like you did in the Pass of Light," said Ainsley.

"Very similar, yes, but this dome will grant you extra privacy. Nobody may enter the circle who isn't already inside when the spell is cast."

"Thank you, Lady Maudred," said Megan with a sigh of relief. Though she enjoyed the kinship of her male companions, the modesty of mixed company had forced her to sleep fully dressed for the better part of three weeks, and she had found herself hurriedly changing clothes behind different random bushes every day.

Lady Maudred approached Megan's circle and repeated her command. Megan closed her eyes. The dome itself wouldn't be enough to trigger Megan's claustrophobia, but watching the walls form around her, cutting her off from the outside world, made her a bit anxious.

"You're all done!" said Lady Maudred.

Megan opened her eyes, pleased to note that while the dome was too frosted to see through, it still allowed outside light. She got to her feet, and her head and shoulders protruded from the dome as she stepped out.

"Hey, Megan." Ainsley grinned at her from his own half-bubble. "Check me out." He tucked in his wings and bent his knees until he was only visible from the neck up. "Ta-da! Severed head."

Megan rolled her eyes. "Can we get rid of what's outside your dome and just keep what's inside?"

"Funny. I was going to ask the same about you."

Megan shot him a withering glance, but a smirk tugged at the corners of her mouth. Ainsley knew she missed their back-and-forth banter as much as he. When they'd arrived in Arylon, they had been enemies, using their words as weapons. Then Ainsley had been stricken with the Illness, and Megan had felt too sorry for him to fight. Now, things were finally comfortable between them again, and Ainsley was happy to give, as well as get, his verbal jabs.

"I think it's time to wash up and get ready for sleep," said Lady Maudred. "If the two of you want to get to the gaming arena before the food vendors waylay you again, you're going to need your rest."

Lapper

"The lift is coming," said Lady Maudred. "Are you both ready?"

Ainsley and Megan glanced over at the rising airpad and its passengers, a dark-haired man with almond-shaped eyes and a handsome, redheaded man.

"What's *Evren* doing here?" Ainsley whispered to Megan as the redheaded man greeted his grandmother.

"What a pleasant surprise running into you again, Lady Maudred." Evren flashed her a luminous smile. "Twice in a single week!"

"Mmm." Lady Maudred didn't appear nearly as enthused as he. "It *is* a small world, isn't it, Sir Sandor?" She turned to Evren's companion. "Master Oh, how are you?"

Master Oh smiled and gave Lady Maudred a slight bow. "I am well, my lady. It is, as always, a pleasure to see you." He shifted toward Ainsley and Megan. "And it is good to see the two of *you* again." He assessed them both. "Your arms are back to normal I see," he said to Megan, "but *you*," he pointed to Ainsley, "seem to have sprouted wings."

"We've been busy," said Ainsley with a grin.

He liked Master Oh, even though he and Megan had only talked with him once. Master Oh was the master mage of the community of Amdor, a group of powerful, retired wizards. He also happened to own a shop that sold knacks, or elemental potions, and knack-making ingredients. Ainsley and Megan had visited him to order image-summoning tablets after Megan had tried to mop a wet floor with them. In the process, she'd also turned her arms purple, for which Master Oh had provided a bottle of whitewashing tonic.

"Did you get the soulfire you were after?" asked Megan. Though she addressed this question to Master Oh, she watched Evren out of the corner of her eye.

When Megan and her friends had been in the frosty Icyll Mountains trying to cure Ainsley's Illness, they had encountered Evren and Master Oh. Evren had explained that they were trying to find soulfire and didn't know where to search, but Megan's Pearl of Truth had told her Evren knew more than he let on.

"I have enough soulfire to avoid freezing my fingers off for a while," said Master Oh with a chuckle.

Evren cleared his throat. "Lady Maudred, I assume Bornias and Rayne have already arrived?"

Lady Maudred nodded. "They're here, as is Governor Tybor. They're in the assembly hall, preparing for tomorrow's summit."

"Excellent." Evren rubbed his hands together and grinned. "I have something rather amazing I'd like to show them . . . and you, if you'll be in attendance."

"We would also enjoy your company at lunch today," said Master Oh. "If you have the time."

"Of course," said Lady Maudred, placing an arm around Ainsley and Megan's shoulders. "Let me just see these two off to the gaming arena."

"We'll wait for you inside the city walls." Evren and Master Oh bowed to the trio and strode into Pontsford with three pairs of eyes boring holes into their backs.

Megan scooted out from under Lady Maudred's arm and faced her. "Be careful at the summit tomorrow, Lady Maudred. Something bad is going to happen."

Lady Maudred clucked her tongue and steered Megan onto the airpad. "I could have told you that myself, darling, but if I don't go, there will be one less person to protect the others from Evren."

"Can we go with you to the summit?" asked Ainsley.

"Don't be silly. Of course, you can't." Lady Maudred sniffed disdainfully. "If you think it's dangerous for *me* to be there, don't you think it would be even more dangerous for you?"

"But I still have a little bit of magic on my own," said Ainsley, "and Megan will be able to point out when Evren is being deceitful."

"I know when Evren is being deceitful," said Lady Maudred, nudging her grandson onto the airpad. "Every time he opens his mouth."

Ainsley would have continued the argument, but the airpad let out a loud hiss and began its descent. Lady Maudred waved to them as they disappeared from sight.

"Watch out for charlatans in the arena!" she called. "Everyone down there is out to make a quick coin. And keep your money well hidden!"

"Great. Thanks for shouting that *last* part!" said Ainsley. Megan giggled.

Before they'd left The Swig and Sleep, Lady Maudred had handed her and Ainsley each a purse containing four gold coins. After Ainsley shook his and didn't hear the familiar chink of metal against metal, Lady Maudred had explained that she'd magicked the bags so any sound their contents made would be restricted to the inside of the bag itself. She'd then gone on to lecture them about not taking their money out in front of strangers and only removing exactly what they needed. Merchants in the gaming arena, she'd explained, could be even more conniving than Evren Sandor.

Ainsley and Megan waved to Lady Maudred, and as the airpad came to rest on the ground, Megan turned to him. "We *have* to get into that summit tomorrow."

"I know," he said, nudging her toward the arena. "Give me some time to come up with a plan."

They zigzagged through the tents of the food vendors who were just setting their cooking fires to blaze for the day. Megan sniffed at the air and sighed, hoping the gaming arena would prove a worthy diversion from chargrilled fillets. The meadow was quiet with the exception of random clinks, clanks, and chops as the food vendors prepared for the impending lunch crowd. Many of the food tents belonged to families with young children still abed, so conversation was minimal, limited to the necessary commands to season the meats and slice the vegetables.

When Ainsley and Megan stepped through a leafy archway into the arena, however, they were almost knocked backward by a multitude of sounds.

"What the hell happened?" Megan fished her earplugs out of her pocket. "How come we didn't hear these people a minute ago?"

"The arena must be like our money bags," said Ainsley. "It's magicked so that no sound can escape."

Megan fitted the beeswax in her ears and followed Ainsley to a man sitting behind a wooden table and puffing on a pipe. On the table sat fifteen bowls that had been turned upside down.

"I know this one," said Ainsley, rolling his eyes. "It's one of those memory games, right?"

The man leaned toward Ainsley and shifted the pipe to the corner of his mouth. "Only charlatans run seedy games like that. Do you want to play, or not?"

"Now, now, Templeton." A man clad in vibrant gold from top to toe strolled toward them. "We don't want to dissuade potential customers with a fussy attitude, do we?" He stopped before Megan and took her hand, bending low to kiss it. "I do apologize for my servant's offensive behavior. I hope it won't deter you from enjoying my games."

"*Your* games?" asked Ainsley while the man pumped his hand heartily.

"Yes, my good sir, yes! I am Lapper, the Arena Master, and this," the man opened his arms in a wide flourish, "is my arena."

Megan saw the man with the wooden bowls roll his eyes and exhale a curl of smoke.

"Now, this game, my good sir," Lapper threw an arm around Ainsley's shoulder and guided him to the bowls, "this game is a game of skill and wits! I call it 'Trash or Treasure.'"

"Um. Okay. How do you play?" asked Ainsley.

"Under each of these bowls," Lapper tapped the one closest to him, "is either an item of value or a piece of rubbish. You choose a bowl. If it's a treasure, you can keep it or you can forego that treasure and try for a different one, one that could be even more valuable. If it's trash, you get the opportunity to choose one more bowl. If you choose trash again, the game is over. If you choose treasure, then good for you!"

Ainsley studied the bowls. "What if I choose a treasure and then choose trash?"

"You still get one more opportunity to choose a bowl. If you choose trash again, the game is over."

"To put it simply, the game is over anytime you choose trash twice," said the man behind the table.

"Care to give it a try?" Lapper smiled, revealing golden teeth. "Only two gold coins."

Ainsley chewed his lip, wishing there was a way to know if the items under the bowls were truly worth anything. He felt Megan shift beside him and smiled.

"Could you excuse me for a second?" he asked Lapper.

He grabbed Megan by the arm and pulled her away without waiting for a response. "Can you use the Pearl of Truth to find out what's under those bowls?" he whispered.

Megan's eyes grew wide. "Ainsley, I can't believe you would ask me something like that. It's cheating!" She paused. "Besides, I already tried."

Ainsley grinned. "Well, is he at least telling the truth that some of the items are valuable?"

"I think so. I didn't get so much as a twinge from him. But two gold's half your money, you know."

"I know, but if I don't lose it here, I'll lose it some-where else." He fished two coins out of his money pouch and walked back to the table, slapping his money down. "Okay. I'll give it a try."

"Splendid!" Lapper scooped up the coins and bit them each to test their authenticity. "And which one will you try first?"

Ainsley stared at the three rows of bowls, then pointed to one. The man behind the table flipped it over.

Lapper let out a long-suffering sigh. "No, no, no, Templeton." He grabbed the bowl from the other man. "Not like that. You need to reveal the item slooowly to add suspense." Lapper demonstrated for him, then shook his head at Ainsley and Megan. "He's new on the job."

"Is that an Abbat?" asked Megan as Ainsley picked up a small jewel-encrusted weapon that had been beneath the bowl. She had seen, and used, a soul-banishing dagger once before.

"It *is* an Abbat," said Lapper. He placed a hand on Ainsley's shoulder. "Would you like to continue playing in hopes of finding better treasure?"

Ainsley turned the Abbat over in his hand, admiring the glimmering gems. "I don't know. This might come in handy, and I know a place where these stones will get me a fortune."

"Come now." Lapper leaned in toward Ainsley. "You can't possibly be content with that . . . shiny knife. Why not try for something bigger?"

Ainsley thought for a moment, then nodded and put the Abbat down. "All right. How about *that* bowl."

This time, the man at the table lifted the bowl more slowly. Ainsley cocked his head sideways and Megan found herself inching closer for a glimpse.

"You see, Templeton?" Lapper beamed. "Part of the game's allure must be the suspense."

"Of course, Master Lapper," grumbled the man, pulling the bowl away entirely.

"Oh." Ainsley frowned at the contents. "I don't suppose it's magical in any way?"

"It's a twig, Ainsley," said Megan, picking up the stubby scrap of wood. "What do *you* think?"

"Don't be disillusioned yet, my good sir," said Lapper. "For you have one more chance to reclaim your dignity and solidify your manhood."

Ainsley raised an eyebrow at the Arena Master. "My manhood's—"

Megan elbowed him. "Pick the one next to the twig. They can't possibly put two crappy items side by side."

"That's the worst logic I've ever heard," said Ainsley rubbing his chin. "But—" Ainsley reached for the bowl.

"Wait, wait!" blurted Megan. "Try one of the corner ones instead."

Ainsley looked at Megan. "Make up your mind! I'm about to lose my money."

"Listen. I'll bet they don't expect anyone to ever go for the corners, so they put good stuff under there. The middle is going to be nothing but garbage."

Ainsley sighed. "The Abbat was in the middle, Megan."

"Uh," said Megan. "Well—"

"I'm assuming you're going to keep the most valuable treasures closest to you in case someone tries to sweep everything off the table and run with it." Ainsley watched Templeton for any hint of affirmation or denial. Then, he tapped the bowl farthest from him. "This one."

Templeton gripped the bowl in one hand and tilted it back, revealing a smooth flat stone the color of a robin's egg.

"Great." Ainsley sighed. He was about to say, "Thanks for letting me play," when Lapper cut him off.

"Oh, blech!" Lapper pinched his nose. "One of those boring stones of shared sight."

Ainsley's eyebrows rose, but he simply said, "By shared sight, you mean—"

"Whoever possesses the stone will see through the eyes of any living creature they touch as long as the two are connected," said Templeton.

Lapper sidled toward Ainsley. "You appear to have traded your two gold pieces for a rock," he said out of the corner of his mouth. "Perhaps you'd like to try for something else."

"I don't think I will," said Ainsley. He picked up the stone and rubbed it between his fingers. Then he reached out and touched Megan's arm. His vision blurred for a moment and then he found himself looking at . . . himself. "Awesome. I'll keep it."

"I'm so glad you like it," said Lapper, but his smile was more of a sneer, and Ainsley noticed the golden glimmer had vanished from his teeth. He let go of Megan's arm and pocketed the stone.

"Are you *sure* you don't want to try for something different?" asked Lapper, all golden smiles again.

Ainsley shook his head and patted his pocket. "I know somebody who could really use this."

They bade goodbye to Lapper and hurried away before he could finagle Ainsley into returning the stone or picking another twig.

"Let's find a game for me, now," said Megan. She reached for Ainsley's arm, and then thought better of it. "Wait. Are you going to keep seeing what other people see every time you come into contact with someone? I bet we can buy magic-binding bags in the city."

"I don't need something like that," scoffed Ainsley.

"Suit yourself." Megan grabbed his arm, and out of the corner of his eye, Ainsley could see himself walking beside her. Then, Megan stopped and turned her head toward a crowd of young men, and Ainsley found himself viewing the rear end of one of them.

"Nice view, huh?" Megan tightened her grip on Ainsley arm when she felt him squirm. "Those pants are kind of snug on him, aren't they? Maybe he'll turn around and show us more if I can get his attention."

"All right, that's enough!" Ainsley broke free, rubbing his eyes before the image he'd seen burned into his retinas.

Megan grinned wickedly at him. "What's the matter? Not liking the world from a woman's point of view?"

"Whatever," said Ainsley. "Women don't normally do that."

"Ainsley if that were true, your fan club back home would be a lot smaller." Megan patted Ainsley on the shoulder, and he lurched forward. Megan grabbed his arm. "Are you okay?"

Ainsley shook her hand off. "I will be if you quit doing that."

"Oh, sorry." Megan clasped her hands behind her back.

They walked a bit farther until they reached an attraction that caught her attention.

"Hey, let's do this!" She ran to what appeared to be an obstacle course.

Lapper emerged from behind a wall laced with vines. "Care to try your luck against Anton the Great?"

Megan stopped in her tracks and blinked hard. "How did you—? Never mind." She pointed over her shoulder. "I thought my friend and I could compete against each other." She eyed Anton, a giant of a man, and shook her head. "I don't think I could beat him."

"Maybe not in his *current* form," said Lapper. "But perhaps as someone . . . more your size?"

He snapped his fingers and Anton's body seemed to melt like candlewax into a figure several heads shorter. Then, he tightened and tucked until he was a young man about Megan's size with a more muscular build.

"Or perhaps something simpler still?" Lapper snapped his fingers again. Anton's features softened and his body developed curves until he'd shifted into a feminine shape. The girl winked at Ainsley who was flattered, then disgusted when he remembered the man who had been standing there moments before. "Anton becomes Antonia."

"Maybe," said Megan. "What are the rules?"

"You start here," Lapper indicated the wall, "and end up down there," he pointed to a pool of water fifteen yards away. "The first person to finish is the winner."

"And what's the prize?" asked Megan.

Lapper clutched the inside of his cape and drew it open, revealing a gleaming collection of various weapons. "You get to choose one of these. All it costs to enter is two gold coins."

"All right," said Megan, fishing the money out of her top.

Ainsley leaned towards her. "Megan, don't do it. A weapon that nice for two gold coins? The course has to be rigged so you won't win."

"You blew your money looking under bowls," said Megan, handing Lapper the coins. "Let me spend mine how I want."

Lapper pocketed the coins and beckoned for Megan to join Anton at the wall of vines. "Let the race . . . begin."

Unforeseen Obstacles

Megan reached for a sturdy-looking vine and started to climb. She raised her right leg to boost herself up, but it caught on one of the vines.

"What the—?" Megan glanced down and saw that the vine had twisted itself around her ankle. She felt something brush against her hand and moved it just as another vine lashed out and tried to entangle her wrist. Megan kicked free of the vine around her ankle and dropped to the ground. The entire wall was a wriggling mass of vegetation. Beyond it, she could see Antonia already moving on to the next obstacle, apparently aware of the pitfalls of the wall. Megan whirled angrily on Lapper. "That isn't fair."

"My dear," he said with a toothy grin. "It's an *obstacle* course. Those vines are obstacles. You can drop out now if you'd like to avoid further embarrassment."

Megan felt an overwhelming urge to knock out the arena master's teeth. She turned her back to him and breathed deeply . . . and that was when she noticed a tiny section of the wall that wasn't moving. In fact, it appeared to be in the exact spot she'd seen Antonia climb earlier. The Pearl of Truth in her chest gave a tiny shudder.

"Ready to give in?" Lapper asked again.

Megan looked over her shoulder at him. "I'm not done yet."

She sprinted toward the immobile section of wall and shimmied up and over the top, landing squarely on her feet. The next object was a balance beam no wider than Megan's hand over a series of steel spikes. At first glance, the beam appeared to be coated in oil, but Megan noticed particular spots that appeared duller than others. She climbed onto the balance beam and leapt from each spot to the next with arms outstretched. When she reached the end, Ainsley cheered. Antonia glanced over her shoulder and gaped at Megan who was fast on her heels.

Megan smiled at the other girl. "Didn't expect me to get past the wall, did you?"

"Megan, watch out!" cried Ainsley, pointing at a gigantic swinging pendulum that was about to knock her off the course. To his surprise, however, Megan waited right in the pendulum's path for the next one in the series to swing by. He winced as the first pendulum drew closer, but it passed directly through Megan and continued moving. The pendulum in front of her swung out of her path and she ran through to the next one where she waited again.

"How is she doing it?" Ainsley heard Lapper mumble beside him. "It's as if she knows which ones are an illusion."

Megan was now past the pendulums and sizing up a collection of rings shooting jets of fire skyward at random intervals. Unfortunately, all the flames were very real, but Megan wondered if the rings had been simply laid upon the grass or if the rings covered holes drilled into the ground. Experimentally, she nudged one with her toe, and it shifted. She kicked the ring to the side and darted forward, kicking two more out of her path. One rolled directly in front of Antonia who was busy moving her own rings aside.

Megan heard the surge of fire and then a girlish scream. She whirled around and saw Antonia rolling on the ground, her pant legs dotted with flames.

"Are you all right?" Megan rushed to her, but Antonia spat in her direction.

"You bitch!"

"Run, Megan!" shouted Ainsley. "She'll be fine!"

Megan turned on her heel and maneuvered around the last few flames before leaping up and grabbing at the closest rung of a horizontal rope ladder. The next rung in sequence had been sawed to a flimsy thread so Megan skipped over it and reached for the one after. Her wide swing carried her to two more good rungs, and from there she jumped down to the next and final obstacle before the water, a 25-foot high climbing net.

To Megan's surprise, this obstacle had no tricks to it, and she started her ascent with trepidation.

"You've got this, MonkeyGirl!" shouted Ainsley. To passersby it might have sounded like an insult, but Megan was an amazing climber, and Ainsley watched as she scrambled up the net with the dexterity of a spider in its web. She paused for a moment to glance over her shoulder at her competition, and Ainsley groaned.

"Keep going!" He cupped his hands around his mouth. "Don't look back!"

Megan felt the net bob beneath her, but she continued to climb. She was almost to the top when she felt her foot catch again. Cursing, she gave a hard yank and looked down. Instead of rope wrapped around her ankle, it was Antonia's hand.

"Let go!" Megan kicked out, but Antonia held strong, jerking on Megan's leg and trying to dislodge her from the net. Megan watched the young woman's features harden until, to her horror, Antonia had morphed back into Anton, complete with extra muscle mass.

"He can't do that." Ainsley turned to Lapper, fuming.

Lapper regarded him with a cold stare. "Your friend tried to light my worker on fire. I say turnabout is fair play."

The burly Anton now tightened his grip on Megan's leg, and Bit darted down Megan's backside to clamp her teeth in

Anton's hand. Anton used his free hand to knock Bit aside. Then, he grinned up at Megan. "Have a pleasant fall."

"No!" Ainsley leapt into the air, but before he could even beat his wings, a snow-white ferret darted up the rope net. It wrapped its front paws around one of Anton's burnt ankles and sank its teeth into his raw flesh. With a bloodcurdling screech, Anton released Megan's ankle and toppled backwards twenty feet to the ground.

A thunderous boom reached her ears, and though Megan half-hoped he was dead, she looked over her shoulder to where Anton lay, groaning and clutching his ankle. The ferret climbed up beside Megan, and she turned to face it, though to her, it appeared in its true form—that of a young man.

"Hi, Brighton," she said with a broad grin.

Brighton smirked. "That's all I get for saving your life?"

"I could give you some of Bit's food pellets." Her smile slipped as she patted her breast pocket and scanned the ground beneath her. "Bit!"

A squeak sounded from above, and Megan glanced at the top of the net where the narshorn sat on its haunches and blinked at her.

"I think she wants you to press on," said Brighton.

"I guess I have to, if I want my prize." Megan ascended the last length of rope separating her from the summit, but when she reached the top, she peered over the edge and frowned. "Um . . . isn't there supposed to be a rope or another net for me to slide down from here?"

"Naw, you have to jump," said Brighton.

"What?!?"

"Don't tell me you braved fire and man-eating plants, and you're afraid of a little water?"

Megan stared at him. "Brighton, that is a twenty-foot drop into . . . a . . . puddle!"

"A deep puddle," he corrected. "Do you want me to go first?" He climbed up beside Bit, leaned back, and did a graceful swan dive. He surfaced a moment later and shook the water out of his hair. "It's all right. You've got a good six feet of depth. Just curl into a ball when you jump!"

"Great." Megan flashed him a thumbs-up and turned to Bit. "Would *you* do it?"

In answer, the narshorn scrambled up Megan's arm and into her pocket.

"Megan!" shouted Ainsley. "Make sure you don't jump too far out. Otherwise, you'll miss the puddle and probably break every bone in your body."

"Thank you!" she shouted back.

"Do you want me to fly up and get you?" he asked.

Staring down at the water, Megan wanted nothing more than that, but Brighton had jumped to make sure it was safe for her, and her guilt outweighed her fear. She took a deep breath, and slid off the net, pulling her legs to her chest. Her stomach gave the same uncomfortable lurch as if she was riding an airpad, and she impacted the surface of the pool with a satisfying splash. The water surged past her ears and overhead, and she felt the tips of her toes touch bottom. Straightening her legs, she burst up and out of the water and wiped the moisture from her face.

Ainsley grabbed her beneath her armpits and lifted her to dry land. "You did it!" he said, his face almost as white as Brighton's hair. Megan pulled open her pocket, and Bit scrambled out, shaking her wet torso and hitting Megan with a tiny spray of water.

"Of course she did," said Brighton, though Ainsley had seen him wringing his paws together nervously the moment Megan had jumped.

Megan twisted her hair, letting the water dribble onto the grass, and watched two men hoisting Anton onto a stretcher. "Is he going to be okay?"

Lapper, who had also been watching the proceedings, turned to Megan with an expression of utmost contempt. "Do you really care?"

Megan blushed but fixed Lapper with a hard glare of her own. "I'll take my prize now, please. The short sword with the leather-wrapped hilt."

Lapper snorted. "You assaulted one of my workers. That is an instant disqualification. You get no prize."

"What?!" Megan whipped her hair back and stood toe-to-toe with the arena master. "That's bullshit! You never mentioned *anything* like that in the rules, and your obstacle course assaulted me first."

"The obstacle course presented obstacles," snapped Lapper. "What do you expect?"

"She expects you to give her the prize she won." Ainsley advanced upon him, thrusting out his wings menacingly.

Lapper glared at Ainsley but raised his cane in a debonair fashion and nudged Ainsley aside. "You'll excuse me. I have other patrons to attend to."

"Perhaps you should tend to that wound on your knee first," said Brighton.

Lapper slid his leg to the side and looked down. "What wound?"

Brighton bared his teeth. "The one I'm about to give you." He leapt at Lapper but his body froze in midair. Glancing around in confusion, he kicked his legs and pawed at the space before him but only succeeded in flipping himself upside down. "Oh, crumb."

"Why is there anger at Carnival?" asked a gravelly voice.

Everyone turned toward the speaker, a thin, stooped man with pointy ears jutting out of his white hair. His bony index finger was aimed at Brighton, and it was clear he had been responsible for the ferret's frozen flight. He lowered his hand and Brighton dropped to the ground on all fours, his skin a slight pink beneath his white fur.

"Good afternoon, Master Nates," said Lapper with a sweeping bow. "Just a little misunderstanding." He gestured to Ainsley, Megan, and Brighton. "These . . . *children* and their rabid pet were just leaving."

The white-haired man turned his attention to Ainsley and Megan. They had met Pocky Nates, one of the city's last surviving Ponzipoo, once before and visited him in his house full of interesting pets. Pocky had helped them find Rayne when he had been under the influence of a dark witch and stolen the Quatrys. At the time, Bornias had told them Pocky sold icicles for a living, but the way Lapper genuflected to him seemed to indicate otherwise.

Pocky recognized Ainsley and Megan as well, for the confused expression with which he'd regarded them had dissipated. "You both appear to be doing well." He nodded to Ainsley. "And *you* appear to have become a bird of some sort."

"Why are the wings the first thing people always notice?" asked Ainsley.

"Sir," said Megan. "I won this contest fair and square and—"

"You little liar!" Lapper pounded his cane against the ground. "I don't know how, but you found a way around my obstacles, and to insult me further, you injured one of my workers."

"Your worker tried to kill me!" Megan shot back. Several passersby glanced over curiously, and Lapper leaned close to Megan.

"You'd better watch your mouth," he raised his cane and shook it before Megan's nose. "I won't have you slandering my good name."

Megan narrowed her eyes. "Your games are deceitful, and you don't care if your workers hurt people. Anything to make a gold coin."

Lapper's hand swung down toward Megan's cheek, but it made no connection. Pocky Nates had yanked on the back of Megan's shirt, pulling her from harm's path.

"I think," he said to Lapper in a serious voice that seemed ill-matched to his Ponzipoo personality, "that perhaps it would be better for you and your workers to leave Carnival tomorrow morning instead of at week's end."

Lapper's hand and lower jaw fell at the same time. "But . . . but you can't possibly," he pointed at Megan, "children will say anything to . . . she's lying!"

"I don't care if she's lying or telling the truth," said Pocky. "You're a grown man, and you should have no reason to resort to violence, especially against someone *much younger* than yourself."

Lapper stiffened at these words. "I'm not leaving. I've paid my fee for using the land."

"The remaining days will be refunded to you, minus the gold you owe our young friend," said Pocky, nodding toward Megan.

"Have it your way," said Lapper with a sniff. "Except . . ." He flung open his cloak and withdrew the sword Megan had been eyeing. "I'll keep my money, and the child can have this."

He tilted the sword point down and released it with the disdain of someone dropping a used ball of tissue. It pierced the grass and wobbled where it had been wedged into the soil.

"I've got dozens of those toys." Lapper turned on the tip of his boot, the grass shredding beneath his toes, and without so much as a backward glance, he said, "You know, Pocky, for someone who's supposed to provide a neutral presence in the valley, you seem to have no problem choosing sides." Then, he bustled after a group of wide-eyed girls in white cloaks. "Ladies, welcome!"

Megan yanked the sword from the ground and sliced the air with it. "Wow. I've never gotten anyone kicked out of a city before."

"He was a marked man," said Pocky, shaking his head. "I've received a few complaints about him since he arrived but nothing so serious as an attempt to assault a visitor." He nodded as Megan inspected the sword's blade. "Despite what he says, that *is* a good weapon, though I doubt he paid anything near two gold for it."

"Really?" Megan flicked the blade with her thumb. "How do you know that?"

"Lapper owns a trading company at the Port of Scribnitch. He allows incoming vessels to use his docks for a merchandise discount."

Megan slid the blade between her belt and pants. "Well, good sword or not, it's better than poking an enemy in the eyes. I'll have to buy a scabbard for it when I get a chance, though."

"You can get it in town while I'm buying my magic-binding bag," said Ainsley. "We're done here anyway." He turned to Pocky. "I'm glad you showed up when you did."

"Yes, thanks," said Megan, reaching for Pocky's hand and shaking it.

Pocky placed his free hand atop their joined ones. "You'll be more careful with that Pearl of Truth, won't you? There are many who would use you for your gift."

"Yes, sir." Megan blushed. "I'm sorry about cheating at the game."

"Balderdash." Pocky's cheeks puffed out. "The only rule was that you had to finish the race. There were no restrictions as to how you overcame each obstacle." He winked at Megan. "Now, if you'll excuse me, I think I'll stroll around a bit and have a look at these 'games of chance.'"

Jealousy

Ainsley, Megan, and Brighton bade the Ponzipoo farewell, and then Megan turned to Brighton. She realized she'd never had a long look at him, the majority of time they'd spent together having been in a no-magic zone where he appeared to her in ferret form.

With her Pearl of Truth unfettered, however, she could see a young man with white-blond hair and dark shining eyes that were almost black, like onyx marbles. One of his eyebrows was positioned higher than the other to give him a perpetual appearance of amusement, and he stood a head shorter than Megan. She supposed his diminutive stature worked to his benefit when he was engaged in thievery, though his last human attempt had failed with the result being his cursed animal form.

"I have to say that it's good to run into you," said Megan.

"You don't *have* to say it," said Brighton, smiling, "but it's nice to hear."

"What are you doing at Carnival, anyway? Isn't your boss watching Master Nick's shop while he's here?"

Brighton nodded. "That's why he sent me. He's going to watch the knack shop and the bookstore while I browse the market for him. He figures I'll be able to get through the crowds faster than he could."

"That's probably true," said Ainsley, looking down at Brighton. It was odd to him that Megan should speak to the ferret as if he were practically at eye level. "I'm Ainsley, by the way."

Brighton extended a paw. "Brighton Stroca, rogue extraodinaire . . . ah . . . once upon a time." He indicated his rodent form.

"Well, we're going back up to the city if you'd like to join us," said Ainsley.

"I'll take you up on that," said Brighton. "It'll be easier for me to make it inside if I'm accompanied by people. A ferret standing at the gates without so much as a nascifriend can seem pretty suspicious."

"Speaking of nascifriends," Megan gauged the location of the sun, "it's almost time for me to meet Garner."

"Garner?" Brighton's right eyebrow rose to join his left.

"The love of Megan's life," said Ainsley, sticking his finger in his throat.

"He is *not* the love of my life," said Megan, pausing to get a pastry sample as they left the arena. "I've only known him for a month, and it's a doomed relationship anyway. He's only interested in being with 'the one.'" She made air quotes with her fingers, then licked the powdered sugar from them.

"The one. I don't believe in such nonsense, myself," said Brighton with a disdainful sniff.

"Really." Megan cleared her throat. "So, your ex-fiancé was—"

"*One* apple in a barrelful . . . and I intend to sample the whole lot."

"Nice," said Ainsley with a wicked grin. He would have given Brighton a high-five had the ferret not been walking on all four paws. "Megan, I like this guy. You should dump his holiness and get with Brighton."

Megan gave him withering look. "No, thank you. I'm not into being used and discarded like an apple core. I'd rather be with a priest than a pig."

"Here now, I take offense to that. I'm not a pig. I'm a ferret." Brighton grinned, and despite herself, Megan grinned back.

"Shut up, then, and act like one."

They reached the airpads surrounding the city just as one was descending. Ainsley ran his hand over the warding post, and the trio boarded the platform, air hissing beneath them as the platform was propelled skyward.

Despite the numerous times she'd ridden the airpads, Megan still felt as if she were leaving her stomach on the ground while she hurtled through the sky on a piece of wood.

"Speak of the devil . . . or angel, I should say. Look who's waiting for us." Ainsley nudged Megan and pointed to the city gate.

A young man with curly brown hair and eyes like emerald chips waved at Megan and smiled. Ainsley wasn't surprised that Garner seemed to be ignoring him. Their last encounter hadn't been a pleasant one.

When Ainsley had been afflicted by the Illness, Garner had tried to convince Megan to stay away from him rather than help him find a cure. Megan wouldn't obey Garner, so he had drugged her and Ainsley and taken them to Hylark, where they'd been separated. In the end, Ainsley and Megan were reunited, but Ainsley had promised Garner an unpleasant end if he ever did anything hurtful to Megan again.

But Megan seemed to think Garner could do no wrong. Even now, she didn't wait for the airpad to draw level before hopping onto the platform.

"Hi." She smiled at Garner and pressed her lips to his. "It's good to see you."

Ainsley noticed that Garner faced Megan but his eyes flickered up to Ainsley's for the briefest of moments. In what Ainsley saw as pure exhibitionism, Garner wrapped his arms around Megan and kissed her hard, all the while glaring at Ainsley.

Ainsley held his hand high enough for Garner to see and let electricity arc across his fingertips. He might not have the Quatrys or the Illness anymore, but he still had magic in his blood. Garner's eyes widened, and he pulled away from Megan, bending down to ferret eye-level.

Placing his tongue to the roof of his mouth, he emitted a series of clicks and squeaks. Brighton blinked at him for a moment. "Not too bad," he said in human tongue. "Yourself?"

Ainsley choked on a laugh, watching Garner straighten with a flustered look. "My apologies. Curse of Sargon, is it?"

Brighton nodded and puffed out his chest. "Tried to steal a horse of royalty. I'm rather fond of the beasts."

"Really?" Garner bent back down. "I am as well. What's your favorite breed?"

Brighton shrugged. "They all taste the same."

This time, Ainsley couldn't contain his mirth, snickering at Garner's bulging eyes. "You . . . you eat those intelligent creatures?"

"Come on, now." Brighton placed a paw on Garner's leg. "They can't be that intelligent if they let themselves get caught. When I see them grazing, unawares, I just can't stop myself."

"You prey on the helpless, then." Garner clenched his jaw. "You deserve to be cursed."

Brighton retreated a few paces, stunned by the verbal slap. Ainsley stopped laughing and balled his hands into fists.

"Garner!" Megan gaped at him. "Don't talk like that to my friends."

"I'm a nascifriend in training," he shot back. "It's my duty to defend the helpless, and he was encouraging cruelty against them."

"It was a joke, dumbass!" Ainsley waved his arms for emphasis. "And I don't think a guy who drugs women and kidnaps them has much room to talk about defending the helpless."

Garner's face turned an ugly shade of red. "I was protecting her from you," he said, keeping his voice even. "She was too stubborn to leave your side, and for the life of me, I *cannot* figure out why."

"Because I care about him," interjected Megan, stepping between Ainsley and Garner. "And I care about you. But if you two don't stop making a scene and announcing all of our biggest flaws to the city, I will forget I know you *both*."

After she said this, Ainsley finally bothered to look around. Sure enough, a small group of people had stopped in their shopping and Carnival merriment to watch Ainsley and Garner go at it.

"Sorry," Ainsley told Garner, more for the sake of the crowd than anything.

"My apologies to both of you as well," said Garner, though he only looked at Brighton.

"Good. Now let's go check out some shops." Megan grabbed Garner's arm and steered him toward the main avenue, smiling apologetically at Brighton.

Ainsley looked down at the ferret whose fur was bristling as he watched Garner walk away with Megan. "Don't listen to him, Brighton. He's just a jerk. You don't deserve to be cursed."

Brighton sighed, and his fur flattened against his body. "I know. Let's just keep up with them. I don't trust that elf."

"Join the club," said Ainsley, as they skirted passersby and fell into step behind the lovebirds. "By the way, do you really eat horses?" he whispered.

"Naw, but our nascifriend doesn't need to know that." Brighton winked. "You suppose I should tell him I killed a motley so I could juggle its eyeballs?"

Ainsley collapsed against a merchant's cart, doubled over with laughter until Megan stormed toward him.

"Stop picking on Garner!" she hissed, kicking Ainsley in the leg and thumping Brighton on the ear.

"Ouch." Brighton massaged his bruised cartilage. "Violent this one, isn't she?"

"Just be glad she likes you," said Ainsley, placing his hands over his eyes. "Man, I *really* need to find a store that sells magic-binding bags. This alternate-sight stone is making me nauseous."

"If you weren't so busy making smartass comments," said Megan, "you'd realize we're right outside a store that sells them." She pointed behind Ainsley, and he turned.

"Oh, excellent. Do they sell some big enough to put over the heads of evil elves?"

"He is *not* evil," said Megan, jerking open the door of the shop and joining Garner.

Brighton padded behind Ainsley. "Why don't you like him, anyway?"

Ainsley explained the incidents of the past weeks, leaving the details of the Illness vague. If anyone asked, he wouldn't deny it, but it seemed too weighty a subject to be chatting about at Carnival.

Brighton shook his head and wrinkled his nose. "He does sound a bit dodgy. Even I couldn't stoop so low."

"Megan's normally so good at seeing the truth." Ainsley held the door open. "I don't know why she can't see it now."

Megan did her best to ignore Ainsley and Brighton, though they were chattering loudly enough for the entire store to hear. "So, have you started back on your nascifriend training yet?" she asked Garner.

When she and Ainsley had met him last in the wooded Folly, he had explained that his test to become a nascifriend was to restore life to the deadened remains of the forest. He had strayed off his path to accompany Megan, however, when she'd explained her search for an Illness cure.

Garner pulled a thick bag from a peg and studied it as he spoke. "I have, though I'm doing more research now than field work. I've seen the devastation in The Folly, and I've been researching what people have recorded about it so I don't repeat their efforts."

"That makes sense," said Megan. "So, you'll be around for a bit?"

"Maybe." Garner smiled and moved closer to her. "Who wants to know?"

Megan leaned toward him, lips puckered, but to her dismay, Ainsley popped up between her and Garner. She gave a guttural growl. "Ainsley, what?!"

"I found my magic-binding bag." He jiggled it in her face. "Could I borrow some money?"

"If you're using it to leave the country, then yes!" Megan pulled a coin from her leather pouch and tossed it to him.

"Thanks!" Ainsley flashed the coin at her, and he and Brighton headed for the salesperson.

When the merchant told him the price of the bag, however, Ainsley wondered if he should have asked for more money. "Considering these bags have nothing in them, I can't believe how much they cost," he said, handing his coins to the merchant.

The merchant snorted. "You think *this* is pricy?" He slid the bag across the counter to Ainsley. "Our most expensive one costs twenty times this."

"Where is it?" Ainsley glanced at the shelf behind the merchant, looking for something that seemed worthy of such a fee. The merchant reached behind the counter and produced a rather plain sack made of black cloth.

Ainsley raised an eyebrow at him. "*That's* the bag?"

The merchant, expecting admiration for his product, pressed his lips together and whisked the bag away. "Keep in mind, sir, it's not what the bag looks like but what it can do that is important."

"Well, unless that one can lay golden eggs . . ." Ainsley shook his head and tucked his own bag away. "Good luck trying to find a fool to buy it."

He turned to walk back towards his friends, but the merchant had to have the last word. "Actually, I sold one just this morning," he called after Ainsley, "and I don't think most people would consider Evren Sandor a fool."

Megan hadn't heard most of Ainsley's conversation, but she did hear the last remark and shot him a meaningful glance.

"Evren Sandor bought one of those bags?" asked Ainsley, turning back around. "What for?"

The merchant gave Ainsley a smug smile. "Doesn't seem so ridiculous now, does it?"

"What was the bag for?" Megan repeated Ainsley's question, stepping up to the counter beside him.

The merchant lifted his chin and sniffed. "It would have been rude of me to ask, wouldn't it? But you can rest assured that whatever he needed it for must have held some pretty powerful magic."

"I imagine so," said Ainsley. He grabbed hold of the hem of Megan's shirt and tugged it in the direction of the door. "Well, thank you again for the bag."

He and Megan headed for the exit, she catching Garner's eye, who in turn nudged Brighton to follow. They tucked themselves into an alley cluttered with packing crates and sat upon them in a half-circle.

"What do you make of it?" Ainsley asked Megan.

She shook her head. "I don't know what magical item he's hiding in that bag, but he can't have good intentions with it."

"I feel as if I'm missing something here," said Brighton. "Who are we whispering about in a suspicious manner?"

"Evren Sandor," said Ainsley. "He used to be the lieutenant commander for the Silvan Sentry."

"I know him," said Brighton. He narrowed his beady eyes. "He's constantly in our cottage trying to flatter Poloi out of one book or another."

"That's the thing," said Megan. "He was in Poloi's cottage about a month ago looking at a book call The Tomdex. Supposedly, it contains certain knowledge that could be dangerous in the wrong hands."

"What was he looking for?" asked Garner.

Ainsley and Megan looked at one another and frowned.

"We don't know," said Megan, "but when we were up in the Icyllian Mountains, we ran into him with Master Nick and they were acting strangely. Master Nick acted like he didn't know us, and Evren pretended to be lost when he really wasn't."

"And that's when we found out . . ." Ainsley paused as one of the cart merchants passed the alley, eyeing the teenagers suspiciously. As soon as he had left, Ainsley leaned in close to the others. "That's when we found out that Evren plans to overthrow the Raklund government."

Brighton laughed until the tip of his tail shook. "You're joking, right? That little sniveler is going to rule Raklund?"

"That's his plan," said Megan.

"I still don't understand how he intends to do that," said Garner. "Even if he can get Captain Kyviel and the entire Silvan Sentry behind him, he's no match for the Kingdom Coalition."

"Unless he has some sort of secret weapon in that magic-binding bag of his," said Ainsley. "For all we know, he plans to poison everyone's drinks over their summit lunch." He snapped his fingers and hopped up from his crate. "Or maybe he plans to slip them all a little ninayet!"

"Hold on," said Garner, raising a hand. "You're suggesting poison and . . . and mind control?"

Ainsley stared at him. "Uh . . . yeah!"

"Do you realize how asinine that sounds?"

"Asinine? Listen—"

Garner pressed on. "You're accusing a man favored to be the newest member of the community of Amdor of high treason!"

"Do you realize how naïve *you* sound?" countered Ainsley. "You don't think treason's possible in your dream world?"

Before the fight could escalate any further, Megan jumped up from her own crate. "Listen. We'll talk to Bornias tonight and let him know to be on the lookout. We'll have the guards inspect everyone's bags as they enter the summit or something."

Garner opened his mouth to protest, but Megan placed a finger to his lips. "Please. Let us try this."

Garner wrapped his hands around hers. "Just don't let these fools talk you into something dangerous."

Megan bit back the harsh reply building on her tongue and nodded. "For now, let's get something to eat. All this action's got me starving."

Garner kissed Megan's forehead and pulled her after him. "Let's go over there." He pointed to a large tent across the street where a man was serving skewered meat, which he flambéed by spewing fire from his mouth.

"Do you think we could convince him to do that to Garner?" Ainsley whispered to Brighton who smirked.

"I don't expect so. Who'd want to eat a jackass on a stick?"

They both busted out laughing, and at a glare from Megan, they hung back until they could regain their composure.

"Do you want a motley skewer or a doodah skewer?" Garner asked Megan as they ducked beneath the canopy.

"Ugh. Neither." Megan made a face. "The last thing I want is food heated with someone's breath."

Garner laughed. "Understandable. Then, what *do* you want?"

"Do they have salad or anything that's just vegetables?" Megan rubbed her throat. "I think I've eaten enough grease for the day, and I'm sure Bit could use something different."

She pointed at the narshorn poking out of her pocket who was nibbling forlornly at a food pellet between her paws. At the mention of fresh vegetables, Bit squeaked and let the pellet drop to the ground.

Garner studied a sign dangling from the ceiling with the vendor's offerings painted across it in sloppy, splotchy letters. "How about the Gardener's Sampler?"

Megan shrugged. "Sure. I'm willing to try a couple new vegetables."

He, Ainsley, and Brighton put in their meal requests while Megan found an open table. Ainsley and Brighton reached her first with their plates of food, and they were both grinning.

"What did you say to Garner *now*?" she asked with a sigh, reaching for a chunk of potato on Ainsley's plate and popping it into her mouth.

"What did *you* say to Garner?" asked Brighton. "How hungry did you tell him you were?"

Megan stopped chewing and got to her feet. "Why?"

And then she saw Garner walking towards her, carrying his plate in one hand and grinning as he gestured behind him. Megan leaned slightly sideways to see past him.

A little boy trailed after Garner, pushing a wheelbarrow filled with vegetables.

"Oh, no," said Megan. "That couldn't be . . ."

The other patrons watched the procession with amusement, and when the boy brought the wheelbarrow to a stop in front of Megan, they all laughed.

"Your Gardener's Sampler, my lady." The boy raised his voice to be heard over the uproar and gave a little bow.

With a gleeful squeal, Bit leapt from Megan's pocket into a bed of lettuce. Megan stared from the narshorn to the contents of the wooden cart to the mirthful faces of her friends, and she began to laugh as well.

Tamtam and Trouble

Megan was almost full to bursting, though the wheelbarrow seemed no emptier, when a golden butterfly lit on her shoulder.

"Ainsley and Megan," Lady Maudred's voice issued from the butterfly, "would you please meet me at Tamtam's on Pedora Avenue?"

"Sure," said Megan while Ainsley murmured his assent through a mouthful of food.

After the butterfly had fluttered away, Megan turned to Brighton and Garner. "What's Tamtam's?"

"I don't know," said Garner. "It's not near any place I frequent, but I'll walk there with you."

"Count me in," said Brighton. "I'll keep you two company."

But as soon as they arrived at Tamtam's, a frosting-pink building with white trim, he changed his mind.

"Have fun in there. I'll catch up with you later."

"But—" Megan turned to Garner with pleading eyes.

He kissed her on the cheek. "I'll see you tonight."

Then, he and Brighton hurried down the street and distanced themselves from Tamtam's House of Bath and Beauty.

"You ready to go in?" asked Ainsley.

It didn't surprise Megan that Ainsley, always preoccupied with appearances, seemed almost eager to enter. She, on the other hand, would rather be running away with Brighton and Garner. "I suppose I could use a bath," she said with a sigh.

When Ainsley opened the door, a handsome man wearing too much pomade and a pretty woman wearing too much rouge were waiting in the foyer.

"Megan?" The woman drew near, smiling through lips stained the color of pomegranates. "This way, please." She walked toward a door on the left side of the house.

"And you must be Ainsley." The man's smile rivaled Ainsley's own in whiteness and sparkle. "To the right, if you would, sir."

"Have fun!" Ainsley called to Megan.

"Don't count on it!" she called back.

The room to which she'd been led served as the bath and, judging by its size, not much more. The tub, sunken into the floor, was shaped like a massive square and filled almost to the brim with steaming hot water. Clear bottles filled with colorful liquids and jars of bath salts and soaps edged one side of the tub. Megan eyed them warily, remembering her first experience with the Arylonian soap flakes that had culminated in a frothy roomful of suds.

Luckily, the ruddy-cheeked woman measured out a pinch of soap for Megan and swirled it around until a cheerful pile of bubbles coated the surface of the water.

"Enjoy yourself," said the woman. "And when you're done, slip on the robe and meet Lady Maudred through there." She pointed to a door opposite the one they'd entered.

"Thank you." Megan locked the door behind the woman and slipped out of her clothes, eager to enjoy at least this part of her Tamtam's experience. She let Bit dip into the bathwater first and stepped in after the narshorn had paddled to the edge of the tub to dry her fur.

Megan scrubbed away every ounce of filth and soaked until her fingers and toes were waterlogged. She dried off and donned the robe, leaving Bit to settle into the pocket of her discarded clothes, but even though she had been instructed to enter the room, Megan still knocked on the door.

"Come in, Megan, dear," Lady Maudred's chirped from the other side.

Megan opened the door but couldn't bring herself to enter into the next room. She knew this would entail the "beauty" portion of the experience. Lady Maudred sat at one end of a wooden counter that ran the length of the wall adjacent to the door. On the wall above the counter hung a mirror of similar dimensions in which Lady Maudred was scrutinizing her own reflection. The left half of her hair had been arranged in tight curls and the right half hung loosely to her shoulder. An empty stool beside hers supported a bucket of milky liquid filled with sticks.

"Why are you changing your hairstyle?" asked Megan. "And . . . what *is* that?"

"It's setting wax," said Lady Maudred, reaching into the bucket. "I wanted something different for tonight's cotillion, and if you don't mind my saying, you ought to have something special as well."

"The Carnival Cotillion?" Megan's eyes widened. "That's *tonight*?"

"Of course it is," said Lady Maudred. She wrapped a section of hair around the stick and rolled it up against her scalp, pressing it in place. "Haven't you seen the dignitaries arriving all day? Don't tell me you've forgotten."

Megan fidgeted with the sash on her robe. "Okay."

Lady Maudred slid the stick free of the strand of hair, and it coiled like a spring. "Oh, Megan," she said with a sigh. "Do you even have a dress?"

"When would I have had time to get a dress?" Megan flopped down on a spare stool at the counter. "When I was trapped in the void between life and death fighting a dragon? Besides . . . Ainsley doesn't have anything to wear either."

Lady Maudred fixed her with a stern gaze. "We have been here three days now. You have had more than ample time."

"Fine. I'll go out and buy a dress in my bathrobe." Megan started to get to her feet, but Lady Maudred pressed a hand to Megan's forehead, forcing her to remain seated.

"There isn't time for that *or* your sarcasm." Lady Maudred unhooked the familiar golden butterfly pin from her dress and held it close to her mouth. She whispered to it, and the butterfly spread its wings and flitted away.

"I'm having Sari create something for you *and* Ainsley," said Lady Maudred.

"Sari's here?" Megan relaxed her shoulders. She'd almost forgotten that the seamstress had planned to sell the new fabric she'd created at Carnival. "How's her business doing?"

"Fairly well, I imagine," said Lady Maudred, grabbing a handful of Megan's hair and twisting it on top of her head. She leaned back to gauge the hairstyle, "but you can ask her yourself when she comes to deliver the clothing. I'm sure she'll be eager to see you and Ainsley." Lady Maudred took one of Megan's hands and used it to replace her own. "Very pretty."

Megan glanced askance at her. "I can't wear my hair up like this. My ears stick out."

"And?" Lady Maudred reached into the bucket and removed two sticks, shaking the excess wax from them. "There's more to you than your ears, isn't there? Or are you just a giant pair of ears with feet attached?"

Megan couldn't help laughing. "No. I guess you're right."

"You're a lovely girl with some very thick hair." Lady Maudred stabbed the sticks through Megan's curly locks and frowned. "You look like you're wearing a bush on your head."

"But there's more to me than my *hair*, isn't there?" asked Megan with a smirk.

"Ordinarily I would agree, but hair is everything at Cotillion." Lady Maudred pulled out the sticks and set them aside. "Tamtam!" she called over her shoulder. "Megan's hair needs a little more help than I can provide."

Megan rolled her eyes toward the ceiling. "I don't *have* to go to the Cotillion if it's this much trouble."

"Of course you do." Lady Maudred picked bits of wax from Megan's hair. "I'm very excited to present you and Ainsley to the country's most prestigious leaders. Ah . . . here's Tamtam."

"Hi!" Megan smiled and glanced over. "I—woah!" She almost tipped her stool backwards in surprise.

If hair was everything at Cotillion, Megan had a feeling Tamtam would be at the bottom of the waiting list for an invitation. The woman was bald from head to foot except for her arms, which were carpeted with hair.

Megan licked her lips. "You're a . . . uh . . . hairstylist?"

"She's one of the best," said Lady Maudred, squeezing Megan's shoulders. "I leave you in her capable hands."

"Great. Thanks!" Megan pasted on a smile until Lady Maudred walked away. She winced as Tamtam reached for a section of her hair. "You style hair and you have none. Should I be worried?" Megan couldn't stop the words from spilling out of her mouth, but Tamtam just laughed.

"Turn away from the mirror and relax."

Megan did as she was told, and after twenty painstaking minutes, Tamtam scooted her around to see her reflection.

"Oh!" Megan leaned toward the mirror, tilting her chin up and turning her head from side to side. "This looks—"

"Beautiful." Lady Maudred's image appeared beside her own. "And just in time for this . . ." She gestured toward the doorway leading to the bath where Sari stood with her arms outstretched. Draped across them was a ballgown sewn from emerald-green fabric.

"I thought this would be an enchanting color for you," said Sari.

"Hello, Sari." Megan hugged the woman awkwardly, not wanting to crush the dress. "How are you? How's business?"

"My cloth cart has been crowded with customers all day, so I think that's a good sign." Sari winked at her. "But conversation can wait. I'm more interested in seeing how this gown looks on you."

Megan took it from her and hid behind the bathroom door before dropping her robe. "How's the aingan selling?" she asked, thinking of the fabric the tailor had designed based on her and Ainsley's denim jeans.

"Sold out within the first few hours!" chirped Sari. "With plenty more orders to keep me busy when I settle into my new shop."

"New shop?" Megan clutched the dress against her and peeked around the door. "So you're finally moving to Pontsford?"

"She has to if she wants to be on the main commerce route," said Lady Maudred. "Now, put on that dress and let's have a look at you."

Megan untied the lacing on the back of the gown and stepped into it, slipping the straps onto her shoulders. She pressed her hands against the bodice, thankful she could fill it, and smoothed the folds of the satiny skirt beneath her fingers.

"Well, Megan, what do you think?" called Sari.

Megan opened the bathroom door wide. "I like it."

Sari and Lady Maudred beamed at her, and Lady Maudred clapped her hands together to cement her approval.

"Let me tie up the back for you," said Sari, twirling Megan so the skirts billowed around her. "Say when." She gave the laces a hard tug that forced Megan's breath out.

"When!" squeaked Megan, wrapping her arms about her midsection.

"Maybe you should loosen them a bit, Sari," said Lady Maudred. "Megan's face is turning an unappealing color."

"Oh! Apologies!" Sari ran her nimble fingers through the laces, and Megan felt her internal organs return to their natural position.

"Much better," she breathed. "Thanks."

Ever the diligent tailor, Sari circled Megan, fidgeting with creases and stray threads until Lady Maudred took her by the arm and pulled her away.

"You can't improve perfection."

Megan wasn't sure if Lady Maudred was referring to her or the dress, but she blushed all the same. She couldn't resist admiring her reflection in the mirror, and she was thankful Ainsley wasn't around to see her do it.

"Thank you so much, Sari." Megan took the woman's hands.

"You're always welcome." Sari squeezed Megan's fingers. "After the cold shoulders I've been getting in Raklund, your appreciation is a nice change."

Megan tilted her head and released Sari's hands. "Cold shoulders? What do you mean?"

The tailor laughed and tucked a stray length of hair behind her ear, pacing the room. "I'm sure it's nothing. I was probably just nervous about Carnival and being over-sensitive."

"I don't believe that coming from you," spoke up Lady Maudred. "What happened in Raklund?"

Sari leaned against the counter. "I had to leave Carnival to go back there after I forgot a special cloak I'd been working on for Pocky Nates. It took longer than usual to get through the entrance and when I managed to get inside, everyone seemed to be ignoring me. Wait. That's not entirely correct."

She waved a hand in front of her as if sweeping away her previous words. "They seemed to be ignoring each other, too. They all just walked around looking a little despondent, wandering back and forth between the different shops." Sari looked at Lady Maudred. "Did someone pass on recently? Is Raklund in mourning?"

"Not as far as I know." Lady Maudred frowned. "But I've been away from the palace for some time. I'll check with the Silverskins this evening at Cotillion."

Sari nodded and traded her troubled expression for a smile. "As I said, I'm sure it's nothing." She squeezed Megan's shoulders. "You look beautiful. Have fun at Cotillion!"

"I will, and thank you again!" Megan waved to Sari as the woman disappeared through the bath door. When she heard it close, she turned to Lady Maudred. "What do you think is really happening in Raklund?"

"Hm?" Lady Maudred, who was staring out the window, blinked and turned to Megan. "Oh, don't worry. I'm sure everything's just fine."

Megan didn't need the sting of the pearl in her chest to tell her that Lady Maudred was lying.

Music of the Night

When Megan returned to the front room, she was surprised to find it jammed with customers, mainly women and teen-aged girls, all clamoring for beautification from Tamtam. The male and female greeters weaved through the throng with parchment and quill, taking down names and breaking up arguments over who had arrived first. All the while, they maintained their glamorous smiles, though his hair now stuck up in odd tufts and her rouge had smeared to her eyes. Several people saw Megan emerge and she found herself being pulled through the crowd toward the female greeter.

"This is how I want my hair," said one girl to the greeter, patting Megan's updo, "but I want jeweled pins to hold it in place."

An older woman bumped the girl aside and gestured at Megan. "I want my face paint to look as natural as hers."

Megan didn't bother to tell the woman that she wasn't wearing any makeup except for a small amount of lip stain Lady Maudred had forced upon her. It had been a hard-fought battle, but Megan had convinced the older woman to set aside the kohl pot and lead face powder by threatening to let down her hair.

Another hand grabbed at Megan, but she stopped resisting when she realized it was Ainsley. He spread his wings to shield her from the maddening crowd and steered her toward the exit.

"I'm guessing we just missed the rush," he said when they had finally reached the outside. He dodged two more girls bound for Tamtam's who paused at the doorway and voiced their admiration of Megan's appearance.

Ainsley couldn't blame them. She did look rather pretty, smiling her lopsided smile at the girls. Her cheeks glowed with a natural blush and the dress hugging her waist gave her flattering curves and an air of femininity. Had he not known what a disgusting tomboy Megan could be, he might have been inclined to flirt with her.

But true to form, once the other girls had disappeared, Megan adjusted her cleavage and said, "I wonder how I'm going to pee wearing this thing."

She wasn't sure why those words evoked a sigh from Ainsley, but while he adjusted his cloak between his wings, she gave him a quick once-over.

"You look nice," she said.

Now that his hair was clean and dried, it had the texture of velvet and the color of soft butter. The tone of his hair brought out flecks of gold in his eyes so they looked like two spheres of lapis lazuli. His skin had darkened from all the time they'd spent outdoors, and Megan could distinguish a few new freckles from the previous specks of dirt. Best of all, the malodorous cloud that had been hanging about him had been replaced by the clean scent of soap.

Ainsley grinned and ducked his head. "You don't look too bad either."

"There you two are!" Lady Maudred squeezed through a crowd at the doorway to reach them. "I have a banquet to attend, but don't forget that you need to be at the assembly house in exactly two hours for the promenade into the ballroom."

"Two hours?" Megan reached for her bodice again but changed her mind when Lady Maudred frowned at her. "What are we supposed to do until then?"

"Get some rest . . . or practice your dancing. Just don't dirty yourselves." She pinched both of their cheeks and bustled away.

Ainsley and Megan looked at one another.

"Dancing?" asked Megan. "I only know the Hylark Blade."

Ainsley placed a hand on her waist and nudged her toward the street. "Well, let's go practice it. Maybe we'll get lucky and sprain our ankles in the process."

———

The two hours passed more quickly than they had expected. Brighton had tracked them down in an empty alley where they were attempting the Hylark Blade with neither rhythm nor grace. Megan convinced Brighton to teach her and Ainsley a few new dance steps, but they couldn't seem to master any of the moves. Ainsley thought they would have done better if Brighton had spent more time correcting their missteps and less time staring at Megan, but since his wings and her feet kept getting in the way, it didn't seem to matter much. And none of them could ever remember laughing so hard.

At half past the first hour, the ringing of bells flooded the streets and spilled into the alleys and through building windows to remind people of the approaching Cotillion.

"We should get going," said Ainsley, running a hand through his hair and dusting off his pants.

"Good idea," said Megan. She gathered her skirts in one hand.

"Have a good time!" said Brighton.

Megan's skirts slipped through her fingers. "You're not coming?"

"Nah. Go on. Fancy dances aren't my kind of thing." Brighton waved them away, but Megan felt a tingling in her chest.

"I know you want to be there. Come with us." She gave him a hopeful smile.

Brighton puffed his chest out a little, then dropped his nonchalant act and sighed. "I . . . I'm not allowed. Criminal and all that."

"But nobody would know it's you," said Ainsley. "They'll just think you're our pet."

"If you want, I can drape you around my neck like a fur stole," said Megan.

Brighton smiled ruefully. "Thanks ever so, but I'd better not risk it. I don't want to extend this curse any longer than I have to."

"Okay." Megan lifted her skirts off the ground and out from underfoot. "Maybe we'll see you afterwards."

"We're going to be late." Ainsley grabbed Megan's arm and waved to Brighton. "Catch up with us tomorrow at least?"

"Of course." Brighton returned the wave and headed off in the opposite direction.

Megan glanced over her shoulder. "I wish he would have come with us," she told Ainsley. "Even if they wouldn't let him inside, he could have watched us through the window."

Ainsley steered her left at the street intersection toward a towering stone building whose roof was supported by thick patterned pillars. "Do you really think he would have enjoyed watching *us* have a good time knowing he couldn't join in?"

Megan shook her head. "You're right." They joined a line that had formed between the building's center pillars. "Tomorrow we'll take him to do something he normally can't do on his own."

A man standing in front of them turned around and nudged Ainsley. "I think the king of Raklund is trying to get your attention." He pointed toward the head of the line where Rayne was beckoning them forward.

"Ah, the royal treatment. Shall we?" Ainsley bent his elbow toward Megan and she draped a hand over it.

"But of course."

They both enjoyed the jealous looks and whispers from everyone they overtook, but when they passed Evren and several members of the community of Amdor, Megan leaned close to Ainsley.

"Remind me to tell you what Sari saw when she went back to Raklund." She pasted on a smile as they continued toward the front.

"Does it have something to do with our redheaded friend?" Ainsley asked out of the corner of his mouth.

"I don't know." Without breaking a stride, Megan curtsied to a young man that bowed to her. "But it bothered La . . . your grandmother enough when she heard it that she lied to me about its significance."

Ainsley wished she would elaborate, but they had reached Rayne who was standing with his grandfather, Frieden, and Lady Maudred.

"I'm glad you took me seriously about your punctuality and tidiness," said Lady Maudred. "Now then, Ainsley you will accompany me and be introduced as my grandson. Since everyone thinks your father died as a teenager, expect some gasps and looks of surprise."

"And Megan, if you'd like, you can accompany me as my niece," said Frieden. "Or you can be Rayne's partner for the evening."

Megan reached for Frieden's arm and smiled at Rayne. "If it won't break your heart, I'd rather enter with my uncle."

Rayne pressed a hand to his chest. "I'll do my best to live on," he said with a grin.

Trumpets blasted from within the building, and the few people standing in line ahead of them marched up the stairs and through the open double doors in a smart line. Bornias and Rayne filed in next, followed by Lady Maudred and Ainsley, then Megan and Frieden.

The last time Frieden had guided Megan into a room, the main hall in Raklund, the aesthetic wonder had robbed her of breath. Now entering the ballroom, she experienced the same sensation of overwhelming awe.

They stood at one of the four entrances to a symmetrically square room. Each doorway was centered on a wall crawling with golden vines, their crystal leaves tinkling together from even the slightest breeze. A staircase on one side led to a balcony level where tables and chairs had been set up overlooking the dance floor. The ceiling lacked any formal lighting, but it still shone bright as the sun, sparkling and shifting as hundreds of fairies drifted in lazy circles, making shadowy patterns far below.

Sealed archways had been carved to either side of each doorway and water cascaded from the keystone of each arch, spilling into a river that circled the inside of the room. Polished wooden footbridges connected the true doorways to the dance floor, and the pale blue water whispered beneath them, its path broken every few meters by a pedestal jutting from the river bottom. Upon these pedestals stood musicians with ocarinas and lutes and zithers, and as the first guests marched into the ballroom, they raised their instruments and played a processional melody.

While Ainsley and Megan took pleasure in being among the first to see the ballroom in all its splendor, they suffered the slight disadvantage of awkward silence from an empty room when their names were announced.

"Let's sit upstairs until the procession is complete," said Bornias. "This could take awhile."

Megan trusted Frieden to guide her up the stairs while she watched the fairies on the ceiling and the glowing light that appeared behind them. "How is the room lit?" she asked Frieden. "It can't be the fairies, can it?"

Frieden drew back a chair and waited for Megan to arrange her skirts and sit down. "I imagine the ceiling is painted with a coat of melted snow from the Icyll mountains. Do you remember how luminous it was?"

"Of course!" Megan brushed a vine with her arm, causing the leaves to jingle. "And is the ivy real?"

"It is, though it isn't native to Arylon."

"So it grows well in foreign places?" Megan could imagine the side of her house shining with golden vines, the leaves tinkling like windchimes in the winter gusts.

"I . . . don't think it would thrive where you imagine planting it," said Frieden with a smile. "Your home lacks the magical energy upon which the ivy feeds."

"Either that or you'd kill it by touching it too much," spoke up Ainsley from the next table.

Megan released the leaf she had been admiring with a sheepish grin. "I'm surprised you're not ripping the plants off the walls. Gold, Ainsley! Walls and walls of gold!"

Lady Maudred leaned toward them. "You're missing the promenade. Pay attention!"

Ainsley and Megan did their best to listen and watch, but the names and titles and faces all began to blur together and soon Ainsley was pulling his chair over to Megan's while the adults discussed the background of various people entering the room.

"So what did Sari see?" asked Ainsley.

Megan told him about Sari's visit to Raklund, and he raised an eyebrow. "Okay, something is *definitely* going on. First, Losen tells us that Evren plans to overthrow the kingdom and then Evren buys this magic-binding bag and now everyone in Raklund is acting like zombies?" He paused. "Are you sure Losen doesn't have anything to do with this?"

Megan rolled her eyes. "The people are *acting* like zombies, they aren't real zombies. Besides, Rayne told me about it when he and Bornias got here, and he told me that as soon as Losen and his mother received their pardons, they fled for some mountains on the coast."

"Oh. Well, then I don't know *what's* going on." Ainsley stood and glanced over the balcony at the ballroom floor. "But almost everyone's in."

"Where's Evren?" Megan joined him and scanned the crowd. "I think I know a way we can get more information."

"There." Ainsley pointed to where the handsome copper-haired man was speaking to a group of giggling women, all of whom were doing their best to position themselves closest to him.

"I have to get down there with him," said Megan, adjusting her cleavage again.

"Um." Ainsley pressed his lips together. "Megan, you look pretty and everything, but you can't compete with women twice your age."

"What? No!" Megan's face twisted into a horrible grimace. "I'm not going to try and seduce him, sicko! I just want to dance with him and ask some questions." She patted her heart. "And get some honest answers."

"Ohhh." Ainsley tapped the side of his head. "Good thinking. But I foresee a hitch in your plan." He nodded toward the base of the staircase where Garner was craning his neck to look over the crowd. Megan was surprised to see that for once, his entire body, even his arms, was clothed in regal-looking costume.

Megan smiled and waved over the balcony to him. "That's okay," she told Ainsley. "I have all night."

As the last person filtered through the ballroom doors, the orchestra struck up an upbeat tempo and everyone on the balcony level left their seats, making a beeline for the ballroom floor.

"First dance," said Lady Maudred, clutching Ainsley's arm.

"With my grandmother?" he couldn't help asking. He had spied two or three gorgeous girls his age huddling together, partnerless.

"With your *escort*," huffed Lady Maudred. "Unless you'd rather dance outside in the streets."

Ainsley placed a hand over hers. "No, here is good."

Frieden held his arm out to Megan. "I promise to keep this short."

She grinned at him and tucked her arm through his. "You don't have to, but you may *want* to the way I dance."

The first song was indeed a short one, for which Megan was grateful. Frieden didn't appear pained, but Megan had counted seven different times that she had stepped on his feet and one time that she had kicked him in the shin. When they parted and bowed, Frieden didn't ask for another dance, and Megan was certain it was more out of fear for his own limbs than out of politeness to Garner who was waiting on the side.

"Hello," said Garner. He grabbed Megan around the waist and spun her onto the dance floor as the next song began with a beautiful lute solo. He bowed his head and nuzzled his cheek against hers to whisper in her ear. "You look magnificent."

"Thank you," Megan kissed him and wrapped her arms around his neck. "You look nice, too. I've never seen you with so many clothes on."

Several people nearby chuckled, and Megan gasped when she realized the image her words had inspired. She hid her face in the curve of Garner's neck. "You knew what I meant, right? Dance me away from these people."

Garner was laughing, too. "But they want to hear the rest of the story . . . and so do I."

Megan scowled up at him playfully.

"I'm moving, I'm moving." He shifted them to the other side of the room.

"So, what were you doing while I was at Tamtam's?" she asked.

"I was being grateful that I *wasn't* at Tamtam's . . . and I was studying at the Pontsford library."

"More on The Folly? Ow!" She had lunged forward at the same time as Garner and they had knocked their knees together. "Sorry. Brighton only taught me the steps he knows, and those are the men's steps."

"I'm just glad my knee was there to protect other parts of me." He lifted Megan's hand over her head and she twirled beneath it. "But yes, I was doing more research on The Folly. In fact, after a couple more days, I should be ready to return there and begin the regeneration process."

"Oh." She lowered her arm with less enthusiasm than the dance called for. "I thought you'd be here longer than that."

"Well, you can accompany me and help me get settled." He pulled her close. "Then we could have some genuine time alone." He let his hands slip down her back, and Megan felt herself melting in his arms. "Just us," whispered Garner. "No annoying ferrets or flying boys."

Megan stiffened and walked to the edge of the floor. "Their names are Brighton and Ainsley, and they're not annoying. They're my friends."

Garner held up his hands. "All right, I was just teasing."

Megan's heart twinged, but she let it go. "Well, I won't be around much longer myself anyway. Ainsley and I have to head home soon. I miss my parents."

"I can understand that." Garner wrapped his arms around her again. "But you'll come back to visit, won't you?"

Megan kissed him and lingered with her lips against his. "Of course."

Another upbeat melody played, and Megan grinned. "The Hylark Blade."

"I know you know this one," he said.

They joined the other dancers and stepped and turned with the best. Megan only trod on someone's toes, a complete stranger's, once. By the end of the song, she was out of breath, but the orchestra started in with another fast-paced song. Since she was sweaty and didn't recognize the dance steps, she convinced Garner to sit out the next one with her.

"I'll get us something to drink," he said. "You go out and get some air." He held open the door opposite the ballroom which led onto a veranda spilling over with fragrant flowers blooming around and overhead amid fluffy, tasseled floor cushions just big enough for two. Several couples were already settled upon the ground, snuggling and kissing, but Megan had a feeling that she wouldn't be able to stand back up if she sat down. Instead, she walked to the railing of the veranda and stared up at the darkening sky, a welcome change from the intense lighting inside.

"How's the cotillion?"

Megan started and glanced to her right. Brighton was perched precariously on the railing, holding a flower between his teeth. He dropped it by Megan's hand. "A bit of lovely for a lovely girl," he said.

Megan blushed and lifted it to her nose. She'd never received flowers from a boy. "Thank you." She inhaled the sweet scent of the petals. "The cotillion's going fine, but I wish you could have joined us."

"I wouldn't fit in around this crowd," said Brighton.

"You fit in around me," said Megan, which brought a smile to Brighton's face.

"Your friend Evren is here, I noticed. I heard him enjoying some female company on the balcony earlier."

"Yeah, I'm going to dance with him in a bit so I can ask some questions."

"Good luck getting to him." Ainsley joined Megan and Brighton at the railing. "I've been watching him since he got here, and those women haven't left his side. *And* I heard him saying something to one of the other dignitaries about leaving early to prepare for the summit tomorrow."

"Dammit." Megan clenched her fist around the flower's stem. "How can we get all those women away from him at once?"

"You could try spilling wine on all of their dresses," said Brighton. "That'd send them shrieking. Course, it would also get you kicked out of the cotillion."

Ainsley watched Brighton run a paw over his whiskers and thump his tail against the railing. "I know something else that would send them shrieking," he said. "Brighton, how would you like to come to the cotillion?"

Ballroom Blitz

Megan was alone on the veranda when Garner brought her an iced berry juice, Ainsley and Brighton having taken refuge behind a rose-covered trellis. Megan smiled at Garner, then proceeded to chug the entire contents of the goblet in one swallow. "Let's go dance some more." She tugged Garner's hand, sloshing his drink on the ground.

"Wait a moment." Garner downed his own drink and set the glass on the railing. "Why don't we stay out here for a while?" He tilted Megan's head up and kissed her. "You taste like berries."

Ainsley turned to Brighton and stuck his finger down his throat.

"Oh, but I . . . really like this song," said Megan lamely.

"All right." Garner took the flower Megan was holding and tucked it into her hair. "Let's go back inside."

He draped his arm around Megan and ushered her toward the door. As they passed the trellis of roses, Megan turned her head slightly and nodded to her hidden friends.

"Are you ready to move?" Ainsley asked Brighton.

In answer, the ferret climbed up Ainsley's backside, slipping under his cloak and crawling between his wings. He flattened himself as close to Ainsley's back as possible, but when Ainsley checked over his shoulder, he could still see a lump. "Great. I look like a hunchback."

"Don't worry, mate," came Brighton's muffled voice. "Everyone's too busy staring at your pretty face to notice anything else."

Brighton couldn't have been further from the truth. While it was true Ainsley had had no shortage of dance partners or attractive girls to talk to, each one had made it a point to compliment him on his wings. The attention had been flattering at first, especially since he was the only person in the room, besides the fairies, who could fly.

After an overabundance of looks and suggestive comments about his wingspan, however, Ainsley began to wonder if he would have been as popular without them. He'd seen several guys just as good-looking as he moping against the wall, the only discerning difference being their lack of wings. Had Ainsley never contracted the Illness, he would have been just like them. He supposed he should be grateful people weren't ridiculing him instead, but he wouldn't have minded if someone pointed out one other good thing, *anything*, that they noticed about him.

"Here we go. Remember, the launch word is 'cotillion,'" he whispered. He strode onto the bridge that led to the ballroom floor but was stopped before he reached the other side by two girls he hadn't spoken to before. He smiled hopefully at them. "Hello."

He considered it a bad omen when both girls giggled, and one pushed another forward. She made a silly slapping gesture at her friend and turned to Ainsley.

"Um . . . is it true you have a wingspan bigger than your body?" Her friend giggled and hit her on the shoulder.

Ainsley sighed. "Yep."

"Can we see it?" asked the other girl in an awed voice.

Checking for clearance on either side, Ainsley spread his wings out to their fullest. When they opened, it sounded like a ship's sails snapping taut as they captured the wind. The girls clapped their hands as if Ainsley had just performed an amazing feat.

"Here's a thought," whispered Brighton. "Dance with one of them and get the other to ask Garner. That frees up Megan."

Ainsley surveyed the ballroom and saw Megan with her head on Garner's shoulder. She was laughing at something he said, but her eyes were on Evren and his entourage. Ainsley refocused his attention on the two girls in front of him, trying to discern which one would be less annoying. His decision was made for him when the girl who had asked about his wingspan placed her hand in his.

"Be my partner," she pressed against him, "and *lift* me to the skies so we might dance among the stars."

The lump on Ainsley's back snickered, and he cleared his throat loudly to mask it. "You know what? My friend over there has been telling me all night how much he wants to dance with you." He pointed to Garner. "That girl he's with just won't leave him alone. I'll bet he'd love it if you cut in."

The girl gazed in the direction Ainsley was pointing, and he could see her eyes light up when they fell upon Garner. "He *does* deserve better than that big-eared frump, doesn't he?"

Brighton stirred beneath Ainsley's cloak. "Listen here, you troll!"

On the guise of scratching between his shoulders, Ainsley reached back and smacked Brighton.

"What did you say?" asked the girl.

"I said . . . uh . . . do you hear trolls?" Ainsley nudged the girl toward the dance floor. "I'll go check for them. You ask my friend to dance."

The girl tugged her bodice a bit lower so her chest spilled over the top, then gathered her skirts and strode purposefully toward Garner.

Ainsley turned to the other girl. "Would you like to dance?"

She smiled at him coquettishly. "I knew you preferred me. That was the real reason you sent her to dance with your friend."

"Wow. Nothing gets by you," said Ainsley with a fraction of a smile. "Come on." He herded her toward the corner of the room where Evren had settled himself. His latest female-charming stunt was proving how strong he was by lifting a woman in each arm. They squealed and kicked, begging to be let down, though their arms were wrapped firmly about Evren's neck.

Ainsley spun his dance partner so he could see the opposite side of the room. Garner and Megan separated, the girl Ainsley had sent working herself into Garner's arms. He protested, but Megan laughed and made a gesture that indicated it was okay for him to dance with the other girl. Then Garner and his new dance partner twirled off and Megan was slipping through the crowd in Ainsley's direction.

When Megan was only a few feet away, Ainsley asked his dance partner in a loud voice, "So, are you having fun at the cotillion?"

Brighton unhooked his claws from Ainsley's back and dropped to the floor. With as loud a growl as he could muster, he launched himself at the dress of one of the women with Evren. She gave a prissy squeal and shook out her skirts at which point Brighton proceeded to climb around to the backside of her dress and journey upwards. All thoughts of propriety lost, the woman shrieked and flailed her arms and legs, shaking her torso in an effort to loose Brighton.

At first, Evren and the other women had no clue what she was upset about and, perhaps assuming she had gone mad, shifted away from her a few paces. Then, Brighton climbed upon the woman's shoulder and hissed at the rest of Evren's entourage. He leapt from his perch and landed among the feet of the other women just as his first victim fainted and crumpled to the floor.

Ainsley, Megan, and others standing nearby watched the spectacle with horrified fascination. There were more screams as Brighton darted between pairs of slender feet in an attempt to send the women fleeing from Evren, and for a moment, Megan thought she had won her moment alone with the redheaded lothario.

Unfortunately, Evren felt the need to rescue his many damsels in distress and reached down for Brighton, snatching him around the middle. Brighton bit him hard on the finger, and Evren flung the ferret away, elbowing one of the women in the process. The blow tipped her off her feet and she stumbled backwards in the direction of the river that snaked around the dance floor. The woman teetered on the edge and grabbed at the sash of one of her comrades for leverage.

The second woman had lifted a leg to let Brighton skitter past and lacked the strength in her remaining leg to support her weight and that of another. Both women toppled backwards into the river, dousing the musicians and their instruments and sending a wave of water onto the dance floor. People scurried out of the water's path, terrified at the thought of ruining their wardrobes. The wet floor combined with the smooth stone became as slick as oil and soon dignitaries and their partners were sliding and tumbling across the room.

Ainsley and Megan looked at one another and burst out laughing.

Megan spotted Evren atop the bridge where the floor was still dry and gestured at him. "I have . . . I have to go talk to Evren!" she sputtered between chuckles. Fixing a serious expression on her face, she walked carefully toward him under the semblance of going for higher ground. As she reached the base of the bridge, she allowed her feet to slide a little. "Whoops!"

Evren caught her beneath the arms.

"Oh thank you, Sir Sandor!" she gushed.

"You're quite welcome. I'd hate to see you ruin that pretty dress." Even amidst chaos, he was ever the charmer, flashing a dazzling smile.

Megan lowered her head and toed the ground bashfully. "You're too kind. I bought it in Raklund. You're from there, right? I hear people talk about you all the time."

"Only good things, I hope," he said with a chuckle.

Megan let out a high fake laugh. "They miss you. They say you haven't been around much recently. When was the last time you were in Raklund?"

"Oh, it's been months now," he said.

Megan's chest began to ache. "That's too bad."

She tried to think of a subtle way to bring up what Sari had seen, but she could tell time was running out. The dance floor was being magicked dry and the poor guests who had gotten wet were being comforted. Someone had managed to find Brighton and he was being carried, in a cage, to Pocky Nates. Megan knew that Evren would be walking away at any moment.

"Uh . . . I ask because," Megan fought for an excuse. She glanced at Ainsley who raised his eyebrows and shrugged. "Because . . . um . . ."

"Excuse me, won't you?" Evren patted Megan on the side of the shoulder. "I have some business to tend to." He smiled at her but his eyes, cold and hard, were on Brighton. "I want that animal destroyed." He stormed down the bridge and across the floor.

"No!" Megan hurried after him. "He didn't know any better!" She stared at Brighton through the cage. "He's just a harmless ferret."

Playing along, Brighton squeaked and chirped, rubbing his fur against the bars of the cage.

"He isn't harmless," said Evren. "He bit me and hissed at these women. Clearly, he's rabid or has some other illness."

"No, he doesn't!" spoke up Ainsley. "He's my pet, and he was just scared."

"Why did you bring him to the cotillion?" asked Pocky. "An event like this is no place for animals."

"I asked him to." The crowd parted, and Garner pushed his way forward. "He told me his pet was sick, and as a nascifriend-in-training, it is my duty to help. I didn't have time to meet with him earlier, so I asked him to bring the animal here."

There were appreciative murmurs from the crowd, and the girl that had cut in while Megan and Garner had been dancing gazed up at him admiringly.

"I think we can overlook this little mishap," said Lady Maudred, "don't you agree, Sir Sandor?"

With an enormous whoosh of skirts and capes, everyone on the dance floor turned to Evren, who flashed his most gracious smile.

"Of course, but I do think it best these young men take their ferret and their business outside of the ballroom."

"Agreed," said Pocky. He handed Brighton's cage to Ainsley. "You may release him once you've reached the street."

Though Garner had explained away the incident, Ainsley still felt all eyes upon him as he walked across the dance floor toward the entrance. When he reached the section of the crowd where his grandmother was standing, she fell into step beside him and he cringed. He had a feeling she didn't plan to overlook his "mishap."

Garner extricated himself from his new female admirer and hurried after Ainsley like a nascifriend with a task. His eyes flickered up to Megan, and her heart sank at the frustrated and hurt way his brows furrowed together.

"Excuse me," she said, elbowing through the crowd that surged toward the dance floor. After Ainsley and Garner's departure, the partygoers were eager for the dancing to recommence.

When Megan finally slipped outside, it was to find Ainsley sitting on a bench where Lady Maudred was chastising him while Garner fiddled with the door of Brighton's cage. The moment he unlatched it, Brighton forced the door open with his body and shook himself vigorously.

"Thanks for that," said Brighton. "I don't care much for tight spaces, and I don't care at all for dying."

"Yes, thanks."

Garner turned around, and Megan was waiting for him with an apologetic grin. "You didn't have to help us, but you did," she said. "My hero." She closed her eyes and leaned toward him, but Garner moved to the side so that she stumbled forward, kissing the air.

"You're welcome," he said. "Good night." He walked away, headed toward the south end of Pontsford.

"Garner! Wait!" Megan spun and got tangled in her skirts, falling face and palms into the dirt. Garner didn't so much as look back.

Ainsley helped her to her feet. "You okay?"

She ignored him and hefted her skirts over one arm, chasing Garner down the avenue. "Garner! Why are you mad?"

"You really have to ask that?" Garner continued his brisk stride which Megan found herself jogging to keep up with.

"I'm sorry I didn't tell you what we were doing, but I didn't think you would like it."

"You're right. I don't."

"Why not?" Megan frowned. She hadn't expected him to agree with her so quickly. "We weren't doing anything wrong."

Garner finally stopped to face her. "You snuck an animal into a formal event to scare guests away from Evren so you could entertain some far-fetched notion that he's evil incarnate." Garner raised his arms to the sky. "*What* about that is *right*?"

"It isn't a far-fetched notion," said Megan. "Ainsley and I—"

Garner pointed towards the assembly hall. "*He* is a bad influence on you. And so is that thief ferret."

"He isn't, and leave Brighton out of this! He's only trying to help Ainsley and me."

Garner snorted. "To serve some purpose of his own, I'm sure. I read about him in the Pontsford library this afternoon. Do you know how many people he's swindled and stolen from?"

"He hasn't stolen from *me*." Megan crossed her arms. "Or Ainsley . . . I'm pretty sure."

"Of course he hasn't stolen from you. He knows you're friends with the king of Raklund, so he's waiting for you to let your guard down so he can use you to get into the Hall of Staves."

"What? Give me—" Megan lowered her voice when she realized passersby were staring. "Give me a break. Brighton's my friend. He's not using me."

"I hope you're right." Garner closed the distance between them. "Because I won't be here forever to protect you."

Megan leaned into Garner, but his arms stayed at his side. Her heart dropped into her stomach. "I don't need protecting. I need you to not be mad at me."

At last Garner made contact with her, but it was only to squeeze her arm. "Just be careful who you're friends with. The ones who seem innocent can turn on you when you least expect it. I'll see you tomorrow?"

Megan nodded. "Of course." She watched Garner stroll down the street, and even though she knew he was wrong about Brighton, she ran her fingers over her heart to make sure the Pearl of Truth was still there.

Rogues in Action

"I still want to know what Evren's up to," said Megan. She, Ainsley, and Brighton were eating lunch in their sleeping area behind the stage, having been restricted to the tavern as punishment.

"Me too," said Ainsley. "Especially after Evren lied to you about being in Raklund. I told Gran everything we knew, but she didn't take me seriously."

"Did you tell her that we think Evren's going to do something at the summit?" Megan tossed a piece of fruit in the air and caught it with her mouth.

"She says there's no way he's going to try something in front of so many powerful people. Powerful, as in magic powerful."

"Well, I think she's wrong," said Megan. "I wish we could find out what Evren was doing right now." She tossed another piece of fruit in the air, but this time Brighton caught it and started to nibble on it.

"After what happened last night, he's probably out shooting ferrets." He looked up at Megan. "Sorry we got you in trouble with Garner."

Megan stuck out her tongue and blew a raspberry. "Don't worry about it. He's just upset that we still think Evren's up to something."

"Well, he is," said Ainsley. "Whether Garner wants to believe it or not.

"I know." Megan offered Brighton the rest of her fruit and wiped her sticky fingers on her pants. "I want to try talking to Bornias. Maybe *he'd* believe us."

"Good luck," said Ainsley around a mouthful of parbar fruit. "He left for the summit first thing this morning."

"Well, what about Rayne?"

Ainsley pulled an oversized piece of fruit out of his mouth and sucked up the excess juices. "Let me rephrase. He, Rayne, and Frieden all left first thing this morning."

Megan cursed and pounded her heel against the floor. "Lady Maudred it is, then."

"Uh . . . no," said Brighton. "I bumped into her when I came here. She was on her way out."

"Wait." Megan jumped to her feet. "So nobody's here to make sure we don't leave?" She bolted for the door without another word.

Ainsley and Brighton looked at one another and scrambled after her, but Ainsley stopped on the porch of The Swig and Sleep. "Oh, great."

Garner stood in the street with Megan, hugging her close.

"If that doesn't bring up breakfast, I don't know what will," said Brighton.

Megan turned to him and Ainsley, all smiles. "Garner's going to help us. Let's go!"

When they reached the assembly house, to Megan's dismay there was an even larger crowd than there had been for the cotillion. She craned her neck and searched for a thatch of short red hair amidst the many women's updos. It took but a second for her to spot Evren, and on the guise of being one of his infatuated fans, she pushed through the throng of giggling women.

Megan progressed at a snail's pace toward Evren until Bit slid down to the sleeve of Megan's tunic and began swinging her spiked tail from side to side. The women around Megan gave her a wider berth, along with several nasty looks, but soon she was standing behind Evren. He had bent close to the ear of a stunning blond whose hand rested upon his arm in a coquettish fashion. Tucked under Evren's other arm was a large black bag. Megan worked her way back out of the crowd and rejoined her friends.

"Whatever he's got in there . . . it's no little bottle of poison. And he's being pretty protective of it. We need to let Lady Maudred or Bornias or *someone* know."

"They're probably already inside," said Ainsley. He flexed his wings and hovered above the crowd. "Should we try and ask someone?"

"I guess so, but I don't think it would do much good at this point," said Megan. "I doubt they'd want to come back out. They'd probably tell us to wait until later."

"We could try to get a message to them," said Ainsley.

Megan shot him a withering glance. "What are we going to tell the messenger? 'Don't drink the water'? 'Evren is going to kill everyone'? We'd be blacklisted from the city."

"There is another option," said Brighton, rising high on his haunches. "We could sneak in and deliver the message ourselves."

Garner shook his head. "We can't sneak in."

"Well, if you want to be a goody-goody, you can wait here, then," said Ainsley.

Garner spun to face Ainsley, jaw clenched. "While it's pathetic that you have no moral compass, I actually meant that we *physically* can't sneak in with all the guards monitoring the exits. It's impossible."

Brighton climbed onto Ainsley's shoulder and stared from the assembly hall to the buildings around it. "Difficult, yes. Impossible, no. You'll end up with a few scratches and bruises before it's over, though."

"I've been through worse," said Megan, rotating her wrist. Weeks earlier, she'd broken it, fighting with Captain Kyviel and his men in Raklund's dungeon for Ainsley's freedom. Ainsley had managed to heal it with magic, but it still throbbed on occasion.

"This way, then," said Brighton, jerking his head to one side. He skittered down an alley that ran the length of the building and emptied into a narrower street. Instead of attempting to enter the building, however, Brighton crossed the street and scurried up to the steps of a candle shop opposite the building.

Megan tilted her head back and noticed a portal window in the candle shop's second story. "I really hope this doesn't involve leaping from one roof to the other."

"This from the girl who jumped twenty-five feet into a pool of water?" asked Brighton. He leapt for the door handle several times before Megan reached out and turned it for him.

"That was different," she said. "Gravity was already pulling me down."

Brighton pushed open the door and struggled to hold it in place. "Everyone in."

Compared to the noise and clutter of the street, the candle shop was a serene haven. The air held a slight warmth and smelled of melting wax. The few patrons of the candle shop spoke in voices that were almost whispers, as if the breath from their regular speech would extinguish the dozens of lit candles festooning every flat surface.

The various hues of the candles corresponded with the décor of each shop room, and separate containers for scented candles allowed for each delicious aroma to be experienced individually.

"What's on the second floor?" asked Megan, removing the lid from a parbar-scented candle and breathing in the cinnamon and citrus.

"The specialty candles," said Brighton, "and us."

He led the way up the stairs, which were draped with a garland of round candles strung on waxed rope. They stepped onto the second-floor landing, and the shop was plunged into darkness.

"Woah!" Megan balked and fell back against Garner. "Brighton?" She felt something grip her leg.

"Don't worry. It's just a bit of magic so customers can see the effects of the candles when there's no light."

Megan squinted and blinked, letting her eyes adjust. She could see a table in the center of the room with an enormous pillar candle sitting atop it. The wick of the candle curved like a horseshoe, and both ends were buried in the wax. The arch of the wick burned with silver flame, and on the top of the arch danced the image of a scantily clad gypsy girl.

"Now, that's a candle *every* cottage needs," said Brighton, scampering over to the table.

Garner tugged at Megan's hand, but she hung back. "You guys go ahead," she said. "I need to wait for my eyes to adjust."

Garner followed after Brighton, but as Ainsley shuffled forward, Megan grabbed his arm in the darkness.

"I should be able to see everything!" she whispered.

Ainsley bent his head too low and smacked it against hers. "What do you mean? You lost your vision?"

"No!" Megan rubbed her skull. "This illusion of darkness shouldn't be here for me. The Pearl of Truth, remember?"

Ainsley frowned. "I thought it revealed the truth of deceptions. I don't think this qualifies as deceptive."

Megan looked out the window, which revealed not even a glint of light. "Are you sure?"

"Well, they're not trying to trick you into thinking it's dark, are they? They just want the cool candle effects to show up better."

Megan considered this. "I guess you could be right."

"Look," said Ainsley in a solemn tone, "if you're concerned, I think you should talk to Garner. He's very wise."

Megan felt a pinching in her chest. "Ouch!"

"And manly," Ainsley added.

The pain increased. "Ainsley!"

"Oh, and did I forget to mention how fond I am of him?"

"Stop!" Megan laughed and clutched at her heart. "You proved that it still works, okay?"

Ainsley nudged her forward. "Let's go join the others before Brighton tries to mate with the dancing-girl candle."

"Everyone, over here." Brighton beckoned them to the windowsill, and they crowded around him. "There's the assembly hall."

"Okay. Sooo, how are we going to use the candles to get in there?" asked Megan.

"Right, well, I figured we could pull the wicks out of all of them, tie them together and *swing* to the other building. As long as the sun doesn't catch the wicks on fire, we should be all right." Brighton stared at Megan until her jaw dropped. He grinned and was rewarded with laughter from Ainsley.

"Hilarious." Megan crossed her arms. "What's the *real* plan with the candles?"

"They actually don't factor in at all," said Brighton. "I wanted you to see my entrance point," he pointed to a small hole in the roof, "and yours." He pointed to a shop beside the building. The second floor had a window, which drew level with a large balcony bordering the building.

Megan bit her lip. "Um . . . you don't think people are going to see a bunch of teenagers climbing out a window and onto the balcony of a government building?"

"Not while Ainsley's creating a distraction, no."

Ainsley had been keen on the plan until he heard those words. "Excuse me?"

"While I'm letting Megan and Garner in, you need to draw attention away from the side of the building," said Brighton.

Ainsley looked out the window at the growing crowd. "How?"

Brighton shrugged. "Pretend you're dying or light something on fire. Enough to make you interesting but not enough to get you kicked out of Pontsford."

Ainsley glanced at Megan who pretended to be fascinated with a loose thread on her collar. It was obvious she wasn't going to protest lest she get left outside instead.

"What about Wilderness Boy?" he pointed at Garner. "He didn't even want to go in the first place."

Brighton shook his head. "It'll be easier for you to escape if the authorities come after you."

"Fine." Ainsley scowled and started toward the staircase. "I'll be your flying martyr."

"Great!" said Brighton, either not picking up on Ainsley's sarcasm or not caring. "Let's get started. We're running out of time."

Ainsley remained in the alley while Brighton scrambled up the roof of the building and Megan and Garner headed for the store beside it.

"I feel bad leaving Ainsley behind," said Megan, looking over her shoulder where Ainsley was leaning dejectedly against a barrel.

"I think he'll be just fine," said Garner. "Looks like he's going to have some company." He pointed at a pretty girl who rounded the corner and approached Ainsley.

Ainsley noticed her as well, and straightened. "Afternoon," he said with a flash of his sparkling white teeth.

"Nice wings." The girl reached out and touched one. "Do you ever take people flying?"

"Depends on the passenger," said Ainsley, holding his arms open.

The girl stepped into them and wrapped her arms around Ainsley's neck. She squealed as Ainsley beat his wings and left the ground. "Don't drop me!"

"Oh, give me a break," said Megan, rolling her eyes. "He'd better not forget what he's here for."

"He won't." Garner grabbed her arm and steered her into the store which, to Megan's chagrin, sold women's toiletries and perfumes.

The merchant hurried to greet her latest customers, but upon seeing the teenagers and their worn, less-than-regal clothing, she slowed her pace to a stroll. "Hello. Can I help you?"

"Um . . ." Megan peeked out the window. She couldn't see Ainsley anywhere. "We're just looking for a gift for my mother. Is it all right if we see what you have upstairs?"

"Of course." The merchant gestured vaguely toward the staircase. "Let me know if you need anything."

Megan grabbed Garner's hand and climbed the steps two at a time. At the top of the stairs, a heady perfume saturated the air and several women turned well-coiffed heads to see who approached.

Megan pasted on a huge smile. "Oh, I'm sorry. We were just looking for my . . . um . . . sister." The wheels in Megan's head began to turn. "She wanted me to let her know as soon as Evren started handing out invitations to his post-Carnival celebration." She shrugged. "Oh, well.

Since there was only a limited number of invitations available, I'm sure she's already waiting at the assembly hall."

Megan heard the boards creak and saw one of the women sway back and forth. "Excuse me," she said, pushing past the others and hurrying down the steps. The remaining women regarded Megan and Garner for a moment, then bustled downstairs after their companion.

"Good plan," said Garner while Megan peered down the stairs after the women.

The merchant stopped one of them at the door. After the two exchanged quick words, she fled her own shop, chasing the other Evren worshipers.

"Yeah, well, they'll be back soon," said Megan. "And they'll be pissed." She approached the window that opposed the assembly hall's balcony.

The door on the balcony swung open, and Megan darted to the side of the window. She peeked around the corner and smiled when she saw a familiar shock of white hair bobbing behind the railing. Brighton raised his head just enough to make sure Megan could see him, then ducked down again.

"Well, Brighton's ready," she said, peering down at the crowd amassing in front of the building. "Now if Super-Ainsley would just quit flying Lois Lane around the city . . ."

She gasped and stumbled backwards as a streak of blonde hair and wings shot past the window, accompanied by flowing dark hair and billowing skirts. A delighted squeal grew louder and faded as Ainsley carried his passenger between the buildings and straight for the crowd.

Ainsley gritted his teeth. He hoped Megan had seen where he was heading for he was beginning to feel the weight of the girl that had wrapped herself about him. The crowd, who had been bouncing up and down on their toes to catch last glimpses of Evren and the master mage, didn't notice Ainsley until his female passenger gave a delighted shriek and clung to him even tighter.

"Faster, boy, faster!" she cried.

Ainsley cringed and wondered if the girl saw him as nothing more than an amusement. He swooped down low over the sea of heads, and the crowd raised cries of alarm, followed by curses as Ainsley climbed skyward again.

"Once more, my winged pet!" squealed the girl.

Ainsley squeezed the breath out of her but said nothing. By now, all eyes of the crowd were fixed on him. He chanced a glimpse between the buildings and saw Garner leap onto the balcony.

"Once more then," said Ainsley. His muscles were starting to shake from carrying so much extra weight for so long, and as he dove down, he faced the horrible realization that he wouldn't be able to pull back up.

The girl screamed again, though this time in fear, and she and Ainsley collided with a few unfortunate crowd members who hadn't the sense to duck. Those people were knocked backwards into others who weren't at all pleased by the rough physical contact and showed their displeasure with a few choice shoves. Hands slapped at faces, fists flew into stomachs, and soon the distinguished crowd had become a maddening brawl.

Ainsley helped the girl to her feet. "I'm so sorry," he said.

The girl, who was now missing a front tooth and sporting a bloody lip, raised her skirts and aimed a forceful kick at Ainsley's groin. He dodged the attack and the girl ended up flat on her back, shrieking with rage. Ainsley debated helping her again when he remembered why he had created the distraction in the first place.

Forcing his way to the edge of the crowd, he glanced toward the balcony where Megan was watching him with a worried expression. Ainsley waved her on, and Megan disappeared into the building.

"Where's the young flying man who started all this trouble?" he heard someone in the crowd yell.

For the first time in a while, Ainsley wished he didn't have wings. He knew there was no way he could duck down and blend in with everyone else.

"Dammit." He sprinted forward a few paces and launched into the air just as someone shouted, "There he is!"

"Well spotted, eagle eye," he muttered. He hoped Megan, Brighton, and Wilderness Boy were having better luck than he.

A Commanding Presence

Megan bit her lip and listened to the mob chasing after Ainsley before she closed the balcony door behind her, drowning out the angry cries.

"I hope he'll be okay," she whispered to Garner. They stood with their backs pressed against the wall, waiting for Brighton to give them the okay to move on.

Garner squeezed her hand. "The worst thing they'll do is oust him from the city."

"Yeah," Megan smiled ruefully, "after they beat him senseless."

"If he has to, I'm sure he'll use magic."

"I don't think he would." A realization hit Megan, and she smiled. "You know, I don't think he's used magic since he got over the Illness. I'm impressed."

Garner snorted and shook his head. "I haven't used magic for that long either."

"And I'm just as impressed by you." Megan blew him a kiss.

Brighton sidled up to them. "There's nobody walking the upper platform. Let's move." He led the way to a vertical support beam that connected to the rafters overhead. "I know you're a good climber, but can you handle this?"

Megan ran her hands over the smooth, painted wood. "With boots on? No. With boots off . . . no." She plucked Bit from her pocket and lifted the narshorn to the support beam. Bit leapt from Megan's palm and dug her claws and tail into the wood, shimmying up to the rafter with ease. "Show off." Megan smiled at her pet.

"Your turn," Garner told Megan. "I'll give you a boost." He knelt and formed a basket with his hands.

Megan stepped into his palms, and he pushed upward until she could wrap her fingers around the rafter overhead. He straightened and helped her onto the plank the rest of the way.

Straddling the beam, Megan lowered her upper body until her chest was touching the wood. She extended a hand to Garner, but he shook his head.

"You're strong, but you're not strong enough to lift me up." With that, he wrapped his hands around the vertical beam and shimmied his way to the top, climbing over the rafter opposite Megan's where she sat open-mouthed.

"That was amazing."

Garner winked at her. "It's not my first time to scale a building."

"So, you're saying you didn't always have a moral compass?" Megan wiggled her eyebrows. "Climbed through a few girl's bedroom windows?"

"Of course not," said Garner, his blushing cheeks split by a grin. "I used to sneak into chapels."

Brighton appeared on the vertical beam between them. "The guards will be making their rounds soon. We should get over *there*."

He pointed over Megan's shoulder to a junction where all the rafters came together. Dangling from the very center was a hooded chandelier the size of a wagon wheel. "If we can make it to the center of that, we can watch everything without being seen. It may get a trifle warm, though."

Megan groaned. "So I'm facing the wrong way?" She lifted her legs and swiveled on her stomach, inching her way forward until the floor below her disappeared. She felt something crawl up her body and froze. Then she heard Bit's familiar squeak and felt the narshorn settle on her back. Megan relaxed and looked down on a mass of people standing around long benches that had been placed behind even longer tables.

Megan scanned the crowd until she saw, with some satisfaction, that Bornias, Frieden, and Lady Maudred were huddled together talking.

"I really hope they're talking about Evren." She whispered over her shoulder to Garner, though with the clamor of voices rising from the floor, there was no danger of anyone hearing her. She knew, however, that people might still see her, so she continued to move toward the chandelier.

Pocky Nates stepped onto a dais at the front of the room. "Ladies and gentlemen, the summit will commence within a moment. Please find your seats."

Bornias, Frieden, and Lady Maudred chose a bench toward the edge of the room and soon the entire audience was seated, their voices quieted to the occasional cough or last-minute comment. Pocky gave an approving nod. "Thank you. And now to introduce our first speaker, I give you the newest member of the Community of Amdor, former lieutenant governor of the Silvan Sentry, Evren Sandor."

"They actually picked him?" Megan's hands lost their grip on the beam, and she smacked down on the hard wood with chest and chin. The applause from the crowd drowned the multitude of curse words she spat, and she massaged her jaw while praying Garner and Brighton had been looking the other way.

"You okay?" a voice sounded beside her ear and Megan almost fell off the beam completely at seeing Brighton's face beside hers. "I'm fine," she gasped.

"Sorry about the fright." He climbed over Megan and watched Evren mount the steps to the dais while he waved at the audience. "He still has that bag with him."

"It doesn't matter," said Garner, crawling forward on a beam parallel to theirs. "I'm sure the guards checked everyone's bags before they were allowed to enter."

The crowd quieted, and Evren flashed them his sparkly, debonair smile. "Good afternoon to you all. First and foremost, I am thrilled to be a part of the Community of Amdor and I thank those wizards for allowing me into their midst. I would say I've been humbled, but those of you who know me, know that's not possible."

A ripple of laughter crossed the audience and Evren waited for it to die down. "Before I bring Master Mage Oh to the stage, I wanted to share something with all of you that played a crucial part in my acceptance into the community of Amdor."

Megan leaned over as far as she dared, waiting for Evren to reach into his bag. Instead, he pushed back one side of his cloak to reveal something golden glinting at his waist.

"You won't be alarmed or surprised to see this," he told the audience. He reached for the golden item, a long, thin cone, and held it over his head. "In fact, you will all respect me for it and bow down before me."

Megan clapped a hand over her mouth to keep a laugh from escaping. She couldn't believe how deluded Evren had become since being asked into the community of Amdor. She glanced over at Garner to see if he shared in the humor, but he was staring open-mouthed at the crowd below. Megan followed his stunned gaze and gasped.

Benches were being pushed back from tables, and men and women stepped into the aisles, dropping to their knees before Evren.

Megan swallowed hard. "No . . . they can't . . ." She looked to where Bornias, Frieden, and Lady Maudred had been sitting, knowing they would never bow to Evren. When she found them by the wall, her heart slipped into her boots.

The men and woman who had helped her battle evil so many times before were now kneeling before it with everyone else, and their heads were lowered. Megan dug her fingernails into the sides of the beam. "No!"

"They can't be serious," Brighton whispered back to her. "This is a bit of show. That's all."

But nobody in the audience appeared to be laughing. They remained in their genuflection until Evren bade them to rise. "You are my servants and protectors. You shall bring forth any who speak against me. Do you understand?"

There was a murmur of assent, and Evren then held his magic-binding bag open before him. "Our powers are now one," he told the audience. "You no longer need to rely on magical staves or charms. Bring them here."

Almost as a singular being, the crowd swept toward the front of the room, reaching beneath capes and garments to drop their magic items into the bag. By the time the last person left the dais, the bag was bulging and Evren was no longer able to suspend it in his arms. But he frowned.

"Bornias, you did not bring me the Staff of Lexiam," he shook the loose fabric at the top of the bag at Bornias. "Do you wish to displease me?"

Bornias dropped to one knee. "Forgive me, Master, but my grandson is now keeper of the staff. Alas, I did not see him enter the chamber."

Evren's frown transformed into his usual smile. "Very well, my servant. Please find him, and bring him here while the rest of us make plans to unite the lands under my almighty power."

Megan cast hate-filled eyes on Evren. "Bornias is *no-body's* servant." She clenched her jaw and grabbed hold of Brighton's ankle. "Let's go. We have to warn Ainsley and Rayne." She swiveled back around on her bag and called over to Garner. "We have to let the others know."

Garner turned to Megan with a dazed expression and nodded. "We must spread the word."

Megan scrambled across the beam as if Evren were chasing her and jumped down after Brighton who was trying to open the balcony door.

"We don't have time for any more sneaking around," she said as Garner dropped down beside her. "We're going out the front door."

Despite her brave statement, they peeked down the staircase before taking the steps two at a time to the bottom floor. Megan led them down a hallway that looked as if it might take them to the outside, but before she reached the end, Ainsley and Rayne stepped into her path.

"Look who it is." Ainsley turned to Rayne with a smug expression. "I told you she was down here."

Megan skidded to a halt and felt Brighton smack into the back of her boot. "Ainsley! You're not . . ." she gulped, "you're not one of them, are you?"

Ainsley and Rayne looked at one another and then back at Megan. "One of who?" Ainsley noticed that she seemed a little pale and her eyes were drawn wide open. On her shoulder, Bit crouched, barbed tail poised to strike. "Are you guys okay?"

Megan placed her hand to her chest and said a quick prayer. "You're not one of Evren's followers, are you?"

Ainsley balked and looked past her to Garner and Brighton, but their faces offered no clue to Megan's strange behavior. "Why would you ask something like that?"

"Please!" Megan's eyes were brimming with tears now. Bit dropped her defensive stance and snuggled into Megan's neck, making a clicking sound in an effort to soothe her master.

But Megan couldn't be calmed. "Just answer yes or no! Are you one of Evren's followers?" She stepped in front of Rayne. "Are you?"

He shook his head. "No."

"Are you?" She took Ainsley's hand and a tear spilt down her cheek and splashed upon his wrist.

"No." Ainsley grabbed Megan by the shoulders. "Megan, what's going on?"

She opened her mouth but only a squeak came out before she burst into tears. Ainsley glanced at Garner, expecting him to comfort her, but he stood against the wall looking dazed. Ainsley pulled Megan to him, and Brighton climbed onto Megan's shoulder, rubbing against her cheek comfortingly.

"Brighton, what happened?" asked Ainsley.

The ferret turned sad, beady eyes to him. "We were right about Evren," he said. "But it's worse than we thought."

Loved Ones Lost

Brighton started to explain what they'd seen, but Megan wiped her eyes and put a hand on his arm. Despite the horror she'd just witnessed, she remembered Rayne was still in danger. "We need to find a hiding place."

Rayne glanced up and down the corridor. "There." He pointed to an open doorway and they followed him, Megan pulling the still-dazed Garner behind her. She pushed him into the room and checked to make sure nobody had seen them before joining the others and locking the door.

"What *happened?*" Ainsley asked again.

Megan took a deep breath and explained how they'd climbed into the rafters and seen Evren at the dais, demanding everyone to follow him.

"At first, I thought he'd gone mental, and I almost gave us away by laughing. But then," Megan wrung her hands together and bit her lip, swallowing hard to clear the cotton from her throat. "But then they, a-all of them, got out of their seats and kneeled down in front of him." She tried to suppress a sob but it still sputtered out. "Even Frieden and Bornias," she looked to Rayne who had turned a shade of green. "They were bowing down to that . . . that monster!"

"Not Gran though, right?" asked Ainsley. "She knew better."

Megan shook her head. "Evren got her, too. I don't know what that cone does—"

"It's a horn."

Three sets of eyes turned to Rayne. Garner was now staring at the wall.

"What's that?" said Ainsley.

"What you're describing . . ." Rayne's eyes took on a faraway look, "it reminds me of something familiar Kaelin and I came across when we were studying the Tomdex." Rayne blinked, as if pulling himself back to the present. "We have to get our things and get to Amdor quickly. If Evren is in possession of what I fear, there is more to be lost than the Staff of Lexiam."

He cracked open the door and peered into the corridor before stepping out. "Quickly, quickly." He waved at the others to follow.

They sprinted down the corridor, but to their dismay, Bornias and Frieden were milling about the foyer that spanned the distance between them and the exit.

"They haven't spotted us," said Brighton. "We should be able to sneak past and act like other dignitaries if you put your hoods up."

"I don't have mine," said Ainsley. "It makes it too hard to fly."

Megan wrapped her cloak around him, and Ainsley pulled his wings as close to himself as he could. While he did so, Megan studied Bornias and Frieden. "Don't you think we should try and talk to them?"

Rayne shook his head. "It's too risky. If they're under Evren's influence, they won't be swayed by simple words. We'll have to find another way to save them."

Megan gave Bornias and Frieden a last wistful glance, and Ainsley placed a hand on her shoulder. "After we save them, we'll make sure Evren pays."

She nodded and pulled her thick mass of curls around her face. "Come on, Garner. We have to go." Megan tugged at his arm, but he didn't move. Then, to her horror, he started walking toward Bornias and Frieden. "Garner, no!" He turned his head toward Megan, and she shrank from the dark look in his eyes. "Garner?"

"Dissenter!" he snarled at her.

He whirled back around and waved his arms over his head to get Bornias and Frieden's attention. When that failed, he opened his mouth to call to them. Before he could utter a word, Rayne shoved him against the wall and Ainsley smacked a hand over his mouth.

"What the hell are you doing?"

Megan grabbed at Garner's arms to pin them down, but he shoved his knee into her stomach. She gasped in pain, and this was what caught the attention of Bornias and Frieden and brought them running.

Ainsley's hand was still over Garner's mouth, and he used it to ram the elf's head against the stone wall. Garner's eyes rolled upwards until the whites were showing and he crumpled onto the floor.

"Help me with Megan!" He yelled to Rayne. They each ducked under one of her arms and the three of them ran for the exit.

Brighton darted out in front and scrambled up Frieden's leg, biting him hard on the thigh. While Frieden battled to extract himself from the ferret, Bornias continued his pursuit. "Rayne, wait!"

Rayne faltered in his footsteps for a moment, but Ainsley kept him moving. "I'm sorry, Grandfather." Rayne's voice was husky, but he didn't look back.

Ainsley heard the hum of magic and felt the air around him change into something much stiffer. Rayne had created a protective shield around them, and in a moment, Ainsley knew why.

"Get back here, traitor!" roared Bornias.

There was a sound, as of a fire roaring to life, and Ainsley felt the forcefield around them shake. He glanced over his shoulder and saw Bornias holding a ball of fire in one hand. Ainsley winced as the old wizard let fly a second ball of fire, striking the forcefield.

"Megan, can you move on your own?" asked Rayne.

Megan's stomach muscles were still spasming from the blow, but she could see sweat beading on Rayne's forehead from the sheer effort of keeping them all protected. She nodded, afraid to speak in case her words might end in a fit of vomiting.

"I'm going to lower the shield," said Rayne, "and we're going to run for the inn without looking back."

"Okay," said Ainsley. Megan nodded again.

"Now!" The air pressure around them returned to normal, and Ainsley, Megan, and Rayne sprinted toward the exit.

Megan felt something grab her hair from behind and screamed.

"Shush. It's just me," said Brighton, scrambling onto her shoulder. "But you might want to duck."

"What?" Megan refused to turn and look back.

"Duck!"

Megan heard fire crackling behind her and screamed again, stooping down just as a flame shot past. Brighton swiveled on her shoulder so he was facing Bornias and Frieden.

"Ainsley, run to your left!" he shouted.

Ainsley veered off his original path and watched a ball of fire shoot out the front entrance, which was now mere feet away. There were a few startled gasps and shrieks from the crowd on the street before they pressed toward the entrance for a glimpse of what was happening.

Ainsley, Megan, and Rayne fought their way through the crowd, which for once was proving beneficial as Bornias and Frieden fell farther and farther behind.

Then someone yelled, "It's that flying boy again! Get him!"

"Shit." Ainsley cleared the doorway and bound into the sky, stretching wide his wings. "I'll catch up with you guys you-know-where!" He called down to Rayne and Megan. "Be careful!" He looked down at the ferret on Megan's shoulder. "And keep them safe."

Brighton touched a paw to his forehead and dug his claws deeper into Megan's shirt.

"Do you know any shortcuts?" she asked Rayne when they finally made their way free of the crowd. Out of the corner of her eye, she could see Ainsley clear a building and for once, she wished she had wings to climb above it all.

"This way." Rayne grabbed her arm and pulled her down a side street that led them past the Pontsford library and in front of an attractive tavern frequented by more devious patrons.

"Ah, the Essential Element. I've conducted many a business deal behind those walls," said Brighton with an almost wistful tone.

Rayne led the way toward the front door, but Megan pulled back on his hand. "Wait, we can't go in there! We'll be trapped!"

"I learned a little secret about this place when I was under Sasha's mind control." Rayne yanked open the door. "Inside. Hurry."

The bartender eyed them warily from behind his post at the polished ebony bar. "See here, now. I'm not looking for trouble from you lot again."

"Great. He remembers us," muttered Megan.

"What's this?" said Brighton. Megan didn't have to look at him to tell he was smiling. "You've got a bit of a wayward past, Megan?"

"It wasn't me!" She blushed. "It was . . . other people."

During Rayne's last visit to the Essential Element, he'd ripped out his hair, smashed a table, and frightened away the customers before the bartender had asked them all to leave.

Rayne's cheeks reddened but he approached the bar. "Show me the secret passage, then, and we'll be on our way."

"Secret passage?" The bartender took a step back and glanced around the room. "We've no secret passages here."

Rayne reached into his shirt and pulled out a bag of coins, spilling the gold onto the counter. "Or shall I start breaking tables again?"

Pursing his lips, the bartender swept the coins into his apron. "Follow me, please." He stepped through a swinging door behind the bar, and Rayne followed.

"Wait a tic." Brighton leapt down from Megan's shoulder and locked the latch at the bottom of the door.

Megan raised her eyebrow. "You really think that's going to keep two angry wizards out?"

"If they're two angry dim-witted wizards."

The door behind the bar opened a crack, and the bartender's head appeared around the side. "Your friend is ready to go."

Megan stepped into the back room and looked around. "Rayne?"

"Down here." Against one corner, Rayne's upper body was sticking out of a trapdoor in the floor.

"What is it with this world and tiny enclosed spaces?" muttered Megan. When she peeked down the trapdoor, however, the tunnel it branched from appeared wide enough for two people to walk abreast.

Rayne climbed down and beckoned for her to follow.

The bartender tapped Megan on the shoulder with a rolled-up piece of parchment and a snow light. "You might need these."

Megan dropped them down to Rayne and then descended the ladder to a dirty, stone floor. Brighton followed behind them, and the bartender closed the trapdoor without so much as a goodbye. Megan could hear scraping across the trapdoor and knew the bartender was sliding something over it. Her heart beat a little faster when she realized there was no turning back.

Rayne didn't seem to notice her anxiety. "Hold this, would you?" He handed her the snowlight and unfurled the parchment.

An intricate mesh of lines ran across it, linking together at different points marked by squares in which minute writing had been scrawled.

"Is this a map of Pontsford?" Megan twisted her head and tried to find their location on the map.

"It's a map of Pontsford's underground, yes. We're here." Rayne pointed to a spot on the map marked with a black dot. "And our inn is here." He pointed to a spot halfway down the map.

Megan's heart dropped. "But that's so far."

Rayne slid the map under his sword belt. "There won't be any crowds or vendors in our way, so we should make quick work of the distance. Let's get moving."

Megan didn't need to be told twice. She was prepared to do anything that would get her back to fresh air and open sky as soon as possible. Holding the snowlight in front of her, she started down the path, taking the turns as Rayne called them out to her.

Toward the end of their trek, they heard voices and footsteps approaching. Megan hid down one of the side tunnels, covering the snowlight with her cape, while Rayne stood in front of her, the Staff of Lexiam clutched in one hand. As the other passage users walked by, Megan got a glimpse of them, a young man and woman, and breathed a sigh of relief, uncovering her snowlight. The man and woman blinked in surprise and fright and continued down the tunnel at a brisk pace, whispering to one another.

Rayne beckoned Megan back into the main path and they continued on their way. After a few more minutes, Rayne directed Megan down a side tunnel and stepped in front of her. He climbed a ladder and cracked the trapdoor above it. Daylight and dust filtered in, and Rayne threw the hatch open the rest of the way and scrambled out.

Megan followed behind him, and he helped her to her feet. They were in the far corner of an alley where street vendors had set up camp. Since it was still mid-afternoon, the area was empty, and Megan, Brighton, and Rayne moved on to keep it that way.

"Our inn is a few buildings up the street," said Rayne, peering around a wagon where several people were admiring leather goods. "Wait here, and I'll bring the bags."

"No need." One of the patrons at the vendor wagon turned around and grinned. "I've already got our things."

"Ainsley!" Megan threw her arms around him. "How did you know we'd be here?"

Ainsley returned her hug and stepped back. "What do you think the shop beside our inn sells?"

"Maps of the underground?" guessed Megan.

"Summoning pools." Ainsley's grin widened. "And they let customers try them out for free."

"Well done, Ainsley," said Rayne. "Though, I suggest we leave here before my grandfather and Frieden find us as well. Back down the alley."

Megan took her backpack from Ainsley, along with a leather belt he held out to her. "Looks like we're not going home any time soon."

Onaj's Horn

Megan breathed a sigh of relief as the portal dropped them at the gates to Amdor. The retired wizard community was just as she'd remembered it; squat cottages surrounded by a fence that separated the magical world from the no-magic zone of Amdor.

She looked to the porch of cabin five, hoping to see Kaelin Warnik, the former governor of the protectors, reading one of his books. Unfortunately, nobody was on the porch and his was the only cabin not spiraling smoke from the chimney.

"Kaelin must be in Pontsford with the rest of the zombies," said Ainsley, his shoulders sagging a little. He had been hoping, when Rayne had mentioned Amdor, that Kaelin would be there to fix everything or at least team his magic with Rayne's.

"It's not him we're here to see," said Rayne. "We're here for the Tomdex, remember?" He stepped through the gate into Amdor and gave a slight shudder as the magic in his body drained away.

The others followed him through, including Brighton, who cursed when he cleared the entrance.

"What's wrong?" asked Megan. She turned to look at him and had to rub her eyes. She wasn't used to seeing Brighton in his ferret form, but now that they'd entered the no-magic zone, her Pearl of Truth had become inactive.

Brighton glanced down at his paws. "Every time I go through there, I kind of hope the magic will reverse itself and I'll be human again." He laughed, but it was feeble and his whiskers were drooping.

He looked so crestfallen that Megan picked him up and hugged him. "Well, *I* see the real you," she said, "and in a few more years, so will everyone else."

Brighton was quiet a moment, then licked her cheek. "Thank you, Megan." He leapt down from her arms and darted towards Poloi's cottage after Rayne.

Megan placed her hands to her cheeks as she watched him push through the front door of the bookshop. Her skin felt warm, as if she'd been blushing, but she wasn't sure why. She fell into step beside Ainsley, and he cleared his throat.

"I have to say I'm glad that you're interested in someone besides Garner," said Ainsley, "even if Brighton is a rodent. I hope he looks better as a human."

"He does."

Ainsley grinned and Megan pushed him. "I mean . . . I'm not interested in him!"

Ainsley snorted. "Yeah, well he's interested in you."

The warmth flared in Megan's cheeks again. "No, he isn't."

They stopped on Poloi's porch, and Ainsley turned to face her. "Megan, if Brighton had been in human form, that lick he gave you would have been the same thing as a kiss on the cheek. When he starts humping your leg like a dog, you know it's getting serious."

"Shut up," said Megan, but she wiped at her face with the edge of her cloak and smoothed down her hair before they stepped inside.

Brighton and Rayne were perched on the window seat with a massive book between them. A dark-skinned man stood over them, studying the pages upside down. He looked up when he saw Ainsley and Megan approach, and a smile seemed to stretch almost up to his warm brown eyes.

"Could I really be seeing Megan and Ainsley?"

"Kaelin!" Megan threw her arms around him and let him squeeze her in one of his bear hugs. "We thought you weren't in Amdor."

"Just because I wasn't in my cabin?" Kaelin held her at arm's length. "I don't spend that much time by myself, do I?" He turned to Ainsley who held up a hand in a halting gesture.

"Let me guess. You want to comment on the wings."

"What wings?" asked Kaelin with a mock serious expression, giving Ainsley a hearty handshake.

Megan nodded to Brighton and Rayne. "So what have they found out?"

Kaelin shrugged. "To be honest, I'm not even sure what they're looking for. I found them a minute before you walked in, and neither one of them has said a word."

Just then, Brighton blurted. "That's it! That's the cone!"

"I stand corrected," said Kaelin, sidling back toward the window to get a glimpse at the book.

Ainsley nudged Brighton out of the way so he could sit beside Rayne, and Megan settled herself on the other side. The illustration on the page was of a marvelous white unicorn with a familiar golden horn spiraling from its forehead.

"That *wasn't* a cone," said Megan. "Evren was holding a unicorn's horn!"

"And it didn't belong to just any unicorn," said Rayne. He moved his hand from where it had been resting on the page to reveal a caption:

Onaj, leader of the White Order.

"Wait, wait, wait," said Megan, leaning back. "Onaj, as in the song about the unicorn that Lodir Novator fought?"

Kaelin nodded. "When a unicorn is defeated, its will is broken and it loses its horn, along with its magical abilities.

The only way for a unicorn to reclaim its powers is by defeating its initial conqueror."

"According to this," said Rayne, scanning the page, "Whoever possesses it can use it to alter the thoughts of others and make them believe all manner of false thoughts. It's even mentioned that Lodir used the horn to resist the temptations of the sirens and best the dragon Arastold."

"But I thought *The Ballad of Lodir* says he defeated Arastold *first*," said Megan.

"His feats are praised in order of their importance," said Rayne, "not necessarily chronologically."

Ainsley was only half-listening to the conversation, trying to remember why the unicorn seemed so familiar to him outside of song. He thought back over the different creatures he'd encountered since their arrival in Arylon, but the only unicorn he could remember was the one Bornias had conjured to keep Ainsley and Megan from going after the Staff of Lexiam with him and Frieden. The thought of Frieden triggered another memory of a conversation Ainsley had shared with the governor about his former love life.

"That's Anala's father!" Ainsley tapped the page with his finger so hard Megan thought he might rip a hole through the paper.

"Who?" she and Brighton asked.

"Anala. She's the reason Frieden's not a nascifriend anymore. She tricked everyone into thinking she was human, and Frieden fell in love with her, but when she finally revealed who she really was, he dumped her."

"Frieden was in love with a unicorn?" Megan made a disgusted face.

"Hey, it's no different than you and—" He faltered at a horrified look from Megan. "Um . . . how you feel about puppies."

"So, why did she reveal herself as a unicorn?" asked Brighton.

"Because she needed his help with something, but he didn't stick around to find out what." Ainsley tapped the page again. "But I bet it had something to do with her father's missing horn. Maybe she can help us."

"Maybe," agreed Rayne. "It says here the only way to reverse the effects of Onaj's Horn is to destroy it, and *that's* only possible by using a more powerful magic."

"So, let's go," said Ainsley, flipping the book shut. "Where do the unicorns live?"

"Well, wait," said Megan. "Shouldn't we warn the people of Raklund and Hylark and the Icyllians and everyone else we can think of before their leaders return home and turn their kingdoms over to Evren?"

"How do we know that hasn't already happened?" asked Ainsley.

Megan gave him a withering look. "You just want to go to the unicorns to see if you can steal some of their magic."

"Actually, he does have a point," said Kaelin. "It's possible Evren has already forced the others into believing *he* is their leader. We should check on a few of our friends in my summoning pool."

"Maybe we can get a message to my dad, too," said Ainsley. "To let our families know we won't be coming home any time soon."

While Kaelin returned to his cottage to gather summoning tablets, the others walked down to his viewing pool outside the no-magic zone.

"I thought you were travelers with the Carnival," Brighton said to Megan. "At least, that's what Ainsley told me."

"We are." She turned to him, prepared to continue the lie, but somehow it wasn't as easy when she could see him in human form with his spiky white hair and puzzled frown. The look on his face was one too innocent to be betrayed. "I mean, we're travelers, but not like you think. We just tell people we're with the Carnival so we can avoid questions."

"So, you live in . . . Raklund, then?"

Megan shook her head. "We live a lot farther away than that.

"Ah." Brighton lowered his gaze to the grass.

"Oh, but it's easy for us to get back here fast," she added.

Ainsley made a sound between a laugh and a cough, and Megan felt herself blushing. "I mean, if someone needs us . . . like Bornias."

Brighton nodded. "Or Garner."

Megan's stomach clenched as she remembered the blow from earlier. "Well, I'm not exactly on speaking terms with him right now."

"He's punched you *and* drugged you," Ainsley reminded her. "You wouldn't take that if we were back home."

"You knew how unusual the circumstances were," snapped Megan. "You normally wouldn't have attacked your grandmother, but you did back in Raklund."

"You attacked an old woman?" Brighton was giving Ainsley the same disapproving look as when he'd heard about Garner's exploits.

"I was *sick*," said Ainsley. "I would have attacked a basket of puppies."

"Fine. Let's just drop it," said Megan. "Here comes Kaelin."

He carried two summoning tablets with him, dropping one into the pool of water in the lipothis-hewn basin and handing the other to Rayne.

"In case you need insight while you're traveling." He stood over the basin and spoke, "*Admis creeba focál.*"

The surface of the water shimmered before revealing Bornias, Frieden, and Garner cowering in front of Evren who glared down at them from the dais in the meeting room.

"You let them get away?" he snarled. "Where are they now?"

Bornias bustled forward and kissed Evren's hand. "Master, I apologize, but we cannot find them . . . any of them. They must be in a no-magic zone."

"Well, then." Evren ripped his hand away. "Since there are only a few *thousand* no-magic zones in the world, I suggest you start looking, beginning with Amdor."

"Yes, Master." All three men bowed and backed away.

Megan turned to Rayne. "Do they have a portal potion?"

"I know my grandfather grabbed at least two before we left Raklund in case there was any trouble," said Rayne. "If Evren still has the Master Mage with him, however, he may not even need the potions to travel."

"Well, if they're coming here, wouldn't it be a good idea for us to *leave*?" asked Ainsley.

"Let's check in on Raklund real quick," said Megan. "If Evren hasn't gotten to them yet, we could have them evacuate the city."

Kaelin waved his hand over the image of their friends and muttered an incantation. The image shimmered again to be replaced by one of Captain Kyviel, commander of the Silvan Sentry. He was sitting at a table, eating with some of his men.

"That doesn't do us any good," said Ainsley. "Everyone knows Kyviel's always been one of Evren's supporters. Try someone who's *respectable*. Try . . . Barsley Inish."

Kaelin passed his hand over the summoning pool, but nothing happened. He frowned and tried it again, speaking in a louder voice. The image of Captain Kyviel faded, and the water cleared, but no image of Sir Inish, Ainsley and Megan's old dwarven friend, materialized.

Ainsley let out a low whistle. "Oh, boy."

"Why," Megan swallowed a lump in her throat, "why isn't it showing him?"

"One of two reasons," said Rayne, placing a hand on her shoulder. "He's either in a no-magic zone . . . or he has passed."

"Passed?" Megan looked to the summoning pool, hoping it might have been delayed in revealing the image, but the water remained calm. "Passed, as in dead?"

"Megan, he's probably safe in some no-magic zone," said Ainsley. "He was smart; he knew something bad was coming, so he probably escaped."

"He was *blind*! Where would he go by himself?"

Megan gasped and clapped a hand to her forehead. "What if he's locked away in the Raklund prison until Captain Kyviel decides to kill him?"

Ainsley grabbed her by the shoulders. "Megan, think about it. If he got captured, then we're going to get captured, and we're the only ones who know what really happened. This is a bad idea!"

"We can just pretend to be followers of Evren and break out Sir Inish and then port to wherever the unicorns are." She turned to Rayne. "Can't we?"

Rayne stared at her for a moment, then sighed. "She's right, Ainsley. As king, it's my duty to save whomever in my kingdom I can. More importantly, I need to get to the Quatrys before my grandfather does."

A silence followed in which fish could be heard splashing in the nearby lake.

"You . . . didn't bring the Quatrys with you?" asked Ainsley.

Rayne reddened as if he'd drank a purple firepot. "My grandfather always kept the Quatrys and staff separate, and I thought it was a good idea. The stone golems are guarding the Quatrys back in the palace so if we were ever to have another fiasco, they'd be safe. I never dreamed that the only other person besides myself who could access them would turn against his own people." The corners of both his eyes and his mouth turned down, making him look a great deal like his grandfather did when he was upset.

"Fine," said Ainsley. "We'll go to Raklund and risk our necks, but I don't think we should all go in case something bad should happen."

"I'll stay behind," spoke up Kaelin. "That way, when Bornias and Frieden arrive, I can attempt to distract them. *And* I'll let your father know what's happened," he told Ainsley who had been about to suggest the same.

"We should leave soon," said Rayne. "Kaelin, do you have an extra basin I can borrow?"

Kaelin held up an iron cauldron. "I thought you might ask that."

Rayne added a portal potion and a few other ingredients from a pouch around his waist. "Everyone going to Raklund, gather close."

Ainsley and Megan stepped toward the cauldron and Brighton joined them.

"You're coming with us?" asked Megan with a hopeful skip of her heart.

"Well, it was either that or stay here and wait for your other friends to skin me alive."

"Good point." Megan smiled. "See you on the other side."

Evren Leaves His Mark

Their portal exit point in Raklund held familiarity with Ainsley and Megan. It was by the same lake outside the kingdom that they'd first been introduced to the new world. This time, however, there were no near drownings and severe blows to the head when they landed in the thick, tall grass surrounding the water.

Rayne straightened his robes and gripped the Staff of Lexiam tightly. "Is everyone ready?" he asked.

"Let's go," said Megan, unsheathing her sword.

Rayne approached the rocky face of the mountain and whistled to it to call forth one of the chitwisps that guarded the city. But several minutes passed and the chit-wisp failed to emerge and begin its usual chatter.

"This is bad." Rayne whistled a slightly different, more urgent tune, still with no results. "This is definitely bad."

"Do you want me to go have a look-see?" asked Brighton. "I could squeeze in that hole."

"Be careful," said Rayne, picking Brighton up and lifting him to the chitwisp tunnel.

They could hear Brighton's claws scrabbling through the loose pieces of stone and an occasional chirp from him in an effort to call the chitwisps. A few moments later, a cascade of pebbles spilled from the tunnel mouth and Brighton's head emerged. He gasped and inhaled deeply, as if he'd been submerged in water. "Phoo! Evren's definitely been here." He made a disgusted face. "All the chitwisps are dead."

Megan gasped while Ainsley looked fascinated. "Are the bodies stacked in a pile or just strewn everywhere?"

"Ainsley." Rayne gave him a look. "Brighton, do you have any idea how long they've been dead?"

"Judging by the smell and maggots, I'd say three to four days." Brighton tucked his snout into his foreleg in an attempt to rub away the stench.

"So, Evren must have been here to charm the citizens right before he left for Pontsford," said Rayne.

"Well, what do we do now?" asked Ainsley. "We can't even get into the city."

"I think there's a lever the chitwisps pull to open the entrance." Rayne looked up at Brighton. "Could you go back in and try to find it?"

"Back in there?" Brighton jerked his head over his shoulder. "With the chitwisp corpses?"

"Please." Megan stepped forward. "If Evren's killed something as harmless as the chitwisps, our friend is in real danger."

Brighton grumbled but took a deep breath and disappeared back into the tunnel.

Megan pulled Bit from her pocket and lifted the narshorn to the tunnel's entrance. "Go with Brighton, and make sure he stays safe."

Bit squeaked and skittered away after the ferret.

Ainsley turned to Megan. "If Evren's already gotten to these people, what's your plan for us sneaking inside? I think they'll notice a bunch of Evren haters."

"We just have to act like everyone else," said Megan, "and hide from Bornias and Frieden if they show up."

"That shouldn't be too difficult for you two and Brighton," said Rayne. "Since you're not from this world, nobody will be able to see you in the summoning pool, and because Brighton's physically an animal, nobody will be able to see *him* either."

"But they can see you," said Megan. Her stomach twisted a little as she realized what Rayne was getting at.

"I'm going to have to separate from you to keep you safe," he said with an apologetic smile. "I'll leave the Quatrys in your care while you go after the unicorns, and I'll visit the other cities in the Kingdom Coalition to warn them. Evren can't have reached them all."

"What if you get caught?" asked Ainsley.

"Then, you'll have to stay one step ahead of me," said Rayne. "Because if Evren has me in his power, he will ask where the Quatrys are, and I'll tell him where you've gone."

"Traitor," said Megan with a weak smile.

At the sound of stone grinding against stone all three of them jumped and saw the entrance to the mountain kingdom of Raklund swinging open.

Brighton and Bit emerged, and Brighton bowed before Rayne. "Your Highness, your kingdom awaits."

"Thank you, Brighton." Rayne stooped and stepped through the entrance. Ainsley followed behind him and Brighton waited for Megan to join.

"Oh, great." She stood in the doorway, remembering how constrictive the walls had felt when she'd walked through the tunnel into Raklund during her first visit. Megan stooped to collect Bit and linger a bit longer outside the kingdom.

Ainsley looked over his shoulder at her. "We don't have to save Sir Inish if you'd rather wait outside."

"No, I'm coming," she grumbled. "We'll be dead soon one way or another, anyway."

The tunnel opened into the antechamber, which was usually sealed off from the main hall and guarded by protectors of the staff. Now, however, the heavy spiked doors stood ajar.

Megan gave Brighton an awestruck stare. "How did you do that?"

Brighton rubbed his nails against his chest and feigned boredom. "Nobody can ever say a ferret makes a poor rogue. I've got built-in lockpicks."

"Inside, quickly, before anyone realizes we don't belong." Rayne ushered the others into the main hall, which glittered and shimmered with the many crystals growing from the walls and ceiling.

"How come there's nobody here?" whispered Megan.

Rayne closed the doors behind him. "They're probably busy doing whatever Evren's commanded of them. My guess would be that they're training for combat."

"Why? Nobody's going to resist him. They can't."

"Some races will be able to resist the horn, and so can others if they're in animal form." Rayne pointed at Brighton. "When people discover that's the only way to keep from falling under Evren's control, he'll find himself facing an army of the most ferocious animals in Arylon."

The thought of a battle between good and evil made Megan both anxious and hopeful, and she quickened her pace. When they reached the intersection of the main hall and the first floor, however, Rayne grabbed her arm and halted her.

Then he cleared his throat. "Er . . . Brighton. I hate to ask another favor of you, but . . ."

"I'll scan the area, your Highness," said Brighton. Dropping onto his stomach, he crawled forward and poked his head around a large clay pot. Then, he darted around the pot and out of sight.

Ainsley, Megan, and Rayne strained their ears for any shouts of surprise or scuffles, but the next thing they heard was Brighton padding back down the hall. They crouched around him.

"The first and second floor are clear," said Brighton, "but I think King Rayne is correct. I could hear sounds from the training arena, like metal against metal. There's nobody on the second floor, and all the people on the first floor are just wandering from room to room like zombies."

"Did they notice you?" asked Rayne.

"They looked at me, but they didn't react at all. Whatever Evren's instructed them to do when they're not fighting must be pretty dull."

Rayne turned to Ainsley and Megan. "I'm giving you a half hour to get Sir Inish and meet me back here. I'm going to the Hall of Staves to get the Quatrys and some more portal potions. While you're around other people, don't do anything overtly suspicious."

"Okay," said Ainsley. Megan nodded.

"I'm not finished yet," said Rayne. He squeezed his hand into a fist and opened it to reveal a ball of sand, the grains of which seemed to be clumped together. "I told you I would give you a half hour. When the last grains separate, your time is up."

Ainsley and Megan watched as one by one, the specks of sand trickled from the larger ball, falling into Rayne's palm. He passed it over to Megan and brushed the loose grains onto the floor. "If I don't see you here by that time, I'll assume you've been captured and will go on without you. Do you understand?"

"Yes," said Ainsley.

Megan opened her mouth as if to protest but grunted and pocketed the ball. She wiped her palms, now sticky with sweat and sand, against her pants.

"Good luck," said Rayne.

They walked across the first floor one at a time. Rayne went first, making a beeline for a mural on the wall, which marked a hidden doorway through which only Silverskin could pass. Ainsley went next, trying his best to stare straight ahead and act uninteresting. His eyeballs couldn't help sweeping from side to side, however, to watch the citizens of Raklund. Nobody he passed said a word, and while they did seem to notice him, their faces remained expressionless and their eyes were slightly glassy, as if they were sleepwalking with their eyes open.

Megan stepped forward last, with Brighton by her side. She inched as close to him as possible without actually standing atop him. While Ainsley appeared to be fascinated by the living zombies, Megan found them unnerving, particularly because she recognized several of them—Stego the portly protector, Healer Sterela, even the hairstylist. She would much rather have been fighting off skeletons than standing amidst people who had lost all will to live.

Brighton tugged at her pantsleg. "Let's go find your friend. We haven't much time."

They caught up with Ainsley and walked down the hall as fast as they dared, all the while scanning the passersby for any signs of cognizance. They had almost reached the stairs down to the dungeon when Megan gasped and clutched her hand to her chest.

"What is it? What's wrong?" asked Brighton, climbing onto her shoulder. Ainsley looked around nervously.

"Someone here is pretending," she whispered. "They're not really under Evren's influence."

"Who?" asked Ainsley, at the same time Brighton asked, "How do you know that?"

Megan took a deep breath and scanned the faces of the people around her. She looked from one blank set of eyes to another until she came across a pair that held emotion. The eyes stared back at her defiantly, but Megan could see moisture welling at their corners.

"Rella?" whispered Megan.

Sands of Time

Despite the gravity of the situation, Ainsley couldn't help but admire the girl Megan was talking to, a beautiful redhead with dewy green eyes. He remembered her as one of the girls who'd ogled him when he first arrived in Arylon, and from stories Megan had told him about her sword practice, he guessed her name even before Megan said it a second time.

"Rella . . . are you with Evren?" Megan asked in a low voice.

Rella shook her head. "No," her eyes took on a fierce glow, "and I will never be, so if you are here to turn me, let us end it now." Rella thrust her cape aside and reached for her sword.

"Woah, woah, woah." Megan covered Rella's sword hand with both of hers. After making sure no sound issued from behind one of the shop doors, she pushed it open and pulled Rella inside. Ainsley and Brighton followed, closing the door and locking it behind them.

"We're not with Evren," Megan continued. "We've come to save who we can." She had hoped those words might assuage the tension, but they did little more than convince Rella to relax her grip on her sword.

"You're too late," was the curt reply.

"Then, how come you're still normal?" asked Ainsley.

Rella snapped her head in his direction, and he could almost hear the air around her crack like a whip. He smiled at her, but she either didn't remember who he was or was in no mood for humor.

Ainsley guessed it was the latter when Rella scowled and said, "There's nothing amusing about this. I survived by the grace of The Other Side." She turned her attention to Megan. "Do you remember that hairstylist who came to Raklund? The telepathic one?"

At Megan's nod, she continued. "He entered Evren's mind and learned of the plan to control all of Arylon. He warned me and told me to escape, but it was too late for either of us. Evren locked the entrance and turned the stylist under his control. I stayed in hiding until Evren left."

Ainsley blushed. "I'm sorry. I didn't know you'd been through so much."

"It's all right." Rella gave him a quick once-over and squinted. "Did you . . . grow wings?"

"By the grace of The Other Side," he said, bowing his head solemnly. Out of the corner of his eye, he could see Rella fighting a smile.

"These are my friends," said Megan. "Ainsley and Brighton. We're here with King Rayne."

"The king?" Rella's eyes lit up. "He can help us free Sir Inish."

Megan's shoulders relaxed slightly. "So, he's still alive?"

"Because he was blind, Evren couldn't turn him. He's downstairs in the Raklund dungeon, but I don't know how to get him out. The warden and the rest of the prisoners have joined with Evren."

"That's why we couldn't see Sir Inish in Kaelin's summoning pool," said Megan. "Those dungeons are inside no-magic zones."

Ainsley didn't share Megan's satisfaction with this news. "Isn't the warden the only person who can get people through the prison doors?" he asked.

Rella shook her head. "Sir Inish's people built this place. If anyone knows a non-magical way out of the prison, it's him. But I can't get to him to do it. With the king's help, though—"

"We're on our own to free Sir Inish," said Megan, "but—" she looked to Brighton who nodded.

"I think I can squeeze through those bars."

Megan pulled the ball of sand from her pocket. "We don't have long until we have to regroup with Rayne. Let's get moving."

If it was possible, the stairwell down to the dungeon had become even filthier and more haunting. Several spiders had taken residence on the ceiling, lacing their webs from wall to wall and a large puddle of fetid, stagnant water ran the length of the floor at the bottom of the stairs.

Ainsley took a larger-than-average step to cross the water but someone grabbed hold of the base of his wings and jerked him back just as a tentacle burst from the puddle and wrapped itself around Ainsley's leg. Megan stabbed it with her sword and the tentacle relinquished its grip, disappearing back into the water.

"I guess I should have warned you about that." The hair on Ainsley's neck rose at hearing Rella's voice so close to his ear, and he realized it was she who had pulled him away from the perilous puddle.

He looked over his shoulder at her and grinned. "I'm just glad you're stronger than a regular girl." His eyes widened. "I mean . . . not that girls aren't strong . . . and not that you're an . . . uh, irregular girl."

Megan snickered and hid it poorly behind a cough. "How many tentacles does that thing have, Rella?"

"Just the one, but it's strong enough to pull in a baby scrambler."

"I'm sure I can get across quicker than it can grab me," said Brighton.

Megan winced, picturing the tentacle grabbing Brighton mid-leap and feeding him to whatever gaping maw waited below the surface. "There has to be a way to get you across without the tentacle springing up."

"Well, we could try covering the puddle with a very large coat," said Ainsley.

Megan shot him a dirty look and pulled off her cape, shredding it into two pieces with her sword. She wrapped one end of each piece around each hand and gestured for Ainsley and Rella to grab the other ends. "Wrap these around your hands, too."

Rella raised an eyebrow but took the piece of silk and twisted it around her fist. "Why are we doing this?"

"So, I can create a distraction for Brighton." Taking a deep breath, Megan descended the last two steps and let her foot dangle above the puddle.

"No!" shouted Rella.

"Are you crazy?" shouted Ainsley.

The tentacle broke the surface of the water and twisted itself around Megan's leg, yanking upon it so that Ainsley and Rella's arguments were lost in their effort to hold onto their silk lifelines to Megan. Bit raced down Megan's body and sank her teeth and tail into the tentacle to no avail.

"Go, Brighton!" shrieked Megan, for he stood on the bottom step, frozen between helping her and completing his task. "We don't have any more time!"

Brighton took one step toward Megan, then leapt over the puddle and slipped through the bars and out of sight.

The tentacle whipped from side to side, dislodging Bit and almost jarring Ainsley and Rella loose.

"Okay." Megan gritted her teeth. "Distraction's over. Now get this thing off me!"

"I have to let go," warned Rella.

Ainsley nodded and tightened his grip on his section of silk. He spread his wings and flapped them to push him away from the hidden creature. Rella unsheathed her sword and took a swing at the tentacle directly below its grip on Megan's foot.

Her blow was more forceful than she had thought, slicing straight through the tentacle, the severed end of which flopped around on the step before splashing into the puddle to disappear with the rest of its former self.

"I'm *so* glad you've got good aim," said Megan, rubbing circulation back into her leg.

She, Ainsley, and Rella waited in silence for Brighton to return, Megan feeling the grains of sand slip away from the ball in her pocket. Just as she was considering calling Brighton back, he appeared with a disheveled-looking dwarf tottering behind him, his hand against the wall for guidance and support.

"Sir Inish!" called Rella, almost forgetting about the creature in the puddle and stepping down toward him. It was Ainsley's turn to grab her and pull her back.

Sir Inish craned his neck to the sound of her voice. "Rella?" His voice sounded raspier than ever, as if it had been days since he'd had a drink of water. But it also held a note of pleasure in it. "Is it you?"

"Us too," called Megan. "Megan and Ainsley. Um . . . Governor Frieden's niece and nephew."

This time, Sir Inish's joy reflected on his face. "I should have known. Didn't I once say you'd been brought here for something great?" He cackled and it changed into a wheezing cough.

He shuffled toward the puddle, but Brighton scurried in front of him and placed his paws against the old dwarf's legs. "There's a creature here. It'll grab us if we try to step over it."

"How did you cross the first time?" asked Sir Inish with a frown.

"Megan distracted it," said Ainsley, "but I don't think she should try that again."

"I may have to," said Megan. She reached into her pocket and pulled out the ball of sand, which had now been reduced to the size of a marble.

"What is this creature of which you speak?" asked Sir Inish.

"It has a tentacle," said Megan, "and it lives in a large puddle."

Sir Inish stroked his grizzled beard and let his blue sightless eyes roam toward the ceiling. "My, my. Evren certainly went out of his way to ensure I wouldn't escape this place. I'm flattered."

"Do you know what it is?" asked Rella.

"It's a dulotte. They hate fire, and that 'puddle' you're referring to is made of an oil base . . . highly flammable so the summoner can easily destroy it once it has accomplished its task. Are there any torches down here?"

The four teenagers glanced around them, but the dim glow in the passage came from a lone snowlight that dangled from the ceiling.

"We don't have anything to make fire with," said Megan, fighting to keep the desperation out of her voice. She could almost feel the last grains of sand shifting apart in her pocket. "Any other ideas?"

"I could give it a shot," said Ainsley.

"What do you mean?" asked Megan.

"I could try to start a fire with magic," he said. "I've done it before."

Megan bit her lip and tilted her head. "Yeah, but Ainsley, before you had the Quatrys . . . and then you had . . . you know."

Ainsley knew she was hesitant to mention the Illness in front of their companions. "Magic runs in my family," he said, "and everyone possesses the ability to use it, remember?" He closed his eyes and concentrated on the ball of silk in his hand, beseeching for just an ounce of magic to spark a flame. A few seconds later, an acrid smoke curled toward the ceiling.

"You did it!" cried Megan.

Ainsley tossed the fabric onto the puddle just as flames began to lick at his fingers. The instant the fire hit the surface of the pool, a massive blaze shot upward and the creature within gave an anguished cry. Everyone stepped back as the tentacle heaved itself onto the steps and began pulling its owner out of the burning inferno. Unfortunately for the creature, its entire body traveled through the oil as it broke the surface and the fire consumed it until it was nothing more than a crisp husk.

"Well, then," said Brighton, as a geyser of smoke bubbled up from the puddle's center, "I think we can cross now."

Rella leaned over the puddle and grabbed for Sir Inish's hand. "Take a big step," she said.

"That's a lot to ask of a dwarf," said Sir Inish, but he smiled. His hand found Rella's and his feet reached the semi-dry ground of the dungeon steps. Brighton leapt across after them and climbed onto Sir Inish's shoulder.

"Mind your footing," he said, as they climbed back toward the first floor. "There's a big chunk missing from that next step."

Megan couldn't help but smile at how Brighton guided the blind dwarf and at the fact that they would make it back to Rayne with time to spare. A quick scan of the first floor by Brighton confirmed that their presence was still unknown, and they hurried through the comatose crowd toward the intersection with the Main Hall.

"Where's Rayne?" asked Ainsley. "He promised he would give us a full thirty minutes."

"I did and I have," said Rayne, emerging from behind a large urn. "Congratulations on accomplishing your mission." He turned to Sir Inish. "It's good to see you're still alive."

"I am honored that you would all risk your lives to return for me." Sir Inish pounded his fist against his chest.

"Megan wouldn't have it any other way," said Ainsley. He pushed his hands into his pockets. "And I had something I wanted to give to you." He leaned forward and pressed the stone of shared sight into Sir Inish's hand.

The old dwarf gasped and stumbled backward, grabbing at his eyes. "I've been down in that dungeon for too long. I almost thought—" And then he seemed to make the connection between the bizarre occurrence and the object Ainsley had given him. He looked in the general direction of Ainsley's voice. "Is this a stone of shared sight?"

Ainsley smiled, turning his head toward the main hall, and placed his hand on Sir Inish's arm. "It is."

Sir Inish drew in a sharp breath, securing Ainsley's hand against his arm with one of his own and looking down a corridor he hadn't laid eyes on in many years. "I haven't . . ." Sir Inish trailed off, his eyes filling with tears.

Sir Inish wiped at his eyes, and Ainsley looked first at the one person he might recognize.

"Rayne?" Sir Inish's jaw dropped. "You've grown in the last ten years."

Everyone laughed, and Ainsley turned to look at Rella. "This is—"

"Rella. I would know her, even without seeing her." Sir Inish beamed and held his arms open, and she stepped into them.

"And this," Ainsley looked at Megan after Rella had stepped back, "is Megan."

Sir Inish cupped her cheek in his calloused hand. "Nice to see you again, Sir Inish," said Megan.

"Nice to see *you*," he replied with a chuckle.

Megan removed Ainsley's hand from Sir Inish's arm and replaced it with her own.

"And this . . . is Ainsley." She turned to look at him.

Sir Inish brought Megan closer to Ainsley, and he squinted. "There's something familiar about you that I can't quite put my finger on." He reached out to touch Ainsley's face.

"You might have known my father Cujark."

"Ah. Of course." Sir Inish grinned and smacked his palm against Ainsley's cheek. "It's that damned cavalier grin of yours. Just like your father." He shook Ainsley's hand. "He raised you well. I can never thank you enough for the stone of shared sight."

"There's nobody else I'd rather give it to," said Ainsley.

"Since we're in such giving mood, I have something for Ainsley and Megan," said Rayne. He held out a leather strap lined with pockets. Four of the pockets held stoppered vials and one held a rolled-up piece of parchment. He handed the strap of vials to Ainsley who secured it diagonally across his chest.

"Because I won't be going with you, these are portal potions. They work on the same principle as the Staff of Lexiam. These are the words you need to say to activate the portal." Rayne pointed to the piece of parchment, then reached into his pocket and pulled out a small leather pouch. "And this is for you, Megan."

She opened it and saw four colored gemstones nestled inside. "The Quatrys?" She gaped at him with wide eyes. "Why do you want *me* to have them?"

"If Evren is looking for me, it isn't safe for me to have the Quatrys *and* the staff." Rayne cleared his throat and avoided Ainsley's eye. "And I think they would be safest with you."

Megan nodded and lifted Bit out of her breast pocket. "Guard these with your life," she told her pet, dropping Bit into the Quatrys pouch. Bit sniffed at the stones and squeaked at Megan before curling into a ball on top of them. Megan slipped pouch and pet back into her pocket.

"And I do have one *last* thing," said Rayne. "Since I had extra time before our rendezvous, I rummaged around Sir Inish's office and found this." He produced an iron mace, the head of which was laden with spikes.

Sir Inish hefted it in his hand and curled his fingers around the handle with a fond look in his eyes. "I never thought I'd be able to use this again."

"And now," said Rayne, "I think we should leave the palace and begin our prospective journeys. You can find the unicorns in the Purefalls Glade."

"Purefalls Glade," repeated Ainsley.

"Follow close behind me," said Rayne, leading the way down the main hall to the cavern exit.

"Take my shoulder, Sir Inish," said Rella.

Megan stepped away, letting Sir Inish and Rella pass down the corridor in front of her. Ainsley and Brighton fell into step beside her.

"That was really nice of you," she said to Ainsley. Then, she looked over at Brighton. "And I can't tell *you* how grateful I am for all the help you've given us. If there's any way I can repay you, please let me know."

"I'm happy to help without any sort of compensation." Brighton grinned. "Of course, if you had the ability to turn me back into a human, I wouldn't refuse."

They arrived outdoors without any incident, and Rayne instructed them to follow him down to the lake. He poured in two bottles of portal potion, and the rest of the party stood around him as he incanted. As the magic began to take its effect, Rayne rounded on Ainsley and Megan.

"Good luck. May the next time we meet be as friends and not enemies."

"Good luck," echoed Ainsley and Megan.

He hugged Megan and shook Ainsley's hand, then shifted a little ways apart from them and closed his eyes.

"Remember everyone . . . Purefalls Glade," said Ainsley.

As the purple light washed over him, he closed his eyes and thought of waterfalls and horned horses.

Horned Horses

There was no herd of prancing, whinnying unicorns to greet them when they arrived in the glade. There was nothing, in fact, but a stand of tall trees clustered together with branches that bent down to the ground.

"Where are the unicorns?" asked Ainsley, examining the foliage in case this might be some strange breed that took to roosting in trees.

"If my memory serves me, they're through the forest," said Sir Inish. "The trees create a protective barrier around the glade itself."

"Okay, then," said Ainsley. He flapped his wings and leapt into the sky, climbing toward the tops of the trees. He caught a glimpse of grassy clearing and flashes of white before a branch straightened itself and swatted him down. He skidded across the ground to a stop at Rella's feet. Sir Inish looked down at Ainsley from where he waited with Rella.

"You can't get in that way."

"Thanks." Ainsley winced as he got to his feet. "I kind of figured that out."

"How are we supposed to get in then?" asked Megan.

"Be patient," said Sir Inish. "Someone will come to speak with us."

True enough, after a moment, two of the smaller branches parted, forming an opening, through which a young woman passed. Her blonde hair was tied back in one long braid which hung to her waist, and she was clad in a simple white shift.

"Greetings." She regarded them all in turn, and as she did so, a golden light flashed across her eyes for each individual. "Why have you come to our glade?"

"We need your help," said Megan.

The woman shook her head. "Unicorns do not meddle in human affairs."

"But this concerns you, too," said Ainsley. "Evren Sandor has used Onaj's horn to control the most powerful wizards in Arylon, and he looks to conquer Sunil next."

A hint of emotion flickered on the woman's face. "He has the horn of our former leader?"

"The very same," said Sir Inish. "We must speak with the new leader of the White Order."

"Or his daughter Anala," said Ainsley.

"Anala *is* the new leader of the White Order," said the woman. "Very well. I sense no dark magic from you." She turned and waved her arms to the trees. The branches swept to either side and created an entrance large enough for the entire party.

Everyone remained silent as they passed through the foliage and onto the verdant dell, for they all knew this was no ordinary grass upon which they walked. Magical beasts had trod there moments before, their hoofprints still pressing the blades of grass to the ground. Even the air around them crackled with magic and smelled of enchantment.

The unicorns Ainsley had spied earlier had disappeared, but out of the corner of his eye, he caught glints of gold from the surrounding trees and heard an occasional whicker.

And then, a multitude of voices, all whispers but no faces, filled the silence of the glade.

"There is great magic."

"From the boy."

"And the girl."

"Hello?" Megan spun a slow circle and called out to the forest. "We're here because of Onaj's horn. We need to speak with Anala."

The voices quieted at once, and there was a rustling of leaves followed by the gentle clopping of hooves upon the ground. An ivory-white unicorn with violet eyes stepped into the clearing.

"I am Anala. What do you know of my father's horn?"

"We know who has it, and we need your help in destroying it," said Megan.

The field was once more awash with the buzz of voices. Anala whinnied, and they ceased.

"Why do you wish to destroy my father's horn?"

"It's being used to control the minds and wills of many people," said Ainsley, "and the only way to permanently reverse the effects is to destroy it."

Anala bowed her head and whickered. "I feared something like this would happen. I should have tried harder to find my father's horn after that horrible human took it."

"Who? Evren?" asked Megan with a frown.

"No. The one you call Lodir. The one you call a hero." Anala snorted disdainfully. "And now his mistake will be the demise of your people."

"But it doesn't have to be," said Ainsley. He approached Anala and she reared onto her hind legs.

"Away from me, human! Your kind has brought me nothing but misery."

Ainsley held his hands up in submission. "I'm sorry about your father, but please don't punish us for what someone else has done."

"You realize that Evren isn't going to stop with just getting the power of the great leaders of Arylon," added Megan. "He'll come for your powers, and these trees won't be able to protect you for long."

The unicorns hiding within the forest snorted and whinnied, but this time Anala did nothing to stop them.

"You know it's true," said Ainsley. "You'll be conquered by humans and your horns will be taken."

"Come with us," said Megan. "We'll find a way to steal the horn from Evren, and you can destroy it."

Anala tossed her head, the hairs of her forelock falling into her eyes. "Impossible. I could never leave the order without a leader."

"You've done it before," said Ainsley. "Frieden Tybor told me about the time you—"

"You know Frieden?" interrupted Anala.

"He's a very good friend of ours," said Megan.

Anala's eyes narrowed. "If he is such a good friend, why did he not come to your aid?"

Megan held her gaze. "Because he's one of the people Evren has under his control."

"What?" Anala's nostrils flared and her eyes widened. "Why would anyone do such a thing to someone so kind?"

"Because Evren's *evil!*" Megan shook her hands in the air.

Ainsley noticed the concerned look in Anala's eyes and decided to take advantage of it. "And . . . when Evren's done using Frieden, he'll probably kill him!"

"He wouldn't dare!" Anala reared up on her hind legs.

"If you won't do it to help *us*, won't you do it to save Frieden?" asked Megan.

Anala stamped at the ground with one hoof, and a male unicorn slightly smaller than she charged out of the forest. "Kinark, can you lead the White Order?"

Ainsley and Megan grinned at one another as Kinark bent low on his forelegs. "It would be an honor, Anala."

Anala touched her horn to his. "Let us discuss our arrangement." She looked to Ainsley and Megan who replaced their giddy expressions with somber ones. "We will remain within the safety of the glade tonight. Find a spot to lay your things and settle in."

"Um . . . what should we do for food?" asked Megan. "I mean, we have a little in our bags but I don't think Sir Inish has eaten for a while."

"Only once a day," said Sir Inish, clutching his stomach.

"We have a few fruit trees," said Anala, "but I wouldn't recommend leaving the glade for anything else. Now, if you'll excuse us." She trotted off with Kinark and disappeared into the forest.

"I'll go gather some fruit," said Ainsley.

"No, stay here with Sir Inish and Rella," said Megan. She dumped the contents of her pack on the ground. "Help yourselves to what I have here. I'll go get the fruit." She slung her now-empty bag over one shoulder.

"I'll help you," said Brighton. "I can make it up those trees quicker."

"If you come across anything with four legs that's not a unicorn, kill it and bring it back!" Ainsley called after them.

"I resent that!" hollered Brighton.

He and Megan were halfway across the glade before he spoke again. "So, who's the pretty redheaded lass we rescued? How do you know her?"

"She was my dueling partner the last time Ainsley and I came to Raklund. Why? Is she an apple you want to sample?" Megan bit her lip, not intending for her question to come out quite so catty. She didn't know why she even cared if Brighton was interested in Rella.

Apparently, neither did Brighton. He blinked at Megan in surprise. "No. I just wanted to know more about your friends. She seems like a nice person."

"She is. Sorry."

Brighton pointed out a cluster of fruit trees and Megan pulled off her boots and stockings. Then, she began to climb, grasping a branch in her hands and planting her feet firmly against the tree's trunk. As she pulled herself up, Brighton appeared beside her, clutching at the bark with his hands and feet, a task she knew was made easier with his ferret claws.

"Why do you care?" he asked.

Megan was thankful she could attribute her red cheeks to her arduous task. "Why do I care about what?" She settled onto a sturdy branch and pulled her rucksack into her lap. Bending down, she snapped a piece of fruit off the branch beneath her. When she straightened to place it in her bag, Brighton's face was inches from her own.

"Why do you care what I think of other women? You're with Garner."

Megan looked down. "I don't care what you think of other women. I just care about Rella is all."

"*Is* that all?"

Megan didn't dare look at him, but she could hear amusement in Brighton's voice and knew that his dark eyes were upon her.

"Yes, of course. As you said, I care for Garner."

"Garner," repeated Brighton.

"Yes." This time, Megan did raise her head to meet his gaze with her defiant one. Still, the expression on Brighton's face, the way his eyebrows knitted together, his rugged cheeks, the smile playing on his lips, intimidated her. And though she had anticipated his next words, they still made her breath catch in her throat.

"Only Garner? Is there no one else you care for?"

Megan did her best to act nonchalant, pulling her hair back into one hand. "Well, Rella, as I said, and Sir Inish and Ainsley and . . . all my friends, of course."

Brighton grinned and climbed up to the next branch. "Of course."

Megan bent back down and plucked a few more pieces of fruit before glancing up at Brighton. "I'm sure you have someone you care about, too." She yelped as he swung down so that he hung by his knees, his face beside hers. Megan stared at his topsy-turvy mouth. His legs were just long enough to position his lips at the same level as hers.

"Isn't it obvious who I care for?" he asked in a quiet voice.

"No." Megan found herself leaning toward him. "Who?" She was now close enough to feel his breath on her lips.

And then he grinned and said in a feminine voice, "All my friends, of course!"

From the opposite side of the valley, Ainsley could hear Megan groan and burst into laughter.

Rella heard it, too, and smirked at Ainsley. "She seems to be having an awfully good time with that ferret."

"He's actually a human who's been cursed," said Ainsley. "Megan doesn't have a weird animal fetish or anything."

Rella laughed, and it sounded to Ainsley like a million tiny bells chiming together. On the ground beside them, Sir Inish snored contentedly.

"I kind of assumed that Brighton was human from the way he talks and carries himself," said Rella. "But what about you?"

Ainsley ran his hands over his hair to smooth it down. "What about me?"

"The wings." Rella pointed over his shoulder. "You don't look like you belong to any of the flying civilizations. You just look like . . . a boy with wings."

"That would be an accurate assessment," said Ainsley with a grin. "The wings are . . . a gift until I return home."

"Ah. A temporary enchantment," said Rella. She reached out to touch one, pulling on it as if to test its authenticity.

"Something like that," said Ainsley, tucking them against his body. For the first time since he had hit puberty, he was beginning to feel self-conscious.

"Will you be glad when they're gone?" asked Rella.

Ainsley frowned and after a moment said, "Yes, and no. I like being able to fly, but I don't like that people seem to admire me just because of them."

"I admire you with them." Rella plopped down opposite him. "But I remember when you first came to Raklund. I also admired you without them."

Ainsley couldn't help grinning. "You did, huh? What did you admire most? My eyes? My smile?"

"Hmm." Rella tapped a finger to her chin. "I think it was your sense of modesty." She laughed at the blush that crept across Ainsley's cheeks. "Actually there's just something about you that's . . . different. You seem very exotic. Where did you say home was?"

"Far away from here," said Ainsley. He gazed out over the glade, watching the unicorns tussle on the grass, which grew dewy with the coming of night. The unicorns' hooves kicked up bits of dirt and grass, brown and green mixing with the gold from their hooves. The sounds of their play mixed with the rustling of the leaves in the trees and the occasional laughter from Megan and Brighton. Ainsley sighed. "Far, far away from here, unfortunately."

"If you love it so much here, why don't you settle down in one of the cities?" asked Rella.

Ainsley sighed again and scratched the back of his neck. "My father wouldn't be able to come, and I couldn't live without him."

Rella tilted her head and smiled. "You really are so different from our people."

"Is that a bad thing?"

Rella shook her head and scooted closer to Ainsley on his blanket. "It's very refreshing."

Ainsley heard Megan holler, "Heads up!" just before a softball-sized piece of fruit smacked into the back of his head. It was soft enough to split open on impact, and Ainsley smelled sugary nectar and felt a cold wet dripping down his neck and into his shirt.

"Oh, sorry!" Megan laughed as she helped Rella pull bits of pulp out of Ainsley's collar. Brighton wasn't picky and gobbled up whatever pieces they dropped onto the grass.

"No problem," said Ainsley through clenched teeth. "I was just thinking that I'm not sticky or dirty enough yet."

"You've got two lovely lasses fussing over you, mate," said Brighton around a mouthful of fruit. "I wouldn't complain."

"Yeah, well . . ." Ainsley was trying his hardest not to snap at Megan who was still laughing as she pressed the back of his shirt against his skin to soak up the juice. "I'm not too thrilled about being chased across the countryside by bees. Do the unicorns have a pond or something? I've got to get clean."

"The Purefalls," said Sir Inish without opening his eyes. He gestured vaguely to the east side of the glade. "Just as you enter the forest, there's a natural spring big enough to swim laps in."

"Then that's where I'll be," said Ainsley. He sauntered away and stepped past a few trees, glancing over his shoulder to see if Rella might be laughing at him with Megan. Not even realizing how close he was to the spring, he slipped on the edge and fell face-first into the water. Sputtering, he surfaced to find a cluster of unicorns staring down at him curiously. "Sorry," he said.

The unicorns whinnied and backed away. Ainsley ducked under the water, and when he surfaced, Megan was sitting in the bank looking down at him.

"Hey," she said.

"Hey." Ainsley pulled his shirt over his wings and head and wrung it out, placing it on the grass to dry.

"Sorry about the whole pelting you with fruit thing," said Megan.

"It's fine." Ainsley splashed water on his face and scrubbed.

"No, it's not," said Megan, holding her chest. "And just so you know, Rella doesn't think you're a dork or anything."

Ainsley stopped scrubbing. "I didn't . . ." He paused when he heard Megan intake a sharp breath. "I mean . . . good. So what are you doing here?"

Megan laid on her stomach. "We need a plan to recover Onaj's Horn. After we find Evren, how are we going to steal it from him when he'll probably have hundreds of guards protecting him?"

"You have the Quatrys," said Ainsley. "He wants them. We'll have to use them as bait to get to him."

Megan frowned. "You mean, we'll have to use *me* to get to him."

Ainsley treaded water for a moment. "You'd be the best person. You're obviously not susceptible to the effects of the horn, you're not really interested in magic so you won't abuse the Quatrys, and you have the ability to see through any deceit."

Megan plucked a fistful of grass and watched it flutter down into the water. "Yeah, I guess you have a good point." She looked at him. "I'm scared, though. All our friends are against us."

Ainsley swam over and put his hands on top of hers. "Not all our friends."

"But what if it comes down to them or us? Could you kill one of our friends?"

"Megan—"

"Could you?"

Ainsley sighed. "If it came down to you or them, yes."

Megan pulled her hands away from his. "What if it came down to you or me?"

"What?"

"What if one of us was turned and stood in the way of finishing the task?"

"*You* can't be turned," said Ainsley softly. "You mean, what if *I* stood in the way."

"Yes." Megan's voice was a whisper. "I don't think I could do it."

"Then, you'll have to give Brighton a tiny dagger and have him stab me." Ainsley grinned at Megan until she cracked a smile.

———

But after everyone had fallen asleep, Megan's thoughts returned to worst-case scenarios. She fidgeted and flipped from facing Ainsley to facing Brighton before finally laying on her back and staring through the canopy of trees at the star-speckled sky.

She sighed, but it turned into a startled gasp when Sir Inish spoke.

"After all the excitement of today, I would have thought you'd be snoring as loudly as Ainsley."

"Sir Inish, why are you awake?" Megan propped herself on one elbow, being careful not to disturb her sleeping companions.

The old dwarf chuckled. "I've done nothing but sleep in the dungeon for the past week. I thought I'd stand guard over all of you tonight."

Though she found this comforting, it still didn't help Megan fall asleep. She settled back into the grass and listened to the sounds of night before she spoke again. "Sir Inish?"

"Hmmm?"

"Do you . . ." Megan plucked a blade of grass and worried it with her fingers. "Do you think we have a chance of success?"

Sir Inish was quiet for a minute. "I've told you before that you and Ainsley were special and brought to us for something great. I believe this is your moment."

"But we weren't brought to you, and we're not special." Megan frowned and took a deep breath. "We accidentally followed Bornias into this world. We're just two ordinary people."

Sir Inish didn't seem surprised by Megan's revelation about her other-worldly origins. "You are certainly *not* ordinary. You've defeated a necromancer and cured the Illness. How many 'ordinary' people could say the same?"

"Yes, but we're not as powerful as Bornias or as skilled in fighting as Frieden."

It was Sir Inish's turn to rise up and look at Megan. "You don't seem to understand the powers you and Ainsley possess."

Megan sighed. "What, that he can fly and perform basic spells and that I can see the truth in everything?"

"Do you really think that is all you're worth?"

Megan stared at him. "Well . . . yeah."

"What about courage, compassion, the ability to tell right from wrong?"

"Oh, yes." Megan rolled her eyes. "When Evren's about to kill me, I'll throw a handful of courage at him." She didn't want to be sarcastic, but Sir Inish's delusions about her and Ainsley's "powers" was beginning to irritate her.

He, in turn, seemed just as irritated that Megan wouldn't believe him. "Do not jest about these powers." His words were short and sharp. "When the necromancer tried to kill you in the Swamp of Sheiran, it was compassion for you that gave Ainsley the strength to defeat him. When Ainsley was caught in the void between life and death, it was courage that allowed you to go after him and save him."

Megan's eyes welled up, and her throat filled with cotton. "Maybe . . ."

"You and Ainsley have what so many others lack." Sir Inish's voice was softer now. "You are born heroes. You will do the right thing because it *must* be done, and you will always find what you need to make it so."

"In the darkest hour, hope finds a way," whispered Megan.

"Precisely."

Megan stared back up at the sky. "So, you really think we can save the world?"

"If I didn't, I would have asked you to leave me in that dungeon," said Sir Inish. Megan could hear a smile in his voice, and she smiled, too.

"Good night, Sir Inish." She rolled onto her side with her back pressed to Ainsley's.

"Good night, Megan," said the old dwarf. "I'll see you in the morning."

"Yes. You will." She grinned to herself and closed her eyes.

A Fight to the Finish

Megan awoke the next morning to someone nudging her shoulder. She opened her eyes and found the young woman in white gazing down at her.

"Good morning," said Megan, rubbing the sleep from her eyes.

"Your friend has arrived," said the woman.

Megan sat up straight and looked around. Brighton lay to one side of her, Rella on the other with Ainsley and Sir Inish at the end. "My friend? What friend?"

"King Rayne of the Silverskin family, ruler of Raklund."

"Really?" Megan leaned across Rella and squeezed Ainsley's arm.

He mumbled to himself and rolled closer to Rella with a sleepy smile.

"Ainsley!" Megan hissed.

He blinked rapidly and then groaned when he realized it was not Rella but Megan that had been reaching for him. "What do you want, Megan?"

"Rayne's here!" She pulled on her stockings. "I wonder if he had any luck talking to the elves."

Ainsley yawned and rubbed his tunic between his fingers to remove the stiffness of the material before slipping it over his head.

"Why doesn't he come meet us in here?" Ainsley asked the woman in white.

She shook her head. "He isn't allowed. His is a dark magic."

Megan stopped in the midst of lacing a boot. "What are you talking about? The Staff of Lexiam is neutral magic. It's only affected by whoever wields it." As she said these words, her stomach turned. "Shit. He's one of them now."

The conversation was causing their companions to stir.

"What's going on?" asked Brighton, stretching like a cat.

"Oh, nothing much. Rayne's turned evil." Megan pulled her laces into a tight knot.

"We knew it was likely to happen," said Ainsley. "I just hoped it wouldn't happen so *fast*."

"Does he have anyone with him?" Sir Inish asked the woman.

"A small band of military men, all with weapons."

"How small is a band?" asked Megan, pulling her sword from her belt. "Are we talking two, or are we talking ten?"

"Both," was the terse reply. "There are a dozen others."

"Shit," said Megan again. She glanced around the glade where the unicorns were stepping out of the forest to enjoy the early rays of sunlight filtering through the break in the trees. "Will the unicorns help us?"

"No." Anala appeared beside the woman in white. "We are already meddling enough in the affairs of man. If you must battle them to complete your journey, then you must. But you will do it without the aid of my order."

Megan turned to Ainsley and the others. "Well, what's the plan? We're looking at a three-to-one ratio."

"A little less than three-to-one," spoke up Brighton. "I can still hold my own."

"Fine," said Megan, "but that still leaves us with at least two people apiece, not to mention Rayne's magic."

"Well, you have the Quatrys," said Rella.

Megan shook her head. "I won't use them. Not against Rayne. I just want to defeat him. I don't want to kill him."

"Agreed," said Ainsley. "So, why don't we just port out of here and avoid them entirely?"

"You cannot teleport into or out of the glade," said Anala. "You will have to step outside the boundaries of the forest."

"Okay. Well, then, let's sneak out the back," said Megan, tossing her pack over one shoulder. "Are we sure they're waiting at the south end of the glade?"

"Let me check," said Ainsley. He flexed his wings and shot up above the treeline. He could make out the almost-bald head of Rayne, accompanied by a group of Silvan Sentry. In one of his hands, Rayne clutched the Staff of Lexiam, which he was pointing at various Silvan Sentry to direct them elsewhere around the perimeter of the forest.

Ainsley followed a pair of the Silvan Sentry toward the west end of the glade and froze in midair. Upwards of twenty men and women, all with weapons and helms, were forming a spaced line along the outskirts of the west end of the forest. Ainsley glanced down the row of soldiers until it disappeared around a bend in the trees, but he had a strong feeling there would be more Silvan Sentry waiting farther along.

He swooped back down in front of the others.

"So, tell me there's not twelve people with him," said Megan with a hopeful expression.

"There aren't twelve," said Ainsley. "There are more like a hundred. They're Silvan Sentry, and they have the entire perimeter of the forest covered."

Megan began to pace, slapping her sword against the palm of her hand. "Rayne probably doesn't know that *we* know how many of them there are." She pointed at Ainsley. "Did anyone see you?"

"Nope. They're too busy waiting for us to sneak past them."

"If everyone is waiting for us," said Sir Inish, drawing his mace from his belt, "why don't we give them what they want?"

"Huh?" Megan curled her lip and resisted the urge to ask Sir Inish if he had gone mad from hunger. "You want us to just surrender?"

"We won't surrender, but we will need the Quatrys."

Megan's hand reached into her pocket, and she fingered the stones. "What did you have in mind?"

"A little wind rustling in the trees here and there." Sir Inish wiggled his fingertips. "Just enough to give the illusion of bodies moving through different parts of the forest. If everyone thinks we're headed their direction, nobody will know where we're truly going."

"If we're lucky, they might even leave a gap where we can slip by," added Rella.

"And if we're not lucky?" asked Megan, crossing her arms. "Because I've been noticing that one thing we've been running short of recently is luck."

"Then, we'll have a much smaller army to face and a much better chance of succeeding," said Sir Inish.

"There's no easy way out of this, Megan," said Ainsley. "And we don't have much time before Rayne starts getting suspicious."

Megan withdrew her hand from her pocket, and held the bag containing the Quatrys out to Ainsley. "Then you have to work the magic."

Ainsley refused to reach for it. "I can't. I need to be able to fight."

"Ainsley," Megan ran her fingers through her hair and clutched it in a giant handful. "As much as it pains me to say this, you're the best one here with magic. That's what you need to be doing. You need to work the wind, and we need you to get the portal going so we can get out of here."

Ainsley glanced at the others, but nobody seemed willing to step forward and take the Quatrys. He grabbed Megan by the arm and pulled her aside. "You know how I can *get* when I have access to that kind of power," he whispered.

"Of course I know, and I know you know, so you'll be extra careful to make sure it doesn't happen. And the Illness doesn't exist anymore, so our biggest concern would be you getting *jidalya*. Besides, there's something I need to do that will involve the Silvan Sentry."

They stood together for a moment in silence before Ainsley sighed and held out his hand, grimacing as Megan dropped the bag containing the Quatrys into his palm. Already, he could feel the magic itching at his fingers to be released.

Megan returned to the rest of the group. "We'll go out the east side by the spring and avoid Rayne entirely. Anala, we'll call for you when we're ready. Ainsley," she tightened her grip on the sword, "let's do this."

Ainsley shook out the Quatrys of Wind and squeezed it between his fingers, ignoring the stone's seductive whispers of power. In his mind, he asked the magic to work with him, to create a wind that could circle the glade and wend through the branches. He felt a tickle to the hairs on the nape of his neck and a moment later, he was folding his wings against his back to keep from being blown off his feet. "Go for it," he told Megan.

Gesturing to the others, she sneaked forward, trying to merge the sounds of her movement with that of the trees. She nudged Brighton with her toe and gestured to her shoulder. He leapt up beside her. "Tell me how it looks out there," she whispered.

Brighton climbed up a nearby trunk and slipped among the leaves and branches, slinking from tree to tree. He returned a moment later, dropping onto Megan's shoulder. "They seem confused by all the noise, so they're scattered. If we move a little farther north, there's a small group of them that we can make short order of."

Megan communicated the details to Rella and Sir Inish, and the foursome pressed onward. Megan climbed into one of the trees edging the forest, crawling to the edge of the branch and straddling it with both legs. Rella kept her hand on Sir Inish's back so he could see where he was stepping.

On Megan's signal, the old dwarf reached through the trees and grabbed the closest man, jerking him backwards. The man cried out and was silenced as Sir Inish's hands twisted the man's neck one way and the rest of his body another. Unfortunately, the man had been loud enough to draw the attention of his companions, and they ran toward the trees, swords drawn.

Hooking her feet together, Megan swung down sideways, plunging her sword between the shoulder blades of a surprised soldier. Now dangling upside down, she jerked free her sword and the man fell to the ground. Another man stepped forward to take his place, swinging his sword at Megan's neck. Bit jumped from Megan's pocket and dug her teeth into the man's nose while Megan dropped to the ground.

The man stumbled about, trying to keep up with Bit's frenzied biting, and Megan ran the blade of her sword across the backs of his knees, severing the tendons. The man screamed, his legs crumbling beneath him, and toppled forward. Unfortunately, when the man fell, he landed atop Bit, trapping the narshorn beneath him.

"Bit!" Megan rolled the man over, but it was too late. Her faithful pet had sacrificed herself to save Megan.

"You bastard!" she yelled at the man, stepping on his groin and grinding her heel down until he screamed.

"Look out, Megan!" cried Rella.

Megan turned just as a soldier charged toward her, using his shield as a battering ram. She waited until he was almost atop her then hit the ground, curling into a ball. A sharp pain coursed across her stomach as the man's front foot connected with her body, but a moment later, he was tumbling over her, shield flying from his hands.

Megan whipped her head toward him and watched the hilt of Rella's sword bash against the man's skull. She winced at the dull sound it produced and saw the man's eyes slide shut.

"No bloodshed?" she asked as Rella helped her to her feet. They both turned and clashed swords with a female sentry. Rella kicked out with the heel of her boot, knocking the wind out of the sentry who doubled over. Rella banged her on the top of the head with her elbow, and the woman collapsed.

"They can't help it." Rella parried a blow from another Silvan Sentry. While they were at arms, Megan slashed her blade across the man's stomach. "They're under Evren's influence."

Megan bit her lip. "Actually, they're not. They've been plotting against the Silverskins for some time."

"Oh! Well, in that case . . ." Rella whipped her sword across the next Silvan Sentry's jugular and pushed him backwards to keep the blood from spraying over her and Megan.

Confident that Rella could hold her own, Megan sprinted off to help Brighton and Sir Inish. Before she reached them, however, she realized they needed no help. Wounded and unconscious soldiers lay in heaps at Sir Inish's feet and the dwarf was striking dangerous and accurate blows with his mace. Brighton clung to Sir Inish's shoulder, providing his shared sight and turning his head this way and that to keep both himself and Sir Inish from ill fortune.

Megan scanned the soldiers on the ground, searching for one that held promise. She spotted one propped against a tree whose left hand had been reduced to a bloody mangled mess, his face a pale whitish green.

Megan dropped down beside him. "Where is Evren?"

The soldier glowered at Megan and spit in her face. "Do you really think I would tell you?"

Megan grabbed the man's good hand and held the edge of the sword to his wrist. "Your left hand will have to be removed by doctors," she growled. "Do you want me to do the same to your right?"

"Do your worst." The man slid his hand back and forth under Megan's blade, cutting his own flesh.

"Stop that!" She pulled her sword away and the man cackled at her.

"Don't threaten me, little bitch!"

Megan held the butt of her sword over his head, but just before she brought it down, she had a thought. Lowering the sword, she asked the man, "Evren's in Amdor, isn't he?"

"Yeah." The man nodded. "Yeah, that's right."

Megan felt a sharp pain in her chest, and an image flashed in front of her eyes of a stone fortress surrounded by palm trees. The palm trees stood just beyond a long line of polished planks that abutted the sand. Megan furrowed her eyebrows.

"Sand? Palm trees?" She looked down at the man. "Is Evren near water?"

The man said nothing but his eyes had grown wide and he shrank back from Megan. She grabbed the front of his tunic. "He is! But where is the water?"

"I . . . I don't know," squeaked the soldier, and Megan winced at the sting in her chest. The next vision was of a dock, hammered from the same polished planks, to which a large ship was tied. Men were carrying large crates down a ramp from the ship to the dock.

Megan gasped. "Is it the Port of Scribnitch?"

The man whimpered and nodded, and this time Megan felt nothing.

She picked up her sword and weighed it in her hand. "Sorry about this, but you can't tell anyone what I know." The man seemed to understand what was coming and bent forward, allowing Megan easy access to the back of his neck. "Sleep tight," she said, slamming the hilt of her sword against the base of his head.

She darted around soldiers and friends in search of Ainsley, but before she could reach him, her feet left the ground and she was propelled into the air. "Help!" she screamed. She knew there was no need for covertness any-more. Rayne had found them out.

She grabbed at passing branches, only plucking hand-fuls of leaves. She struggled through the air, though it did her no good. "Ainsley!" she screamed.

Something shot out of the trees, and then Ainsley was beside her, his arm secured about her waist. They stayed suspended for a moment as Ainsley battled with Quatrys and wings against a forceful gale Rayne had created.

"Is the portal ready?" Megan shouted above the winds.

Ainsley nodded. "Where are we going?"

"Just keep your mind in tune with mine!"

The air pressing against Ainsley and Megan halted abruptly, and they looked down to see what had drawn Rayne's attention from them.

The remaining Silvan Sentry had gathered around Brighton and Sir Inish who was facing Captain Kyviel with mace in hand. Behind him, Rella watched with a helpless expression.

"Oh no," whispered Megan.

"Stand down, Kyviel," said Sir Inish in his gruff voice.

Captain Kyviel smirked at him. "Why should I listen to a pathetic blind fool like you?" He swung at Sir Inish who blocked the strike with his mace.

Ainsley lowered himself and Megan to the ground, and Megan grabbed Rella's arm.

"Call for Anala and wait by the portal," she said, pointing to a glowing circle half-hidden behind the branches. "We'll get Sir Inish out of here."

Rella nodded, wincing at the jarring sounds of metal against metal before she disappeared into the woods.

But retrieving Sir Inish was easier said than done. Megan couldn't call him to her, nor could she interrupt the fight. Sir Inish and Captain Kyviel were locked together by mace and sword, their arms shaking as they each battled for control.

With enraged shouts, they both jumped back at the same time, panting. Sir Inish swung his mace like a baseball bat at Captain Kyviel who attempted a flying parry. Sir Inish's blow was too forceful and sent Captain Kyviel sprawling on his back.

Captain Kyviel leapt up, his blade splitting the air and connecting with Sir Inish's mace arm. Sir Inish grimaced but did not relinquish his grasp, instead reaching with his other hand to grip Captain Kyviel's wrist. He yanked Captain Kyviel toward him and rammed his head against the other man's.

Both of them stumbled apart, and Captain Kyviel blinked through the blood that dripped into his eyes. "Surrender, old man. I can fight far longer than you."

"I don't have to fight longer," grunted Sir Inish. "I just have to fight better." With another cry, he dove for Captain Kyviel's legs and flipped the man head over heels. His nose firmly planted in the dirt, Captain Kyviel lay still for a moment before rolling onto his back. He felt around for his sword, but Sir Inish had kicked it out of range.

"I regret that it had to come to this," said Sir Inish.

Captain Kyviel closed his eyes, waiting for the death-blow, and Sir Inish raised the mace high overhead in his calloused hands.

But then a Silvan Sentry stepped forward, dagger in hand, and with an almost casual air, he plunged it into Sir Inish's heart.

"No!" Megan tried to run to Sir Inish, but Ainsley, grabbed her arm. He could do nothing to comfort her except hold her upright, his eyes riveted on the horror they had just witnessed. Brighton appeared over Sir Inish's shoulder, looking from Megan to the wound to the old dwarf's face. Even Rayne appeared shocked, and though it was the perfect opportunity to attack Ainsley and Megan, he did nothing.

Sir Inish's eyes widened in surprise and he glanced down at his blood spilling a red waterfall onto the ground. The mace fell from his hand and his fingers curled around the dagger's handle as he dropped to his knees at the feet of Captain Kyviel.

Megan's screams were drowned in the cheers of the Silvan Sentry who hoisted Sir Inish's attacker onto their shoulders. One of them tried to help Captain Kyviel to his feet, but he refused, his gaze transfixed on Sir Inish. He nudged Sir Inish onto his back, forcing Brighton to scramble for safety, and retrieved Sir Inish's mace.

"You monster!" screamed Megan. "One of your cowards has already ended him! Let him die with dignity!" She broke free of Ainsley and lunged at Captain Kyviel who knocked her aside.

He glared at Megan and tucked the mace under Sir Inish's arm. The crowd of Silvan Sentry shifted toward him, bouncing the attacker on their shoulders.

Captain Kyviel smiled up at the other man while he collected his sword. "Come down here."

The soldier was lowered to the ground, grinning. "I helped finish him for you, sir."

"That you did," said Captain Kyviel, his smile twisted into a frown. "But I didn't need your help." Then, Captain Kyviel whipped out his sword and severed the man's head from his body. It rolled to a stop at Megan's feet, and this time, there were no other voices to quiet her screams.

The Silvan Sentry stood mutely watching the headless torso flop over, and Captain Kyviel slid his sword back into his scabbard.

"Let that be a caution to anyone else who cares to 'help' me," snarled Captain Kyviel. He pointed to Ainsley and Megan. "Now, grab them and get the Quatrys!"

There was no more time for mourning. Ainsley tightened his grip on Megan and stretched his hand out before him. A tempestuous wind issued from his fingertips, knocking into the soldiers and sending some of them flying while others were laid flat on their backs. Only Rayne withstood the gale, holding the Staff of Lexiam before him.

"Come on! We have to get out of here!" Ainsley started to back away from the scene, but Megan resisted, almost stepping into the wind's path.

"We can't leave Sir Inish here!" she cried, laying on her stomach and crawling toward her fallen friend.

"Dammit!" Ainsley raised his hand a little higher so Megan wouldn't be impacted by the wind and increased the velocity.

Megan grabbed hold of the shoulders of Sir Inish's shirt and tugged with all her strength. Unfortunately, it wasn't enough. All she could do was inch Sir Inish's body across the grass. Then, Rella appeared beside her. They exchanged a teary-eyed glance and both took hold of one of Sir Inish's arms, dragging him toward the portal where Anala was waiting. The unicorn saw the distraught faces of the two girls and the body they supported between them and bowed her head in sympathy.

Ainsley and Brighton joined them a moment later. "Everyone into the circle, and focus your thoughts on where Megan's going!" shouted Ainsley, pulling the portal instructions from his pocket to make the final incantation. Before he could utter a word, Rayne was upon him, wresting Ainsley's arms behind his back and digging through his pockets.

Megan and Rella tried to help him, but they struck Rayne's shield of energy and were knocked onto their backs.

"Give me the Quatrys!" Rayne growled at Ainsley.

Ainsley did his best to resist, but Rayne's shield limited his movements. At one moment, he felt the pouch of Quatrys in his chest pocket, and the next, it was gone.

"You'll stay away if you know what's good for you," Rayne hissed in his ear. He shoved Ainsley's face in the ground and released him. When Ainsley rolled onto his back, Rayne was darting away through the trees and his friends where staring down at him.

"He took the Quatrys," said Ainsley, though he could tell this wasn't news to the others.

Getting to his feet, he finished the chant to activate the portal. "Remember to focus your thoughts on Megan," he said.

"We're not going to try and get the Quatrys back?" asked Brighton.

Ainsley shook his head. "We need to get out of here before we lose anything else." Out of the corner of his eye, he could see Sir Inish's limp, bloodstained corpse. "Or *anyone* else."

16

The Blame Game

Ainsley let himself relax against the movement of the portal as it shifted through space, and when it finally eased to a stop, he opened his eyes.

They had come to rest in a gully flanked on both sides by tree-topped mountains. At the near end of the gully was a cottage surrounded by a fence that appeared to be made of white sticks.

"Why don't I think this is Evren's hideout?" asked Ainsley as Megan hurried toward the cottage. He chased after her. "Megan, where are we?"

Instead of answering him, she scooped up a rock and threw it at the house. Before it could even reach the walkway, however, something wraithlike drifted up from the ground and snatched it out of the air, hurling it back.

Ainsley shielded himself and Megan with a wing, squinting his eyes at the floating object. It was pale and wispy, almost ethereal in appearance.

Anala's nostrils flared, and she bared her teeth. "I'll go no closer to the den of a bonemaster. Call for me when you are ready to leave this place." Before anyone could protest, she galloped into the trees.

"Oh, no," Ainsley groaned. "Megan, please tell me we're not here to see who I think we are."

The front door of the cottage was thrown open and a tall figure filled its frame. "Who's there?" The figure stepped out of the darkened cottage and into the sunlight. Though he was still pale, his skin had gotten a bit more color since Ainsley and Megan had last seen him, and his dark hair had filled in to a thick stubble.

"Losen," said Ainsley under his breath.

The necromancer stopped when he recognized his visitors. "What are you doing here? I've paid my penance."

"We need your help." Megan climbed over the fence, which Ainsley realized was not made of sticks but bones, and swatted aside the spirits that circled her. "My friend's been killed." She grabbed Losen's arm and pulled him away from his cottage.

"Killed?"

Ainsley was glad Megan couldn't see the eager expression on Losen's face.

"Yes, so I need you to bring him back to life." Megan stopped in front of Sir Inish's body.

"Yes, well . . ." Losen scratched his head and bent beside the corpse. "I don't think you really want that."

Rella, who had been doing her best to straighten Sir Inish's clothes, glanced up. "Yes, we do. Please bring him back."

Megan kneeled beside Losen. "Please just do this. I'll arrange for King Rayne to give you as much money as you want. I'll even try to get you reinstated into society. Look, I have a little money right now." Megan started fishing through her pockets for her coin purse.

Losen shook his head and placed a hand on her arm. "You don't understand. I can't bring your friend back to life for the same reason I couldn't bring my father back to life."

Megan paused in her searching. "What do you mean? You're a necromancer. Your specialty is the dead."

Losen sat beside Sir Inish's body and rubbed his temples. "I can reanimate him, but all he would be is a walking corpse . . . a zombie. In order to be a living person, he needs his soul back, and that I cannot provide."

Megan bit her lip, as if she was considering the offer, and Ainsley crouched down on her other side. "Megan, you need to let him go. Sir Inish wouldn't want this."

She shook her head, blinking back tears. "It's not fair. He just got his sight back."

Brighton, who had remained quiet until this point, crept up to Megan and placed a hand on her knee. "At least you gave him his freedom."

Megan jerked away. "Shut up! You didn't even know him, and it's your fault he's dead, you stupid ferret! Why didn't you warn him?"

With each of her vitriolic words, Brighton ducked his head lower and lower. With her final accusation, "His blood is on your hands!" Brighton slunk away.

"Megan, don't attack him," said Ainsley. "He helped Sir Inish when he didn't have to. He risked his life to help us, and he's done it several times before."

Megan's shoulders, which had been heaving with anger moments before, now drooped as she watched Brighton walk by himself to climb a tree. Ainsley bent his head close to hers. "It's too late to save Sir Inish. Let it go."

She nodded and bowed her head, letting her entire body shake with sobs. Rella, who had been silently crying over Sir Inish, wrapped her arms around Megan's shoulders and the two of them cried together while Ainsley fought down a lump in his throat.

He couldn't look Losen in the eye when he asked, "Will you help us give him a proper burial?"

Losen, who had been staring intently at the ground, nodded.

Ainsley cleared his throat. "Thank you. I'll be right back."

It didn't take long for him to spot Brighton, the ferret having chosen to roost in a tree with patchy branches. He lay with his back to Ainsley, the only movement coming from the rise and fall of his furry middle.

"She didn't mean it, you know," said Ainsley.

"I know," came the solemn reply, "but she said exactly what I've been thinking . . . what everyone's been thinking. I saw the soldier with the dagger. I just thought he planned to volunteer his life for Captain Kyviel's."

"You made a mistake," said Ainsley.

Brighton turned to face him. "A mistake that cost someone his life. I don't even deserve to be a *ferret*. I should have been turned into a pile of dung."

"Yeah," said Ainsley. He tried to lighten the mood. "Then maybe Megan wouldn't always be complaining about how bad *I* smell."

The corner of Brighton's mouth didn't so much as twinge. "I was fond of her, you know."

"I know," said Ainsley, "but don't hold what she said against her. She was angry when she said those things."

"She called me a ferret."

"You *are* a ferret."

"Yes, but the way she said it . . ." Brighton sighed and slipped down from the tree. "Let's go bury your friend. We still have the world to save."

Megan, Rella, and Losen had migrated toward the base of one of the mountains, and Ainsley noticed that Sir Inish's body was no longer laying on the ground. Megan had dried her tears and was fashioning a cross out of sticks tied together with fabric from her cape while Rella sprinkled liquid from a bottle on a plot of upturned dirt.

"You've buried him, then," said Ainsley. "Sorry we weren't there."

"That's okay. Losen was able to do it quickly. It was better that way," said Megan, keeping her head bowed over her work. She had watched Ainsley coax Brighton back, but she wasn't ready to face Brighton after what she'd said. She was afraid that if she acknowledged what she'd done, Brighton would see it as an invitation to end their friendship. She knew he wouldn't retaliate with harsh insults of his own, though she wished he *would* to make things even between them.

"Do you need any help?" asked Ainsley.

She wished it had been Brighton who asked. "No thanks. I'm all finished." She forced the cross into the ground at the head of the dirt mound. "Here." She tossed something to Ainsley, and he caught it in one hand.

"The stone of shared sight? Megan, why didn't you leave this with his body?"

"Because . . . because . . ." Megan's lower lip quivered and she pointed to Losen.

"Magic scavengers," said Losen. "If you bury a body with any items of power, they'll sniff it out and loot the grave. I didn't think you'd want your friend's body desecrated in that manner."

"Oh." Ainsley returned the stone to its magic-binding bag. "You're right. Thanks."

"The blessing is complete," said Rella, handing the now-empty bottle to Losen. "His journey to the Other Side should be swift and easy." Tears brimmed in her eyes. "If you'll excuse me for a moment." She started to walk away, but Ainsley grabbed her arm. "You stay. We'll go." Rella smiled at him and settled onto the ground beside Sir Inish's grave.

"Come on, guys," said Ainsley, heading into the shade of the trees with Brighton and Losen.

Megan hung back, gazing at the mound of dirt and thinking of the grizzled, old dwarf resting beneath it. Just the night before he'd watched the treetops brushing against the stars for the first time in so many years, but now he would no more. Even without his eyesight, he'd been an exemplary man and a skilled fighter. He'd given Megan strength and hope to save a world in which he no longer existed. Megan placed her fingertips to her mouth and blew a kiss to Sir Inish's grave. "I won't forget you."

"Megan, are you okay?"

Her heart crumbled a little more when she realized it still wasn't Brighton speaking to her. She smiled up at Ainsley through blurry eyes. "Yeah. I'll be fine."

He hugged her and steered her away from Rella. "Come on. We told Losen about our situation, and he thinks he has a way to help us."

Evil Lends a Hand

Losen nodded at Megan when she and Ainsley stepped amidst the trees. Megan returned it and chanced a glimpse at Brighton, but he was staring at a patch of leaves in front of him.

"Ainsley and Brighton have been telling me what's happened since I left Raklund. Evren has the kingdom under his control?"

"For all we know, he could have all of *Arylon* under his control," said Megan, "but yes, he definitely has Raklund and I'm guessing the Port of Scribnitch as well."

"The Port of Scribnitch?" asked Ainsley. "What makes you say that?"

"That's where he's headquartered," said Megan. "That was the information I was able to get from the Silvan Sentry."

"How do you know he wasn't lying?"

Megan stiffened. It was Brighton now who addressed her, but only to question her knowledge. "I have a Pearl of Truth lodged in my heart, and it reveals any deception to me." She ignored his stunned gaze. "That's how I know."

"It makes sense," said Losen. "He'll be able to control anyone who enters the country from the east: dignitaries, merchants, all manner of brigands. He could commandeer entire fleets and send out raiding parties. Before long, he could have the entire world under his control."

Ainsley and Megan frowned at one another. They both knew Evren wouldn't stop with just his world, especially not since he would soon have both the Staff of Lexiam and the Quatrys.

"So we have to make it into Evren's headquarters and steal the horn and break it," Megan told Losen. "Ainsley and I already thought about that. We have the unicorn and everything."

"Yes, but you won't be able to port directly to him," said Losen. "He'll have soldiers and magical barricades set up to keep out intruders. Where in the Port of Scribnitch is he?"

"I'm . . . I'm not sure," said Megan, staring at her lap.

Ainsley grunted in exasperation. "Megan!"

"What?" She shrugged. "I figured we would look around when we got there."

"If Evren has the port under his control, that could be dangerous," said Losen. "And the port is considerably large. You'll need to find out where he's stationed and quickly."

"Do you have a summoning pool we could use?" asked Megan.

Losen shook his head. "By order of the Kingdom Coalition, I'm not allowed one."

"Then we have to stop by Amdor before—"

"Megan, we're not on a family vacation," interrupted Ainsley. "We can't keep making these detours. Now that Evren has the staff and the Quatrys, the situation's more dangerous than ever before."

She bit her lip. "Okay, you're right. We'll have to split up when we get there, though."

Ainsley groaned, and Megan snapped at him. "What?"

"How are we supposed to let each other know if we find it? Holler down the beach, 'I've found Evren's hideout'?"

Losen held up a hand and got to his feet. "Actually, I may have something that can help you." Without another word, he walked back to his cottage.

"Are . . . we supposed to follow him?" asked Megan.

"You can," said Ainsley. "I'm with Anala. I'd prefer to stay as far away from his house as possible."

"He doesn't seem too bad of a fellow," said Brighton, "for a necromancer that is."

"He's a monster," said Ainsley, "but he seems to like Megan. We've battled with him a few times, and each time he gets worried when he thinks he's killed her."

"A compassionate necromancer?" Brighton snorted. "Why?

"Who knows?" Ainsley shrugged. "Maybe he's in love with her."

"*Her* is sitting right here," said Megan. "And he doesn't like me either. He just dislikes you more because you get into pissing contests with him."

"Pissing contests?" asked Brighton, making a disgusted face.

Ainsley rolled his eyes. "Not *real* pissing contests. We just try and . . . kill each other is all."

"Here we are," said Losen, walking toward them with two hairless black creatures wriggling in his hands.

"What the hell is that?" Megan jumped up and stumbled backwards. Ainsley snorted but scooted a bit farther away himself.

"They're messenger bats." Losen held out his hands, palms up, and Megan ducked, expecting them to fly at her.

But their wings remained folded against their bodies, and the bats did nothing more than hop around, their oversized ears making them teeter back and forth with every movement.

"Huh." Megan stepped closer. "What's the command to get them to fly?"

"They can't fly," said Losen. "These bats were born with lame wings, but instead of letting them die, we use them as messengers."

"Okay." Ainsley prodded one of the bats with his finger, and it toppled onto its belly. "And how do they do that exactly? Please tell me it's not by walking."

Losen gripped the tip of one of the bat's ears. "These aren't sausages, you know."

"So, they call to each other," said Megan. "But how will we understand what they're saying?"

Losen thrust his hands toward Megan. "Take one."

"Um . . . okay." She grabbed a bat around its middle and squealed when it fidgeted in her fingers.

"Now stay there." Losen clutched the remaining bat in one hand and trotted several yards away. He stroked the bat until it opened its mouth, and when it did, he spoke into its ear but his words were too soft for Megan to hear.

The bat she was holding stiffened, and for a moment, Megan thought she had squeezed it too hard and killed it. But then it shifted and opened its mouth. Out came Losen's voice.

"Can you hear me?" it said. Then, the bat closed its mouth.

Megan did as she had seen Losen do, stroking her bat's head until it opened its mouth again. "Yes, I can," she whispered in its ear. There was a pause and then Losen's bat opened its mouth. Megan could hear her own voice emitting from it.

Megan turned her own bat around and studied it. It blinked tiny black eyes at her but seemed like any regular bat. "How do they do that?" she asked.

"It's complicated," said Losen, running back over, "but they send the words we say to one another using sound waves and translate the waves back into words we can hear." He held the other bat out to Ainsley. "Just make sure its mouth is open when you're sending, or you'll lose part of the message."

He then produced two mesh bags from his pocket. "You can keep them hidden away until you need them. They prefer the dark and can survive with minimal air."

Megan dropped her bat into the bag and pulled her chest pocket open. She sighed and fought back tears, seeing Bit's food pellets lying at the bottom. "Goodbye, Bit," she whispered. "Thanks for everything." She sprinkled the pellets on the ground and deposited the bat bag into the newly vacated pocket. Ainsley placed his in his pants pocket.

"Be careful not to squash them," said Losen. "Or they'll make a racket that everyone in the port will be able to hear."

"Thanks," said Ainsley. "I should probably start setting up the portal." He pulled the potion and parchment from his belt.

"I'll go get the unicorn," said Brighton.

"I guess I'll go get Rella," said Megan.

Losen accompanied her part of the way until he reached his front gate. "So, we're *completely* even now, right?"

Megan grinned and bowed her head. "Yes. Completely. Sorry for intruding like that."

"I can honestly say I didn't mind," said Losen. "Nobody ever travels through here, and my mother and I aren't quite brave enough to venture into society. It was refreshing to have people . . . *living* people . . . to talk to."

Megan caught Rella's eye and waved to her. Rella dusted off her knees and walked toward Megan, but before she got too close, Megan asked Losen, "Why *have* you always been worried about what happens to me? Aren't we supposed to be on opposite sides?"

"Well," Losen gave Megan a quick once-over and smiled, "since I can't really lie to you, let's just say you remind me of someone special whom I tried to keep safe but couldn't." His smile faltered a little.

Megan extended a hand to him. "That's good enough for me. Take care, Losen."

He shook it. "You, too, Megan, and good luck." He nodded to Rella and strode up the path to his cottage, spirits swirling around him.

"Are we ready to go?" asked Rella.

Megan embraced her. "That portal will take you anywhere you want to go. It's only going to get worse from here."

"I know, but it wouldn't be right of me to let Sir Inish have died for nothing." Rella lifted her chin and set her jaw. "I have to help you see this through."

"Okay, then." Megan explained their plan. By the time they reached Ainsley, Brighton, and Anala, the portal was ready. Megan couldn't help but notice that Anala seemed a little ill-fitted with the group. "Um . . . is walking through the port of Scribnitch with a unicorn going to be a problem?"

"Not if they see me as a human," said Anala. "I've already cast the illusion, but the pearl allows you to see through it."

"She looks as human as us," confirmed Ainsley. "Now, let's focus our thoughts on the middle of the Port of Scribnitch, preferably where nobody will see us arrive."

"Under the boardwalk," said Rella.

"Under the boardwalk then." Ainsley read the final words from the parchment, and they all closed their eyes.

———

The first thing Ainsley sensed when they arrived at the Port of Scribnitch was a cold wetness seeping into his pant legs and dribbling into his boots.

"Oh, crap," he said, opening his eyes and looking down. They were beneath the boardwalk, but it appeared to be high tide. Beside him, Brighton's furry head bobbed above the surf as he treaded water with his paws to stay afloat. Ainsley lifted him onto his back.

"Okay. I'm really not liking this," said Megan as the water began to rise and her boots began to sink into the sand.

"Apologies," said Rella. "I forgot what hour it was. This way." She pointed toward a break in the boardwalk where stone steps had been carved leading from water to pier.

"Everyone be on the alert," said Ainsley, creeping up to the boardwalk level. He glanced down the length of polished planks on either side, overwhelmed at the number of shops housed beside and on top of one another. He was impressed, but also a little disheartened. As far as he could see in either direction stretched boardwalk and buildings. "Losen was right. This could take a while."

He moved aside so the others could join him and turned around to look out over the ocean. Ships with impressive masts were anchored at each dock butting against the boardwalk. *Lady Luck*, the ship nearest them, had three masts and appeared almost ready to embark. The last few carts of goods were being pushed up the gangplank and several men on board were turning the capstan to raise the anchor.

Ainsley licked the sea salt off his lips and ran his fingers through his hair. "Well, let's start looking." He pulled his messenger bat bag from his pocket and held it up. "Megan, you'll let me know as soon as you see anything."

She produced her bag as well. "Of course."

"Do you want Anala to go with you?" asked Ainsley.

"Nah. I've got the Pearl of Truth, so I should be okay. Good hunting!"

Ainsley waved to her and started down the boardwalk with Rella and Anala. He couldn't help looking at the people they passed. "Some of these people seem so normal," he murmured.

"They are," said Anala. "Evren hasn't affected all of them yet."

They walked in silence for several minutes more until Ainsley began to feel like someone was walking behind him. He glanced casually over one shoulder and then did a doubletake. "Brighton! What are you doing here? You're supposed to be with Megan."

"Well, I didn't think she'd want my company," said Brighton. "And the unicorn's with her anyway, so—"

Now Anala turned around. "No, I'm with you."

"But—" Brighton pointed at her. "You—" He clapped a paw to his forehead. "I forgot you were in human form," he said through clenched teeth. "I thought that maybe you were some lady Ainsley had picked up along the way."

Anala snorted. "I wouldn't dream of it."

Ainsley chose to ignore her comment. "Wait . . . so Megan's wandering around by herself?"

Brighton and Rella stared at one another then at Ainsley. He sighed and removed his bat from his bag. "Megan, where are you?" he spoke in its ear.

There was no response.

"She'd better not be off eating somewhere." Ainsley frowned and pressed a hand to his yawning stomach. He pocketed his bat and hurried back down the boardwalk where they'd left Megan, but she was nowhere in sight. "Damn."

"Um . . . Ainsley?" Brighton tugged at Ainsley's pant leg. He glanced down and cursed again.

Lying on the ground was a wriggling mesh bag containing one flightless bat.

Megan Goes Missing

"Everyone off the boardwalk," said Ainsley, pushing the others into an alley. "Now."

"Where's Megan?" asked Brighton.

"I don't know, but whoever grabbed her is probably looking for us, too." They were now all huddled in front of a shop facing the alley. Ainsley tried to pull up on the door's handle, but it wouldn't budge "Dammit!"

"I think I can get that for you," said Brighton.

Rella kept watch for passersby, while Brighton balanced on Anala's back and picked the lock with one of his claws.

"Here we go," he said.

Ainsley cracked the door open and poked his head into the room. There was nothing inside the shop but racks and racks of barrels and a small desk which was unoccupied. Ainsley beckoned to the others and they all followed him inside, Rella latching the door behind them.

"Okay. About Megan," said Ainsley. "The only guess I have is that Evren or one of his henchman snatched her."

Rella held up her hand. "But if that were the case, why wouldn't he have come for us, too?"

"Probably because we don't have a Pearl of Truth." Brighton climbed to the top of one of the barrel racks. "But 'why' isn't important now. We need to find Megan." His entire body wriggled with nervous energy. "Whoever grabbed her can't be far away, and every moment we waste takes her farther and farther from us."

"Right," said Ainsley. "Now, whoever took Megan didn't go past us, or we would have seen them. That means we start searching in the direction Megan was headed. Let's split up again, but this time *nobody* goes alone." He handed Megan's messenger bat to Rella. "You go with Brighton and I'll go with Anala."

"Why don't I go with the ferret?" asked Anala. "He could climb on my back and we could gallop . . . er . . . run toward the end of the boardwalk and start from there." She reached for Rella's messenger bat.

"No, you have to go with me," said Ainsley. "The Silverskins are familiar with Megan and . . ." He paused, knowing he couldn't mention the real danger of him and Megan being from a different world. "Just trust me. They'll be looking for me, too, and I'll need you to disguise me with magic."

Rella pocketed the bat bag and shifted her sword so it was within easy reach. "Brighton and I will look in the first two buildings closest to the pier where we started. You and Anala search numbers three and four, and we'll continue alternating like that." Rella held her arm up to Brighton and he leapt onto it, crawling to her shoulder.

"Good luck," Ainsley told Rella. "Keep your guard up. If someone comes after you, just run. Don't be a hero. Don't—"

Rella stepped toward Ainsley and grabbed his hand. Not for the first time, he found himself slightly mesmerized by her. Her eyes were fixed on his in a playfully defiant way and her lips were set in a light smirk. He was starting to regret choosing Anala for his search party.

"I'll be fine," said Rella. "I survived in Raklund when I was surrounded by nothing *but* evil, didn't I?"

"Well, yeah," he said. He shifted his weight forward, closer to her, reveling in the way her chest lifted and fell with every breath. "But—"

Brighton reached out and patted Ainsley on the cheek with a paw. "Thanks for being so concerned about *me*," he said. "We'll both be fine."

Ainsley shot Brighton a warning look, and Rella laughed. "Yes, don't *you* get caught," she told Ainsley. She squeezed his fingers with a firm, almost masculine grip.

"I don't want to have to rescue you, too." She nodded at Anala. "Good luck."

"And you."

Rella unlocked the door and strutted out of the shop. Ainsley watched her coppery hair swish from side to side with every movement until the last tendril slipped around the edge of the door and disappeared from sight.

Ainsley sighed, thumping his fingers against the doorframe. Behind him, Anala cleared her throat. "Should I wait here until you complete your mating ritual?"

"What?" Ainsley blushed and turned toward Anala. At the serious expression on her face, however, he laughed. "No. I don't think now would be a good time for that."

"I agree," said Anala. "Let us begin the search for Megan."

They slipped out of the shop and hurried past the two buildings Rella and Brighton were to cover. They could already see Rella speaking to the shopkeeper who sold fishing supplies in the first building while Brighton shimmied up the wall to the second floor.

Ainsley and Anala entered the shop on the bottom floor of building three and were startled by two gargoyles, which waited just inside the doorway to greet them. After surmising that Ainsley and Anala proved no threat, they circled the room and planted themselves on diamond doors at the opposite end of the room, hardening into their stone forms.

The shop appeared to be a bank of sorts where merchants could exchange currency and store their belongings in tar-coated boxes behind the diamond doors. There were only a few people in the bank, but they all seemed eager to get in and out as quickly as possible. The banker behind the counter looked up at her current customer with a dazed expression, going through the motions of her job without so much as a smile. A man in a large floppy hat stood directly in front of Ainsley and Anala, shifting his weight from one foot to the other.

"Excuse me." Ainsley tapped him on the shoulder, hoping he might have a spark of life in his eyes. "Can I ask you a question?"

The man spun around and beamed, the corners of his smile lost beneath the hat. "Oh, thank the Other Side!" He clapped Ainsley on the shoulders. "Someone with a personality." He leaned back and admired Anala with a low whistle. "Does your beautiful mother have a personality as well?"

Anala narrowed her eyes. "He is not my colt."

The man gave Anala a strange look, and Ainsley edged his way in front of her. "She's my sister, not my mother."

The man removed his hat and bowed to Anala. "Apologies. It was not my intent to insult your age."

Anala opened her mouth to protest but changed it to a sigh when Ainsley gave her a pleading look. "Apology accepted."

"You must have just arrived to the port in the last few days," said the man. "All the townspeople are acting strange, but a friend of mine who got here two days ago is as normal as you or me."

"We got here just today, actually," said Ainsley. "And we're looking for a friend of ours . . . a girl with curly brown hair that would have passed by here in the last half hour. She might have been with a red-haired guy?"

The man in the floppy hat frowned. "I wish I could help you, but I've been waiting in this line for almost an hour now, so I haven't seen anyone come and go except through these doors."

"You've been here for an hour?" Ainsley peered around the people in line to the banker's table. The banker was counting out coins to a customer, then scooping them into her palm and recounting them.

"Look, I trust you. Just please give me my money!" The man reached out to grab it, but the gargoyles affixed to the diamond doors shrieked and flew at him. They each clutched one of his arms in their claws and lifted him off the ground.

"All right, all right!" cried the man. "Count it again for the tenth time!"

"She's been doing *everything* ten times," the man with the floppy hat told Ainsley. "That's why it's been taking so long. It's almost like she's been hypnotized to do it that way."

"Huh." Ainsley raised his eyebrows at Anala. "Well, good luck with this. We have to keep searching for our friend."

"Same to you," said the man.

There were groans from the front of the line. "She dropped the coins on the ground! Now, she's starting all over again!" The customer who had been accosted by the gargoyles was sitting on the floor, sobbing.

"Let's move on to the next shop," said Ainsley, holding the door open for Anala.

There was nothing above the bank, so they proceeded to the fourth building, Tipsy's, which had combined two buildings to make a modest-sized tavern. It seemed to be the spot where all those unaffected by Evren had gathered.

When Ainsley and Anala stepped through the doorway, everyone seemed to freeze, their hands reaching for assorted weaponry. Ainsley raised a hand and waved, smiling. "Hello. We just got here today," he said.

The other patrons relaxed, as if those words confirmed the normalcy of the newcomers, and returned to their drinks and conversations. Ainsley, noticed, however, that wary eyes were still upon him but especially on Anala who moved among the tables with an expression of complete indifference. She approached a gruff-looking man in an apron who sat at a table with several other men of questionable appearance.

"Are you the owner?" she asked the man in the apron.

"Nay. That's Tipsy, but she'd be useless to you." The man frowned and pointed to a woman standing over a vacant table in the corner. She held a pitcher at an angle over an empty stein but nothing flowed from the pitcher.

Ainsley frowned. "Uh . . . does she realize she's not filling that stein . . . and that there's nobody sitting there?"

The man in the apron shook his head. "Tipsy's been bent over the table like that all day. She seems to have it in her head that she's supposed to fill the stein with the contents of the pitcher. But since there's nothing in the pitcher, she can't ever fill the stein."

The man patted the apron. "So, I took it upon myself to assume her duties until she eventually comes to her senses. Is there something I can get for you?" He leaned forward confidentially. "If you're having trouble getting your money from the bank, I'm willing to barter."

"We're looking for someone, actually," said Ainsley. He described Megan, but to his chagrin, all of the men at the table shook their heads.

"I haven't left the tavern all day," said one of them. "It's too eerie out there for my tastes. But the girl you described never came in here."

"I've been here since last night," said another. "She wasn't here last night either."

"No, no. Is there anyone who's been outside *recently*? Like in the past half hour?" asked Ainsley.

"Well, you have," said the man in the apron.

Ainsley ran his fingers through his hair. "*Besides* us."

"You can question them until the sun sets and you'll never get the answer you want." A woman sitting at a nearby table laughed, her voice hoarse and scratchy from the pipe she smoked.

"Do you know of anyone who's just arrived?" asked Anala.

"I'm certain I do," said the woman, chewing on the end of her pipe. "Me."

Ainsley pulled out a chair at her table and settled himself across from her. "And did you see a brunette girl?"

The woman leaned back in her chair. "I did. And I might know where she went if the price is right." She took a draw from her pipe and blew smoke circles toward Ainsley.

He coughed and fanned the air in front of him. "Well, I don't have any money—"

"Then I don't have any information." The woman licked her lips and drew closer to Ainsley. "But, like my good friend over there, I'm also willing to barter."

Ainsley crossed his arms over his chest. "Okay, that's just sick. You're two . . . maybe twelve . . . times my age!"

The woman laughed again, ending in a hacking cough that produced a disgusting amount of phlegm. "Don't flatter yourself, boy. Magic's what I'm after." She pointed to Anala. "Give me your magic, and I'll tell you what happened to your friend."

It was all Ainsley could do to not reach across the table and jam the pipe down the woman's throat. "I told you, we—"

"Here." Anala held a sparkling purple object out to the woman. "To turn starlight into gold dust."

The woman put down her pipe and reached for the object with both hands, her eyes shining. "Yes, *this* is powerful magic. I can feel it." She glanced at the other patrons with narrowed eyes, as if they were all preparing to jump her for her newfound treasure.

Ainsley pounded his fist on the table. "Now, tell us where our friend is."

"Of course, of course." The woman slipped the purple object down the front of her blouse and grinned at Ainsley with blackened teeth. "I just hope you're good swimmers."

A Dish Best
Served Cold

Megan awoke to a sharp pain between her temples and felt as if the ground were quaking beneath her. "What the hell?" She rubbed her head, then her eyes, and lay on her back, still feeling slightly woozy.

It took a moment for her vision to clear, and when her eyes focused, she found herself staring at planks of wood. At first, she thought she must have fallen under the boardwalk, but when she put her hands down to either side, she felt more wood beneath her fingertips.

Megan shifted, drawing her legs toward her, but her right leg felt much heavier than usual. She heard a clank of metal and froze. The noise stopped and she pulled her left leg to her chest. When she raised her right leg again, however, the chinking sound returned.

"Oh, please no," she whispered, panic setting in. She twisted her torso so she could see her right leg. What she saw made her whimper and dig her fingernails into the floor.

Her right boot had been removed and replaced with an iron cuff secured around her ankle. A chain ran from the cuff to a plate fastened against the wall. The wall appeared slightly warped, curving inward and damp in places from the sea air.

Megan whimpered and turned her head to the other side. A few feet away, more iron held her captive in the form of bars stretching from floor to ceiling. She reached for one of them and jerked her arm back and forth. The bar didn't so much as creak. Megan rolled onto her hands and knees and crawled up to the bars, still feeling herself sway to and fro.

A hallway separated her cage from one across the way, but there was nobody imprisoned opposite her. Megan pressed her cheek against the cold metal and peered down the hall-way. She couldn't see far, but there was nothing but more cells. She turned the other way and saw more of the same.

Megan screamed at the top of her lungs and pulled on the cell bars. "Help! Let me out!" She stopped for a moment and listened. The only thing she could hear was her own breathing and the walls creaking around her. She screamed again, kicking at the bars with her feet and letting her chain rattle and smack against the wood floor. "Please! Someone help me!"

And then she heard footsteps in the hallway, striding toward her at a brisk pace.

She reached through the bars and waved her arm. "Ainsley, in here! What's—" She cut off when she saw the hem of a golden cape and a pair of polished boots.

"You!" Megan growled and grabbed for the man, but he stepped back a pace and was out of her reach.

"I *knew* there was something different about you," said Lapper the Arena Master. "Nobody your age . . . or gender," he curled his lip, "has ever made it through my obstacle course." He crouched down to Megan's eye level. "But you've got a little something special, haven't you? You've got a Pearl of Truth."

Megan backed away from the bars. "How . . . how did you know that?"

"I didn't have to." Lapper sneered, flashing his yellowed teeth. "I heard you boasting to your friends about it at the Port of Scribnitch, and it gave me an idea for how you could repay me for my servant and sword."

"You can have the sword back," said Megan. She reached for it but realized it was missing.

Lapper held it up. "I've already taken it back, thank you."

Megan clenched her jaw. "So, what, you're going to hold me for ransom until you get the money to buy another servant?"

Lapper examined his fingernails. "Oh, I don't need a ransom to get the money I need. I plan to sell you at auction."

Megan narrowed her eyes. "You can't sell people in Arylon. The Kingdom Coalition wouldn't allow it."

"Oh dear!" Lapper clapped his hand to his mouth, feigning shock. "Then it's a good thing we're not in Arylon anymore, isn't it?"

"What?!" Megan staggered to her feet, but this time she realized the off-kilter feeling she experienced wasn't her. The creaking wood, the damp walls, the rocking motion all made sense now. She was on one of the ships they'd seen at the Port of Scribnitch.

"I'll wager you'll fetch a lovely price in Obonia." Lapper leered. "A pretty girl like you with a magical gift."

"You asshole! You can't do this!" Megan thrust a hand through the bars at Lapper, but he grabbed it.

"After the humiliation and revenue you cost me, you have no idea how much I would love to slice off each and every one of your fingers." Lapper pressed the edge of the sword against Megan's thumb, and she winced. "But that would hurt your resell value." He slid the sword under his belt and kissed Megan's hand. "And we wouldn't want that, would we?"

Megan jerked her hand from him and cradled it against her. "You won't get away with this."

"Famous last words of everyone I've sold at auction."
Lapper smiled at her. "I've been kind enough to leave you
with most of your personal belongings." Lapper pointed to
Megan's backpack, which had been thrown in the corner
of her cell. "We should arrive on the island a little after
nightfall. You'll scream if you need anything in the mean-
time, won't you?" Whistling to himself, he strolled away.

Megan wedged her face between the bars. "My friends
are coming for me!"

"They don't even know you're missing." Lapper called
back with a laugh. "I saw them walking away."

"They *are* coming!" she hollered, her voice shaking.
"They'll find me!" Her throat felt tight and tears pricked
her eyes. She heard a door close and the sound of a
wooden crossbeam sliding against it.

Megan checked her pocket for the messenger bat, but
it wasn't there. She choked back a sob.

For the first time since she'd arrived in Arylon, she
was completely alone, and by the time anyone knew to
look for her, she would be traded off to her new owner
and gone forever. Pressing her back against the bars of her
cell, she slid to the floor and cried.

The ship sliced through the ocean, carrying her farther and farther from Arylon and the Port of Scribnitch.
She listened for a while to the water pushing against the
hull and the ship's respondent creaks of protest, mingled
with the shouts of the men on the deck above. The sounds

of the sea calmed her somewhat, and she wiped her eyes on her sleeve.

She knew there was nobody to help her, and she would need to keep her wits about her if she was to escape when the ship arrived in Obonia. She hoped she could use the darkness to her advantage or perhaps enlist one of the islanders to help her. For all she knew, however, they were cannibals and would love to help her out of her leg cuffs and into a big kettle of human stew.

Megan remembered *The Traveler's Tales* that she had packed in her satchel. She couldn't imagine Lapper taking it from her, but she still said a silent prayer when she reached for her bag. She felt the shape of the book before she even pulled it out and kissed the cover. If nothing else, the book brought her comfort and memories of her friends. She had found *The Traveler's Tales* after her first meeting with Brighton and had read it to Ainsley when he'd been stricken with the Illness.

She sniffled and flipped through the pages in search of the Os, realizing she'd never actually read anything in that section. After the first few listings about oakmoss eaters and obnoxious elves, which were cross-listed with Ponzipoo, she'd skipped ahead to the Ps. Now, she was thankful to find several pages devoted to Obonia. She settled on her stomach and began to read.

When Simeon Drake first set foot upon the tropical isle, he greeted the chieftaness with a hearty "Raylu!"

The chieftaness greeted him in return with a swing of her sword that sent his head rolling into the ocean. For instead of using the Obonian greeting of "Rylu," Simeon had called the chieftaness a raylu, or prostitute.

Megan grimaced. "Rylu, rylu, rylu," she chanted.

Drake's men were smarter than he and used the proper greeting, lavishing the chieftaness with gifts. When they spoke of commerce, however, she found their wares unappealing and challenged them to a contest of skill with Drake's ship as the prize.

The rocking of the boat and stuffiness of its bowels were having a soporific effect on Megan. She yawned and blinked hard, forcing herself into a sitting position against a corner. She propped the book on her knees and returned to the story, but after reading about Drake's men choosing their strongest, she nodded off.

She spent the remainder of the voyage to Obonia asleep with her head lolling over *The Traveler's Tales,* her fingers gripping the pages. The ship lurched to a halt as the anchor was lowered, and Megan's body fell forward, the book slipping from her lap. She jerked herself awake and tried to catch the book but only succeeded in ripping out the pages she was holding.

"Crap." Megan wedged the loose papers into the book and tucked it into her backpack. She heard a door open and then footsteps as Lapper stepped in front of her cell with a smile.

"Are we ready to meet our new owners?"

Megan just stared at him as he fished keys from his pocket and unlocked her cage. She sized him up, confident she could tackle him to the ground once he removed her foot cuff. As soon as Lapper removed the lock, however, a burly man clad in spiked leather opened Megan's cell door and stepped inside.

Instead of unlocking Megan's shackle, the burly man gave one strong pull and jerked the chain from the wall. "Move," he said.

Megan trudged down the hallway, trapped between him and Lapper, with the weight of the iron clinging to her foot so that she hobbled awkwardly. "You don't think you could remove the cuff from around my leg, do you? I don't think my new owners would find me as valuable with a broken ankle."

"You're a strong girl," said Lapper, pushing open the hatch that led to the main deck.

Megan breathed in the fresh air and tropical scents of the island, letting her eyes adjust to the dark of night. Around her, the crew worked to unload cargo and bring in the sails, scarcely giving Megan a second glance. She had a feeling she wasn't the first person Lapper had brought aboard to be auctioned.

The gangplank had already been lowered to rest on a sandbar, and the burly man forced Megan onto it, following her onto shore. Lapper stayed behind to speak with some of his men but called out after Megan, "I'll be along shortly to tuck you in for the night!" He and the men cackled, and one of them yelled in a high-pitched voice, "Tell me a story, Papa Lapper!"

"Assholes." Megan was rewarded with a hard shove from her warden.

"Keep mouthing off, and you won't get any food until morning."

"Oh, dear. No bread and water," said Megan. "Poor me."

"Actually, your dinner *was* going to be *that*." He pointed to where the sandbar widened into the island. When they drew nearer, Megan could see a long wooden table laden with fruit and vegetable platters. At one end, several fire pits had been dug with large boars roasting above them.

"That's fine," said Megan, swallowing the saliva that was filling her mouth. "I'm not hungry anyway."

The warden produced a pair of cuffs linked together with a long chain. "Then, let's get you settled for the night."

At the end of the sandbar, a beautiful dark-skinned woman waited for them. From the rich color of her gown and the bejeweled wrap atop her head, Megan guessed she must be the chieftaness.

"Rylu," said Megan's burly warden, bowing to the woman. He grabbed Megan by the hair and forced her to bend at the waist.

"Rylu," Megan said to the ground. When she was allowed to straighten, she gave the warden a dirty look.

The woman frowned but returned their greeting.

"If you'll excuse me." The warden stepped around the chieftaness, pulling Megan with him. He dragged her away from the table and fire pits and situated her beneath a fruit-bearing tree. He clamped one of the new cuffs around Megan's left ankle and unlocked the old one on her right.

"On the ground," he told Megan.

Before he could force her, she sat, and he dragged her toward the tree until she fell onto her back and her rear-end hit the trunk. Then he took the chain dangling from her left cuff and ran it around the backside of the tree before clamping the connecting right cuff to her newly unfettered ankle.

"Oh, this is *so* comfortable, thank you," said Megan, staring up the warden's nose.

The warden grinned down at Megan and gave the tree a hard shake. She squealed and squirmed as fruit rained down on her, lobbing her in the face and stomach.

"Just a little something to tide you over until morning," said the warden. He picked up a piece of fruit, took a bite, and strolled back down the beach toward the ship and supper.

Megan cursed and hurled another fruit after him, but with the added difficulty of throwing upside down and backwards, it missed its mark and splashed into the ocean. Though she could no longer see the warden, she could hear him laughing. With a resigned sigh, she wiped the sand off one of the remaining pieces and bit into it.

It was delicious, and she devoured all of it save the stem, wishing she could enjoy the other foods set out for Lapper and his crew.

She ate a few more of the fruits and then pulled the loose pages of *The Traveler's Tales* from her book and held them up to the dim light of the fires.

> *The challenge the chieftaness proposed was one of intelligence, ability in which Drake's strongest man, Zeller, was lacking. To win, Zeller would need to reverse her spell. She began to chant and a circle of fire engulfed one of Zeller's shipmates.*
>
> *Zeller was quick to come to his aid, but when he stepped within a few feet of the other man, the flames shot high into the sky, forming a veritable wall of fire. As Zeller vexed his mind trying to conjure a way around the obstacle, the chieftaness spoke another word and another of Zeller's crewmates sank to his waist in the sand. The more the man struggled to free himself, the more buried he became.*
>
> *Zeller abandoned the crewman caught in the ring of fire and reached down to help the man trapped in sand. He halted, however, when the sand spilled over the tops of his boots and pulled at his legs.*
>
> *"Stop this, witch!" Zeller cried at the chieftaness. "I know not your magic! You've set me an impossible task."*

The chieftaness smiled. "Does this mean I have won our challenge?"

Zeller gnashed his teeth and looked from one dying crewmember to the other before glaring at the chieftaness. "Through no manner of honesty, yes. You have won."

The chieftaness spoke the words, "Erifria retawdnas," and all she had done became undone. The fire extinguished itself, and the sand ceased to stir.

While Zeller dug out his crewmate, the chieftaness said, "Ever was I honest with you. If you assumed the contest would be one of physical strength, that was your folly. I will have my reward now."

The chieftaness took Drake's ship, and his crew were forced to bargain for travel back to the Port of Scribnitch with the next vessel that arrived in Obonia. Upon returning home, they relayed their story to anyone who would listen, and those who did scoffed at the crew's misfortune, believing them to have given up too quickly on a simple task.

Thereafter, fleets of ships would travel to the island to challenge the chieftaness. Always they were defeated, for the chieftaness never posed the same challenge to each. She could peer into the souls of men and knew their greatest weaknesses that could be turned against them. Only one man ever possessed the power to defeat the chieftaness, and he did so by deceiving her of his weakness. When she conjured

a circle of sirens to seduce him, Lodir Novator was
able to resist their charms and claim his reward.

Megan couldn't help laughing to herself. Even though she
had banished him to the other side, Lodir still lived on in
stories.

"It sounds as if you're enjoying yourself a little too
much." Lapper appeared beside her. "Should I tighten
your chains?" He caught sight of the book pages before
Megan could think to hide them. "Or, perhaps I should
take away your reading material." He snatched the papers
from her and glanced at them with a smirk. "The Traveler's Tales of Obonia?" He tossed the sheets back at her and
they fluttered in various directions. "Planning to challenge
the chieftaness for your freedom?"

"No, I just thought I'd read up on my new home."
Megan gathered the strewn papers and folded them in half.
"Thanks for the idea, though."

Lapper sneered at her. "You're not skilled enough to
defeat the chieftaness, and even if you could, you have
nothing to offer her as a reward."

"I have myself," said Megan.

Lapper's laughter was like the braying of a donkey.
"You don't even have *that*. You're in *my* shackles, and you
belong to me."

"Not if I escape," said Megan.

This made Lapper chuckle even harder. "Please stop! I've just eaten dinner, and all your silly hopes and dreams are hurting my stomach."

Megan placed the folded pages under her head and lay upon them. "Whatever."

She flinched when Lapper dropped a heavy bag by her head, spraying sand into her face. "What's in the bag?" she asked. "Your soul?"

"The chieftaness feels you should be fed, though I can't imagine why. It's not as if you'll starve if you don't eat for a night." A stoppered gourd hit the ground beside the bag. "She also thinks you might like more than salt water to drink."

Megan sat up and glanced over her shoulder to where the rest of Lapper's crew were gorging themselves and ogling the island women. The chieftaness sat in the midst of it all, surveying the newcomers to her island. Megan wondered if she was analyzing the weakness of every man in preparation of a challenge. "Tell her thank you," said Megan.

"I'm sure your lifetime of servitude will show her how grateful you are. Enjoy your stories of this place. By tomorrow, they'll be fueling the fire." Lapper walked away.

Megan waited until he had rejoined his men before opening the bag he had left behind. The scent of roasted meat and sweet glaze wafted toward her nostrils, making her mouth water. The fruit she'd eaten earlier had only curbed her appetite, and she now reached for the meat, ravenous.

Before she could even bring it to her lips, however, the Pearl of Truth pulsed against her heart. The meat she held wasn't pure. It was laced with poison. Megan unstoppered the gourd and found its contents also tainted. She was being sold to a woman who wanted her dead.

Megan suddenly felt very vulnerable and inched as close to the tree as possible, hugging the bag to her chest. She settled onto her back again and gazed up at the stars, wishing on as many as she could that there might still be some hope left for her.

Battle Royale

It was shortly before dawn when Megan heard a soft voice in her ear that roused her from sleep. She shivered from the chill of evening and felt a sticky combination of briny air and sand on her skin. Some time during the night she had rolled onto her side, still clutching the bag, and had started drooling.

She wiped at her mouth. "Go away, Lapper. Tell the chieftaness that her plan didn't work."

Much to her annoyance, she was now being prodded in the shoulder. "Wake up, Megan. It's me."

The voice did not belong to Lapper.

She opened one eye. Her vision was still a bit blurry, but there was Brighton, kneeling beside her. His hair was matted down and scratches marked his hands and arms, but his dark eyes showed concern only for Megan. Her vision blurred even more, a lump filled her throat, and she smiled weakly. "What took you so long?"

Brighton grinned back. "Apologies. I was frolicking in the waves and searching for seashells."

Instead of laughing, Megan burst into tears and hugged him close. "I'm sorry . . . for . . . for hurting your feelings," she gasped between sobs. "I shouldn't have said those horrible things. I'm really really sorry." She choked on her last words. "I don't deserve to be rescued."

Brighton nuzzled his cheek against hers while she cried. "Of course you do, and I'm sorry, too. I shouldn't have left you by yourself on the boardwalk."

"It's okay," said Megan, sniffling. She wiped her eyes on the inside of the tunic. "I mean . . . it's as okay as it *can* be under the circumstances." She indicated her shackles.

"Well, luckily, your predicament can be easily remedied." Brighton went to work on Megan's right ankle cuff. His fingers nimbly shifted the tumblers inside the lock, and the cuff clanked open.

"You are *dangerously* good at that," said Megan. She rubbed her free ankle as he started on the other cuff.

"Would you think any less of me if I told you I'd been in irons like this before?" he asked. The other cuff popped open and fell into the sand.

"Of course not . . . but I'd wonder why." Megan stuffed the papers she'd been laying on back into her pocket. To her disgust, they were still moist from drool.

"If we make it off this island alive, I'll be sure to tell you the story." Brighton looked down the beach toward the sandbar where Lapper's boat was docked. "For now, though, we'd best be moving."

Megan picked up the bag of poisoned meat and shoved it into her own backpack. "Okay. Let's go."

Brighton led her into a jungle of trees that curved behind the thatched cottages of the islanders. Megan battled branches and gigantic leaves in her path until soon her arms looked like Brighton's.

"So, Ainsley teleported you here, right?" Megan kept her voice lower than the birds in the trees performing their morning calls. "Did he come with you?"

Brighton nodded. "Rella, too." They reached a clearing in the jungle, and he stopped.

Megan looked around. "Well, where are they?"

Brighton rubbed his hands together. "Well, the thing is . . . *we* have to rescue *them* now."

"What?!" Megan's voice sent nearby birds scattering into the sky. "Why didn't you tell me this earlier?"

"Because I knew you'd yell like that," said Brighton.

Megan placed a hand to her forehead. "So, they came to rescue me and got captured?"

"Not at first," said Brighton. "But when the chieftaness wouldn't help Ainsley," he paused, "I believe his exact words were 'Listen, lady, if you don't help us, things are going to get ugly.'"

"Wonderful." Megan rolled her eyes. "At least he didn't get beheaded."

"She didn't have a sword handy," said Brighton. "Otherwise, I think she would have. But Ainsley and Rella are being held in her servant cottages."

Megan sat on the ground. "I don't suppose she'd just let them go, would she?"

"I don't think so, but I thought we might find a way to break them out or offer her an exchange for their freedom."

"An exchange," repeated Megan, feeling the wad of paper in her pocket. "We can challenge the chieftaness."

Brighton sat down opposite her. "Didn't you hear what I just said happened to Ainsley?"

"No, no. I mean a formal challenge." Megan chewed her lip. "What would you say is my biggest weakness?"

———

Ainsley couldn't ever remember being in a human habitat that reeked so much like a barn. The dirt floor of the cottage he'd been taken to was lined with stiff straw pallets of sleeping men, all of whom had varying degrees of poor hygiene. When Ainsley had arrived, one of the servants, a particularly odoriferous man, had informed him that they refused to bathe out of spite. The chieftaness reviled foul odors, so it was the theory of the servants that if they were offensive to her nostrils, they might not find themselves under her watchful eye.

Their silent but smelly protest seemed to be working since the chieftaness and her officials tended to avoid the servants in general, issuing commands from afar. But Ainsley wished they could at least burn some candles or keep fragrant flowers in the cottage. The air around him smelled of body odor and musk, and whoever had used the pallet before him had been particularly flatulent. Ainsley couldn't bear to lie down and sleep, so he sat with his knees folded to his chest and his face buried within his tunic.

But even if the stench hadn't kept him awake, his worries would have. Rella had been sent to another cottage and Brighton had disappeared to find Megan, but he had no idea if Megan was even still alive or if Brighton had been captured. Any thoughts of escaping to find them were out of the question since the servant's quarters were magically sealed at night and the guards stood watch during the day.

Ainsley regretted threatening the chieftaness the afternoon before, but he'd had no idea they would take him so seriously. He was thankful that he'd at least been smart enough to leave Anala at the port and out of the whole mess.

After Anala had given the pipe-smoking woman the charm, the woman had revealed that Megan had been hauled away on the Lady Luck, a merchant vessel owned by a man in a gold cape. Ainsley hadn't needed to hear any further description to know it was Lapper of whom she spoke, and it didn't take much asking around the tavern to learn that Lapper made trade runs from the Port of Scribnitch to the island of Obonia every few weeks.

Ainsley and Anala had rendezvoused with Brighton and Rella back in the shop of barrels and decided that they would teleport to the island ahead of Megan. When she arrived they would be waiting to rescue her. Anala had refused to leave for the island, and everyone agreed it was best for her to stay behind.

He wiggled about on his pallet, trying to find comfort on the thin patch of dried grass that separated him from the ground, but only managed to rip a hole through the center of his mat. "Great."

Ainsley noticed that one of his bunkmates had rolled halfway off his own pallet. With a sly glance around, he grabbed the free corner of the other man's bed and started to rip out a chunk of hay.

"Ainsley!" From behind him, a voice barked at the entrance to the cottage.

Ainsley opened his hand and dropped the hay. "I was just . . ." He swiveled to face the speaker.

A muscular island man, warden of the servant's quarters, filled the doorway. "Come with me. The chieftaness demands your presence."

The moment Ainsley stood, the man he'd been about to steal from rolled onto his stomach and pulled Ainsley's pallet to him, stacking it under his own.

"Hey! That's mine!"

The warden grabbed Ainsley by the wings and dragged him toward the entrance. "After what will happen this morning, you will not need it anymore."

Ainsley jerked himself free of the warden's grasp. "What is *that* supposed to mean?" He blinked against the early morning sunlight and shielded his eyes with his hand.

"It means you will either die or go free, but you will not sleep here tonight."

The warden led the way to the main beach where the chieftaness sat upon her throne, watching their approach. To her left stood Rella, and to her right stood Megan and Brighton. She waved at Ainsley and hurried over to hug him, squeezing him tight around his neck. Though not entirely fresh and clean, hers was a welcome scent after the earlier assault to his nostrils.

"Thanks for coming to get me," said Megan.

"I'm just glad you're still alive," he said. "I'm surprised Lapper didn't try to kill you."

"Oh, he did." Megan pointed to a bulging bag at the chieftaness' feet that was wet with liquid dripping onto the sand.

"Woah. Is that his head or something?"

Megan snorted. "I wish. It's poisoned meat. At first, I thought it was the chieftaness out to get me, but after I talked to her, I learned the truth. I also talked to her about you and Rella."

"Oh." said Ainsley. "And did you say something that's going to get us all killed?"

Megan shook her head. "Brighton and I are free. We challenged the chieftaness for yours and Rella's freedom."

"Oh, so you said something that's just going to get Rella and me killed," said Ainsley. He turned to the warden. "Can I go back to my cottage?"

"Ainsley, you won't die if I win the challenge!" said Megan. She smiled hopefully at him. "And then you'll get to go free."

"What's the challenge then?"

Megan grimaced. "Well, I'm not sure exactly, but it will be something based on my greatest weakness."

Ainsley crossed his arms. "Oh, this should be interesting."

"Trust me. Brighton and I have been going over scenarios in our heads, and we think we know how to combat anything she throws at me."

Ainsley rubbed his eyes with his hands. "Well, good luck to all of us, I guess." He looked at the chieftaness. "Except for you."

The chieftaness smirked at him. "And apologies for any pain you might feel."

"Pain?" Ainsley frowned.

The chieftaness lifted her hand toward him and balled her fist, making a punching motion. The air between her and Ainsley rippled and then he was sent sprawling backwards, skidding across the sand.

Ainsley brought his hand to his chest, wheezing, and studied the ground around him. He couldn't find anything large enough that she could have thrown to strike with such force.

"Great. So she's a witch." He staggered to his feet and positioned them shoulder-length apart, crouching with his hands on his knees. "I'd like to see you try that again."

The chieftaness bent her fingers like claws and slashed them through the air. Ainsley yelped and collapsed to his knees, clutching his stomach. When he pulled his hand away, it was dark with blood.

"Stop this!" Megan grabbed the chieftaness' arm. "You're supposed to challenge *me* for *my* greatest weakness."

"I am." The chieftaness chuckled but didn't look away from Ainsley. She clapped her hands together and he screamed again as a sound like a sonic boom hammered against his eardrums. Ainsley writhed on the ground and rolled onto his back, revealing ten deep lacerations oozing with scarlet sludge, a combination of blood and sand.

When the chieftaness finally turned to Megan, Ainsley's torture ceased, and he lay still on his back, panting and blinking the sweat and tears from his eyes. "Your greatest weakness is your loved ones," said the chieftaness to Megan. "Without them, you would be destroyed."

She balled her fist again and punched it toward Ainsley. This time, her energy ball struck him in the chin and sent him spinning head over heels through the air before he landed facedown in the sand. Ainsley struggled to his hands and knees, spitting out a mouthful of grit and blood.

"Megan," he croaked. "I'm touched that you love me, but *please* love someone else right now." He placed a hand over the wounds on his stomach and closed his eyes. He asked the magic to heal his body, though he knew he would age it by speeding up the process. The magic trickled through his fingertips and into the lacerations, and he sighed as the searing pain quelled.

"Ah, but she does." The chieftaness lowered her gaze to Brighton. Raising one hand, she lifted him off the ground. With the other, she made a clenched fist, constricting Brighton's throat until he gasped and flailed in midair, clawing at his neck.

"Megan, do something!" shouted Rella. She hoisted one of Ainsley's arms over her shoulder and helped him to stand.

"I don't—" Megan ran her fingers through her hair and squeezed handfuls of her curly locks. "I don't know what to do!"

"Getting her to let go of Brighton would be a start," said Ainsley. "Punch her or something."

Megan shook her head. "I'm not allowed to engage her in physical combat."

"Well, nobody said *I* couldn't." Ainsley yanked Rella's sword from its sheath and spread his wings, launching himself at the chieftaness. She focused her attention on Ainsley, and Brighton flopped onto the sand, gulping down huge mouthfuls of air.

Megan kneeled beside him. "Are you okay?"

Brighton nodded and coughed. "We didn't plan well for this challenge, did we?"

They both watched as Ainsley drew closer to the chieftaness, thrusting the sword out in front of him like a jouster's lance. The chieftaness crooked one finger, and at the same time Rella's sword curved in on itself as if it were made of rubber.

"My sword!" cried Rella.

Ainsley tossed it aside and propelled himself forward with his wings. At the last moment, he tucked them against his body and spun around, launching a back kick to the chieftaness' midriff. She raised her hands in a halting gesture, palms toward Ainsley and fingers to the sky. Ainsley saw a wall of energy appear between himself and the chieftaness and tucked his kicking leg back in. Unfortunately, he wasn't quick enough to stop his forward momentum, and he crashed into the wall with the length of his body.

The chieftaness levitated Rella's sword and straightened the blade before launching it toward Ainsley who was sprawled upon the ground. Brighton and Rella looked on, horrified, while Megan squeezed the Pearl of Truth lodged in her chest. She willed it to reveal a clue or some hidden lie that she could use to save Ainsley.

But as she ran her fingers over the bump in her skin, she remembered how it had come to be there in the first place. She had been willing to give up her own life to save Ainsley's.

She knew she had to do so again.

Rella's sword plunged downward toward Ainsley's heart and Megan ran at him, flinging herself over his body. The blade pierced the skin of her back and slid through her torso with ease. The pain was unbelievable, like so many lies at once to the Pearl of Truth in her heart. But this raw aching was lower, puncturing her lung, making every breath a struggle.

Ainsley, who had shut his eyes, opened them to find Megan's face inches from his own. Her eyes bulged and her nostrils flared as her face took on a pained expression. "Megan?" He lifted himself onto his elbows.

Brighton appeared beside them, resting his paws on Megan's leg, his brow furrowed and his jaw clenched. Megan opened her mouth to answer and blood spilled from her lips. Brighton cried out in anguish, and somewhere to their right, Rella fell to the ground, weeping.

Ainsley hugged Megan to him. "Please, no." He helped her to sit up, and his eyes filled with tears when he saw the blade jutting out from between her ribs. "Oh, Megan."

She fingered the blade that had run her through and forced a smile. "Just like Sir Inish." She tried to laugh but it turned into a gasp for air.

The chieftaness kneeled beside them. If Ainsley hadn't been holding on to Megan, he would have ripped the woman's throat out with his bare hands. "Why the *fuck* did you do this, you evil bitch?"

Brighton snarled at the chieftaness and attempted to maul her with claws and teeth. She immobilized him with one flick of her wrist. "You should ask this of her," she said in an even tone. She studied Megan. "Why did you take the blade?"

"I . . . I'd trade my life for his." Megan struggled with the words as blood filled her lungs. The edges of her vision darkened and she could scarcely hear her own voice over her pounding heart.

"Your loved ones are your greatest weakness," said the chieftaness, "but they are also your greatest strength. They give you compassion and selflessness. The only way to save them was to sacrifice yourself." She touched the tip of Rella's sword, and it melted away. "You have won the first challenge."

The sword fell to the ground behind Megan, and the wound in her chest gave one last spurt of blood. Megan's lungs cleared and the searing pain subsided. She glanced down in confusion and brought her fingers to her wound. She felt it shift and shrink beneath her fingertips. Experimentally, she took a deep breath and then another.

Ainsley gaped at her. "You're . . . you're healed!" He hugged Megan tight.

"What?" She looked at the chieftaness while Brighton and Rella joined Ainsley, throwing their arms around Megan. "I'm not going to die?"

The chieftaness shook her head. "You will need to be alive for you next challenge, won't you?"

Everyone froze in their celebration and turned toward the chieftaness.

"Uh . . . say that again?" said Ainsley. "Megan won her challenge. We get our freedom."

"She wishes to free two of you," said the chieftaness. "That requires two challenges. You," she pointed to Ainsley, "are free to go. She is not." She pointed to Rella.

Megan and Rella looked at one another.

"I know you don't love me as much as these two, but please don't abandon me."

Megan squeezed her arm. "I won't." She stood and ran a hand over the spot where her wound had been to make sure it had truly healed. Then she nodded at the chieftaness. "I'm ready for the next challenge."

Once More, With Feeling

"Very well," said the chieftaness. "I will draw upon another of your weaknesses."

"Thank God," said Ainsley. Megan shot him a dirty look and he shrugged. "What? I didn't really enjoy being the focus of your last one."

"You should be flattered," said Megan. "Rella didn't even get a cut."

"Um, I hate to interrupt," said Brighton from behind them, "but I could use a little help here."

Ainsley and Megan turned to find him buried to his shoulders in sand.

"What'd you do, fall into a hole?" Ainsley walked toward him.

"Ainsley, wait!" cried Megan.

He'd already reached Brighton and stooped to pull him out when he noticed that the sand around the ferret seemed a bit . . . runny. "Uh-oh." He tried stepping backward but only succeeded in stirring up the sand and water mixture and sinking deeper.

"It's quicksand, mate," said Brighton. "You can't just walk away."

"Yeah, thanks for the advice," said Ainsley. He beat his wings, but the hold of the sand was too powerful. He tried to swim to solid land, but it always stayed a little out of reach, a bit of the chieftaness' magic he was sure. "Well, it looks like we're screwed." He twisted around to face Megan, cursing when the sand sucked him a little deeper. "Why don't you and Rella think of a way to get us out?"

"I would," said Megan, "but I'm really hoping something will happen to her."

"What?" cried Rella.

"Oh, not something *really* bad," appeased Megan. "I'm just hoping for—" Rella squealed as the sand around her ignited, forming a circle of fire, "that," finished Megan.

She took an experimental step toward Rella, and the flames roared high. Both of them threw their hands up to shield their faces and backed away from either side of the fire. Only Megan was smiling when the flames died down.

Rella scowled at her. "Have you lost your mind?"

"Nope." Megan let the word pop from her lips. Then, she stuffed her hands in her pockets and twisted on her heel to face the chieftaness. "You picked the wrong girl to challenge."

"She *has* lost her mind," said Ainsley, looking over at Brighton. To his surprise, the ferret had managed to float atop the quicksand on his back and was wearing a grin almost as smug as Megan's.

"She knows *exactly* what she's doing."

The chieftaness cocked her head. "You know your weakness?"

Megan pulled the folded pages of *The Traveler's Tales* from her pocket. "I know my weakness, and I know how to reverse your spell."

"All right, Megan!" Ainsley punched his fist into the air.

With a bow and a big flourish, Megan selected one of the papers and let the others drift to the ground. She snapped it open and began to read.

"The chieftaness . . . that would be you," she nodded to the chieftaness. "The chieftaness spoke the words eri-fria retaw . . ." Megan stopped talking and frowned. "Um . . . let's see here." She held the paper up to the sunlight and squinted.

"For cripe's sake, Megan, quit showing off and just finish the spell." The combination of smothering sand

and smoldering sun was making Ainsley perspire, and the moisture was trickling into his eyes. He shook his head vigorously and sank a few inches deeper.

Megan lowered the paper, and to Ainsley's chagrin, she no longer had a confident smile. "I . . . I can't! The ink smeared. I must have gotten it wet somehow." Megan shook her head, remembering the puddle of drool in which she'd awakened that morning. "Should I just guess?"

"Yes!" chorused Ainsley, Brighton, and Rella.

"Megan, please hurry. It's getting really hot over here!" added Rella.

"Uh . . . okay . . ." Megan twisted a strand of hair around her finger and licked her lips. She tried to picture the rest of the text in her mind. "Erifria retawlna? Retawlda? Retawdla?"

"What does it look like it says?" asked Brighton. "I've helped Poloi restore damaged books. Maybe I can help you decipher it."

"Okay, well, there's the erifria part . . . and then there's either an 'l' or a 'd' and then the rest is a smear until 'had become undone.' It was something about how the words she said reversed the spell."

"How is the first part spelled?" asked Ainsley. He tilted his head back to avoid a mouthful of sand and wound up with ears full of ooze. "Not that it'll help much. The whole thing sounds like backwards gibberish."

Megan started spelling the words out loud but stopped on the second "i." "Wait a minute. This *is* backwards. Erifria. Air and fire." She pointed to Rella who was sitting inside the fiery ring looking pale and nauseous. "So retaw is water. And the last word must be—"

"Hurry!" blurted Ainsley. He took a deep breath as the quicksand finally reached his mouth and nostrils.

Megan's hands shook so hard the paper rattled. She did her best to ignore the burbling sounds coming from the sand. Her eyes lit up. "Sand. That's it! Erifria retawdnas!" She grinned at the chieftaness. "I win!"

But the chieftaness didn't move. Ainsley began to flail about in a panic and Rella had collapsed onto the ground. An ocean breeze altered the direction of the fire, bringing it closer to her unconscious form.

"Dammit!" Megan scanned the paper, her lips moving as she reread the story. "I'm right. I know I'm right." She bent over the other pages and sifted through them.

"Megan, hurry!" said Brighton. "Ainsley doesn't have much time."

She read about the man surrounded by fire and the man who fell into the quicksand, both of which were identical to their current situation.

"Except they happened in a different order," murmured Megan. "The fire and *then* the quicksand. Erifria retawdnas." Megan repeated the words to herself several times and then stood up, looking at the chieftaness with shining eyes. "Retawdnas erifria!"

With a crunching sound like snow being crushed, the sand shifted away from Ainsley and Brighton. It solidified into a bowl shape, leaving them to bob in a pool of water that had been left behind. Brighton swam downwards and grabbed a handful of Ainsley's hair, yanking hard.

Ainsley's eyes shot open and he raced to the surface, letting the breath he'd been holding explode from his lungs. Megan helped him out of the water and onto solid ground.

"Thanks," he said.

"You're welcome. Can I borrow your shirt?"

Ainsley glanced down at his bloodstained sandy tunic. "Uh sure." He pulled it off and Megan dunked it in the water, swirling it around. Then she carried it, still dripping, over to Rella and squeezed its contents over Rella's head. After a moment, the cooling water had its effect and Rella opened her eyes.

"Please tell me we can go now."

Megan smiled at her. "We can go now."

"Correction," said a man's boisterous voice. "*They* can go. *You* cannot."

Megan rolled her eyes and glanced over her shoulder to where Lapper was standing beside the chieftaness' throne. "Um . . . no. I'm not your captive anymore. I escaped from you, remember?"

Lapper smacked the flat of his hand against the arm of the throne. "Then the chieftaness owes me money."

"No, she doesn't." Megan sneered at him. "She doesn't own me either."

"Ah, but . . . but . . . she cared for you as one of her own! That food and water she offered you the night you arrived sealed the agreement." Lapper looked pleased with himself.

"Oh, really?" Megan strode up to him and the chieftaness and grabbed the bulging bag Ainsley had noticed earlier. "You mean *this* food and water that you had poisoned so I would die after the chieftaness purchased me?" Megan shook the bag at him.

Lapper smoothed down his eyebrows and wiped the perspiration from his forehead. "Yes, well . . ."

The chieftaness scowled at Lapper. "Why did you want to poison one of my servants? I thought we had a mutual partnership without deception."

"Oh, we do!" Lapper tittered nervously and patted the chieftaness' hand. "The girl would have brought you nothing but trouble. I was just looking out for your best interests."

"Woah!" Megan staggered backwards, clutching her chest. She had known the next words out of his mouth would be a lie, but the truth that had shown through was not what she'd expected. Lapper seemed to realize that she knew, and he pressed his hands together in a pleading gesture. Megan was compassionate, but not that compassionate.

"He didn't want to kill me," she said. "He poisoned the meat even before you'd asked him to give it to me." She pointed to the chieftaness. "He wanted to kill you."

"What?" roared the chieftaness. A sudden gale force hammered the beach, whirling the sand to sting their skin and making Megan's hair whip about her face.

Lapper dropped to his knees, genuflecting and kissing the chieftaness' sandals. "Forgive me. I am but a humble messenger. I have no ill will against you, Chieftaness."

"At least he's honest about *that*," muttered Megan.

The chieftaness kicked Lapper in the face. "Who gave you the poison to kill me?"

Lapper whimpered and held his nose but said nothing. He avoided Megan's eyes lest she glean information from a dishonest thought.

The chieftaness made a gesture in the air, and the hand Lapper held to his face twisted around to an unnatural position. "Who wants me dead?" she shouted over Lapper's crunching bones and screams.

"I can't tell you," he sobbed. "I'll die if I do."

"You'll die if you do not," said the chieftaness. She leaned close to him. "And I promise it will be slow and painful."

"She means it, too," said Ainsley, indicating the reddish scars across his stomach from the chieftaness' earlier attacks.

Lapper's lower lip trembled. "S-sanctuary," he told the chieftaness. "You must offer me sanctuary if I tell you."

The chieftaness pursed her lips and said, "Very well. If you tell me who sent you and why, I will give you sanctuary."

"It was Evren Sandor, wasn't it?" asked Ainsley.

Lapper nodded. "He didn't think the chieftaness would ally with him or succumb to his magic, so a few weeks ago, he invited me to his fortress and offered me a deal."

"Wait," said Megan. "His fortress at the Port of Scribnitch?"

Lapper nodded again. "At the north end, behind the waste dumps."

Megan wrinkled her nose. "Gross."

"Smart though," said Ainsley. "Nobody would think to look for someone like him in a place like that."

The chieftaness silenced them with a glance. "So, Evren wished to have me killed, did he?"

"He gave me a vial and told me to poison you on my next trip to Obonia. He said once the task was complete, I would receive a new ship." Lapper bent and kissed the chieftaness' feet again. "I am so glad the vile deed was never done." He looked up at her with tear-filled eyes.

"As am I," said the chieftaness, cupping Lapper's face in her hands. Her grip tightened and she jerked his head to one side until his neck snapped. Then, she shoved his lifeless body away with her foot.

Ainsley, Megan, and the others just gaped at her.

"You just told him you'd give him sanctuary," said Ainsley.

"If he told me who and why," said the chieftaness. "He only told me why. *You* told me who. Besides," she made a disgusted face, "his shiny clothing was beginning to make my eyes sore."

Megan kicked Lapper with her boot. "You can't argue with that kind of logic."

The chieftaness spread wide her arms. "You have bested me in your challenges. I give you my respect and your freedom."

Megan, Brighton, and Rella grinned at one another, but Ainsley chewed on his lip, formulating a plan. "What are you going to do about Evren?" he asked.

"*He* is a new issue I will have to deal with." The chieftaness frowned. "I must meet my council at once." She rose from her throne, but Ainsley stepped in front of her.

"What if we could help you?" he asked.

"Hold up!" Megan grabbed his arm and pulled him aside. "Ainsley, we don't have time to fight other people's battles," she whispered. "We have our own problem to deal with, remember?"

"Yeah, but *her* enemy is *our* enemy." Ainsley freed himself from her grip. "If we go in with *her* army, they can take out anyone standing between us and Evren and we'll be able to go for Onaj's horn."

Megan's eyes widened. "Ooooh. I like that." She spun back around to face the chieftaness. "How *would* you like our help?"

The chieftaness regarded Ainsley and Megan with a appraising eye. "You are skilled, to be certain, but I don't think you are capable of handling Evren."

"But we have a unicorn back at the port," said Megan.

"A unicorn?" The chieftaness leaned forward. "That is willing to help humans?"

Megan nodded. "Evren stole her father's horn."

The chieftaness leapt to her feet. "What!?" Megan and the others braced themselves for another tempestuous wind, but it didn't come. "Evren has Onaj's horn?"

"He's already used it on the leaders of the Kingdom Coalition and I'm sure more people as we speak."

"So what is your plan?" asked the chieftaness.

Ainsley bowed his head and cleared his throat. "Well, we were hoping your and your warriors could handle Evren and his men while we go after the horn to destroy it."

A gust of wind struck him in the chest, and Ainsley fell backwards into the pool of water.

"Or we could try something else," Megan said quickly.

"I do not like the idea of my people dying while you get the glory," said the chieftaness.

"We're not after the glory," sputtered Ainsley. He crawled out of the water for a second time. "We just want to stop Evren and go home."

"How can I know you don't want the horn for yourself?" asked the chieftaness.

Ainsley drew an arc in the sand with his foot. "We'll destroy Onaj's horn if you'll help us."

The chieftaness stared at the etching on the ground. "You realize how severe the consequences will be if you do not keep your word."

Ainsley nodded. He had seen Frieden forge a similar agreement with the dragon Arastold. If the chieftaness drew an arc opposing his to form a complete circle, she and Ainsley would both be bound by their words. Whoever failed to fulfill their side of the agreement would perish.

The chieftaness stepped down from her throne and finished the circle Ainsley had started. The sand of the circle sparkled and shone as if it had absorbed every ounce of sunlight, and then Ainsley felt as though a white-hot flame was scorching the flesh on his shoulder.

He screamed and reached for his back, though he knew this was only part of the process. The chieftaness cried out as well and gripped the arm of her throne for support. Megan, Rella, and Brighton stared at one another, uncomfortable with the ritual but unable to interrupt it.

The agonizing pain in Ainsley's shoulder subsided and he lay in the sand on his stomach, panting. The chieftaness waved away the guards who had come running when she screamed, and she took a stabilizing breath.

"We will leave for the Port of Scribnitch when the sun reaches its apex. Will you travel with us?" She indicated Lapper's ship, which was still anchored on the sandbar.

"We have our own way back to the port, and we have to retrieve our unicorn," said Megan.

"Then we will meet you at the docks by the waste dumps," said the chieftaness. "Until that time, farewell."

She stepped over Lapper's body and disappeared through the trees.

The four teenagers faced one another.

"Well, we have our own army now," said Ainsley. "It's time to end this. I'll get the last portal started."

"I'll help," said Rella.

"I'm going to wash up and get out of these nasty clothes," said Megan.

Brighton grinned mischievously. "I'll help."

The Final Countdown

"I think I see Lapper's ship," said Megan. "It had three sails, right?"

She, Ainsley, and Brighton were sprawled atop the roof of the weapons shop where Rella and Anala were trying to mend Rella's sword. Megan had already borrowed a new one from a merchant too entranced to notice, but Rella preferred her own weapon, even if the tip had been melted away. She and Anala had found an extra ingot of iron and were busy using unicorn magic to melt and solder it to the existing blade.

Ainsley, Megan, and Brighton could have waited in the shop with their friends, but the eerie behavior of the other shoppers had become somewhat overwhelming. Since they'd returned to the Port of Scribnitch, they hadn't seen a single person unaffected by Onaj's horn. Even the man in the floppy hat that Ainsley and Anala had met at the bank ambled along the boardwalk in a daze. The closer they moved to Evren's lair, in fact, the more palpable his presence was. Any ill mention of his name drew frowns and grumbles from the affected, all of whom Evren had no doubt bade be loyal to him.

Ainsley low-crawled to Megan and squinted at the vessel approaching the dock. "Yep, that's the Lady Luck all right." His heart pounded a little faster. Their last minutes of peace were slipping away, and he was grateful for it. The anxiety building in his mind was beginning to upset his stomach.

Earlier, they'd sent Brighton to scout Evren's fortress, and from what had been described, the entire Silvan Sentry had arrived to support Evren. Guards were posted around the fortress, on top, and no doubt inside it. If Ainsley and the others sought to reach Evren, blood would have to be spilled, and he hoped none of it would belong to his friends.

Beside him Megan fidgeted, adjusting her sword and pulling at the shirt that she'd changed into *without* Brighton's help, much to his disappointment. She'd layered her damaged tunic over the clean one when they couldn't find an armor merchant at the north end of the boardwalk. Despite the warmth of the doubly thick clothing, though, she still felt exposed. Ainsley had suggested she just borrow the armor off someone's back since they would be too spell-bound to care, but anyone who looked of fighting caliber was protecting Evren's fortress. Megan wondered if Garner was one of them.

Ainsley nudged her shoulder. "This is a bad sign," he muttered. The Lady Luck floated beside the dock while two of the chieftaness' men, sporting only loincloths and necklaces, pulled in the sails and lowered the anchor.

Brighton joined them. "What's a bad sign? Their lack of weapons or their lack of armor?"

"Maybe that's just the . . . um . . . sailing crew," said Megan. "And all the warriors are waiting in the hull with spears and machetes and things."

The "sailing crew" lowered a wooden ramp onto the dock and one of the men hurried down it. He secured the ramp to the dock posts with rope, then cupped his hands to his mouth, cooing and cawing.

A rumble like thunder came from the ship as eight more men clambered onto the deck and down the ship's ramp. They all made similar birdcalls and were as scantily clad as their fellows.

"Wonderful," said Ainsley. "They're going to lift their loincloths to shock the Silvan Sentry and then choke them to death with their necklaces."

Megan bit her lip. "Well, at least the chieftaness is a good fighter."

But when the last of the men stomped down the ramp, the chieftaness was nowhere to be seen.

"That bitch went back on her word!" Ainsley pulled up the sleeve of his tunic. "Is the mark on my shoulder gone?"

"No," said Megan, "and she didn't promise she'd come. She promised she'd help."

"I can't say I blame her," said Brighton. "With fighters like those, this is going to be one short, ugly battle. Best to stay as far away as possible."

"Unless you're fools like us." Ainsley pressed his lips into a thin line. "Well, let's get this over with." He stomped on the roof a little harder than necessary to get Rella and Anala's attention. Then, he picked Brighton up with one hand, wrapped his arm around Megan, and glided down to the boardwalk with both of them. In one fluid motion, he released them and closed the distance between himself and the chieftaness' warriors.

"Who's in charge here?" he asked.

The man who had served as Ainsley's warden on Obonia elbowed his way through the group of warriors. "You are in charge . . . as is she." He pointed to Megan who was running toward them. "The chieftaness has commanded us to follow your orders."

"Why isn't *she* here?" asked Ainsley.

"We would not be effective fighters if she were among us," said the warden.

Megan jogged to a stop and paused to catch her breath before speaking. "The men we're going to be facing have swords."

"You need some sort of armor," added Brighton. He leapt down from her shoulder.

"We would not be effective fighters with armor," said the warden.

Ainsley clapped a hand to his forehead. "Oh, for shit's sake."

Megan nudged him and smiled up at the warden. "Um. What *would* you be effective with? Maybe some spears or blow darts?"

The warden crossed his arms, which rippled with an impressive amount of muscle. "We require nothing. We fight with our hands and the chieftaness protects us."

"The chieftaness . . ." Megan peered past him to the ship.

"She is not here. She is safe in Obonia."

Ainsley paced in front of the warriors. "Okay, I can understand that you want to fight without weapons." He punched a fist into the palm of his hand. "I'm a big fan of unarmed combat." He stopped in front of the warden. "But this isn't a fair fight you're entering."

The warden and the other warriors laughed at this. "You are right," said the warden. "They will not survive."

Ainsley didn't bother trying to correct him. "If the chieftaness is in Obonia, how can she protect you?"

"Hers is a strong magic," said the warden. "It casts an aura to protect us from missile attacks."

"Missile," said Ainsley. "You mean, arrows."

"Yes," said the warden. "And we have fists of stone."

Ainsley glanced at the man's normal-looking hands and sighed. Even though he thought them crazy, he had to admire the confidence of the warriors. "Okay. I guess we should get moving." He beckoned to the others and they followed him back to the boardwalk where Anala and Rella were emerging from the weapons shop.

"Perfect timing," said Rella. She brandished her sword at them, the blade of which was restored to pristine condition. "I'm ready for battle."

"I'm not sure we are, though," whispered Megan. She nodded toward the warriors, but to her surprise, Rella beamed.

"Oh, we get ten of them. Excellent!"

"But . . . but they don't have any armor," said Megan. "And they plan to fight with their fists."

Rella shrugged and sheathed her sword. "What did you expect from Obonian warriors?"

Megan opened her mouth but realized she didn't know enough about the people to assume they couldn't fight. "Come on. Ainsley's going over the attack plan with them."

The warriors had huddled around Ainsley, and he was speaking in a low voice to avoid the suspicion of pass-ersby. Rella and Megan wiggled their way into the group.

"We need someone with Anala at all times," Ainsley was saying. He placed a hand on the unicorn-turned-human's shoulder. "She's our key to victory."

The warden raised a hand. "I will guard her myself."

"Excellent. We should have one other warrior accompany you, though," said Ainsley. "Can eight of you handle the Silvan Sentry?"

"Of course," said the warden. The warriors mumbled and nodded.

"If they can't, I can help them," said Rella.

"I'll try and do what I can as well," said Brighton.

Ainsley pointed to Megan. "You and I will enter with Anala and the two warriors."

"Do you know where in the fortress Evren will be?" asked the warden.

"I'm hoping that he'll come to us once things start getting out of control. He'll most likely try and use Onaj's horn. When he does, we grab it from him, Anala turns back into a unicorn and," he smacked his hands together and everyone jumped, "the horn gets destroyed and everyone's back to normal."

The warden nodded his approval. "We shall prevail. When do we begin?"

Ainsley's heart pounded a bit faster, and he took a deep breath before looking around the circle at everyone. "Now's as good a time as any."

Megan wiped her hands against her pants and gripped the handle of her sword. "Good luck, everyone."

They all turned as one and marched down the board-walk. The warriors moved with a hulking swagger, eyes focused on their target, while Ainsley, Megan, Rella, and Brighton glanced around nervously, hearts pumping to match the rhythm of their feet on the wooden slats. Those on the boardwalk under Evren's control seemed to recognize something was amiss, though it was obvious they couldn't determine what it was. They ducked into shops and gave the party a wide berth, increasing their pace to get as far away from the strangers as possible.

This deviation from the usual threatening behavior heartened Ainsley and Megan, and soon they were strutting down the boardwalk with the determination of warriors.

"When this is over, will you and Megan really go home?" Rella asked Ainsley, falling into step beside him.

"I think we have to," said Ainsley. "Our parents have missed us like crazy."

Rella was quiet for a moment. Then, "But you'll come back, won't you?"

Ainsley's heart quickened again, though this time it had nothing to do with the mission they were about to undertake. "Of course we will. We have family here and plenty of friends we'll always want to visit."

Out of the corner of his eye, he could see Rella tuck her hair behind her ear and thought he saw a blush creep into her cheeks. "Do you have any particularly special friends you look forward to seeing again?"

Ainsley felt his own cheeks warm. "Of course."

"Oh," said Rella, though it wasn't with the emotion he'd expected to evoke with his answer. She frowned and Ainsley found himself slowing down to keep pace with her.

"What . . . um . . ." Ainsley scratched his neck. "Was that not the right answer?"

From behind him, he could hear Megan, "You don't tell a girl you're interested in other girls, dummy!"

Ainsley frowned and glanced over his shoulder. "First of all, mind your own business. Second of all, I'm not interested in other girls. I was talking about *her*."

"You were?" Now Rella's voice sounded like Ainsley had earlier expected, and he grinned almost shyly at her.

"Of course. But I can't guarantee I'll have wings the next time you see me. You know, with them being a temporary enchantment and all."

She smiled, and Ainsley watched a freckle on her jaw disappear into the dimple that formed. "If you came back as a head living in a jar, that would be fine with me."

"But then you'd be getting rid of the only tolerable parts of him," said Megan.

Rella and Brighton laughed, and Ainsley unfolded his wings and flexed them straight back so that Megan had to duck to avoid being smacked in the face.

The warden, who had been leading the warriors, turned around and stood in place. He waited for the four teenagers to draw even with him. "We are not going to a celebration," he said. "You should be solemn and respectful of battle."

Megan, Rella, and Brighton stopped laughing and did their best to appear somber, but Ainsley said, "If I'm entering a situation where I might die, I'd rather face it standing tall than bent over."

Brighton snickered, and the warden raised an eyebrow. "Then, if you cannot be grave, be quiet. We are almost to the fortress."

At those words, Megan's steady gait became a foot-fumbling lurch that almost knocked Ainsley to the ground. "Sorry," she said. "Just got a little stage fright."

The warden motioned for her to be silent and veered left off the boardwalk, leading them through an alley. He stopped them just short of where it opened into a natural clearing. The ground changed from wood to scrubby grass, and thick-trunked palms identical to those on Obonia replaced the buildings.

The trees were spaced apart from each other and not in the useful clumps Ainsley had been hoping for. There would be no opportunity for them to approach Evren's army without being seen.

The fortress was a massive stone building much more like the castles Ainsley had expected to find in Arylon, complete with towers and a circular barbican. He could see men stationed around the entrance of the barbican and walking the parapet above. The entire structure stood less than fifty yards away with no townspeople wandering between it and the boardwalk. A handful of Obonian warriors, a woman, a ferret, and three teenagers would definitely raise an alarm.

Ainsley jumped at the sound of a seagull screeching directly overhead. The members of his party glanced up and shifted about to avoid being the target of a bird bomb. Ainsley laughed to himself, wondering if the chieftaness' magic shielded her warriors from short-range attacks.

"What's funny?" asked Megan, not taking her eyes off the seagull. It seemed to enjoy circling above *her* in particular.

Ainsley watched her attempt to shoo it away and smiled. "Nothing. But you've given me a great idea." He grabbed the warden's arm. "Don't do anything. I'll be right back."

"Where are you going?" asked Megan.

"To get some ammunition." He turned and ran back down the alley to the boardwalk, reading the various signs outside the shops until he spotted "She Sells Seashells." He peeked through the window and saw various bins of conch and abalone shells.

"Perfect!" Ainsley dashed inside and grabbed an empty bag from behind the counter where the merchant stood wiping a rag over an abalone shell. Judging by the worn spots, he'd been doing it for some time.

Ainsley filled the bag with the largest, lightest shells he could find and hefted the bag over one shoulder. Then he took the merchant's highly polished shell and replaced it with a dull, dirty one. "Now we're even," he told the merchant. "Thanks for the shells."

When he reached the alley, everyone was crowded around the entrance waiting for him. "Okay, slight change in plans." He held the bag open so the others could see the contents. "I'm going to fly above the fortress and create a distraction by dropping these seashells on the guards. If I can get their attention, you should be able to move in before they're even prepared to fight you."

Everyone except Megan nodded and moved toward the opposite end of the alley. "And if you can't get their attention?" she asked.

"Then, we'll be no worse off than we were before," said Ainsley. "Except I'll be safe in the sky." He grinned when Megan scowled. "I'm kidding."

She shook her head. "I'm not worried about us. I'm worried about you. You don't have the chieftaness' magic to deflect the Silvan Sentry's arrows."

"Well, I have *some* magic of my own. And it doesn't have to last me very long before I'm back on the ground with you guys."

Megan was quiet for a moment. When she finally spoke, her voice was soft and the corners of her eyes and mouth were turned down. "I'm really scared. I wish Bornias and Frieden were normal again and here with us."

Ainsley hugged her tight and she sniffled on his shoulder. He pulled away and held her at arm's length, but she stared at the ground, letting her hair fall around her face. "Megan," he lifted her chin with one hand so that she was forced to look at him, "there's nobody else who can do this but us. Bornias and Frieden and Gran . . . they can't help this time."

She exhaled a shaky sigh, and her lip quivered. "I know. I just . . . I never wanted this fight, and now there's an army of evil waiting to kill us all." Her throat tightened and she fought to ask the question that had been plaguing her since Sir Inish's death. "Ainsley, what if . . . what if good people don't always win? What if this is the one time that evil wins? What if—"

"Listen to me." Ainsley placed his hands on either side of her face. "Good will prevail. It will because it *has* to. If we're going to make it through this, you need *courage*."

His words reminded Megan of her last conversation with Sir Inish, and she began to understand what the old dwarf had meant. She took a deep breath and steeled herself. "Okay." This time, her voice was stronger. She stepped away from him and nodded firmly. "Okay. Go."

Ainsley smiled and pinched the tip of her nose. "Bombs away," he said, twisting the strap of the bag around one arm.

"Wait!" Rella ran towards them. She stopped in front of Ainsley. "I want to loan you something."

He held out his hand, but Rella pushed it aside and leaned in, kissing him on the lips. He tried to kiss her back but she pulled away with a smile. "You can return that later."

Megan rolled her eyes at the giddy grin on Ainsley's face as he rubbed his lower lip. "Don't start flying loopy now," she said. She pointed toward the sky. "Bombs away, remember?"

Ainsley gave Megan a mock salute and winked at Rella. Then, he flexed his wings and climbed into the sky, swinging a big circle around the boardwalk so the sentry wouldn't suspect where he'd come from.

Megan and Rella squinted against the sunlight, watching him before Megan slid her arm through Rella's. "Come on. He's going to need us to move in quickly."

Shells and Stones

The salty sea air was a little heavier than Ainsley was used to, but his wings quickly adjusted and he glided over the palm trees toward the fortress. He'd seen Megan and the others waiting to charge across the field once he'd begun his aerial attack, so he readied his defenses.

Seeking out the magic within himself, he let it leak from his pores and coat him in a thin layer of energy. He knew it would be difficult to maintain for long, especially while he was busy throwing missiles and dodging others, so he moved in for the attack.

At first, the Silvan Sentry didn't seem to notice anything was amiss. The ones on the ground strutted before the barbican, and the ones atop the parapet were clustered in groups, no doubt gossiping about how slow the day was passing. Ainsley removed the first shell from his bag, a conch the length of his hand, and hurled it down at the guards on the parapet. He laughed and sucked in his breath as it struck one of the soldiers in the back and knocked him into the arms of another.

The Silvan Sentry who caught the first man shoved him away with a few choice words while the first man gestured to his back and down at the conch shell. Ainsley took another, slightly smaller, conch from his bag and lobbed it at the group. He missed, and the shell shattered at the men's feet, startling them all into looking up.

"Hi!" Ainsley waved and reached into his bag. "I've got a little present for you." His next shot struck a man in the shoulder and the one after smacked his unfortunate first victim square in the face.

"Get him!" One of the Silvan Sentry reached over his shoulder for an arrow and nocked it on his bowstring. The others came to their senses and followed suit.

With one push of his wings, Ainsley flew above their volley of arrows, which fell innocuously to the ground. "Oh, this is too easy." He dove back down within range and catcalled to the guards. "Is that all Captain Kyviel trained you to do? I don't have any training, and check *me* out!" He tossed down two more seashells and sent the Silvan Sentry ducking for cover.

At the other end of the parapet, more soldiers took aim and fired at Ainsley. He relaxed his wings and dropped down below the lead-tipped missiles. "You guys are pathetic!" he hooted. "Maybe your friends down below can do better." Ainsley dipped down in front of the barbican and swung his bag of shells like a flail, striking several of the men to the ground.

They struck at him with swords and axes, but Ainsley launched himself up to parapet level and shoved the bag of now-broken seashells at one of the guards. "Maybe you'll have better luck hitting me with these." With the man's arms now full, Ainsley reeled back his arm and punched the man in the face. The other guards grabbed for Ainsley but his limbs were quicker than theirs and he eluded their grasp.

"On second thought, I still need those." He took back the bag and flipped it upside down, dumping the jagged shards on the heads of the guards on the ground. "Oops!" He smiled at the men on the parapet. "Guess my grip was as slippery as yours."

"That is *enough* of that." Out of the corner of his eye, he saw one of the soldiers from the other end of the parapet standing beside him with an arrow aimed at Ainsley's heart. The man let fly the arrow, but instead of shooting through fabric and flesh, it struck Ainsley's chest and clattered to the ground. The man lowered his bow and gaped at Ainsley.

Ainsley smiled back. "Nice try." He grabbed the man by the shirtfront and jerked him over the barbican wall, letting him fall onto the Silvan Sentry below. "Who's next?"

Another soldier raised his bow and arrow but was stopped from shooting by one of his fellows. "Leave him for now. He can't be alone. There must be others."

"You've got that right," said Ainsley. He grabbed the soldier's bow and jabbed it into the man's chest, pushing him over. Clutching the bow's string in both hands, Ainsley swung the wooden arc over another soldier's head and yanked on the string so that the man's face collided with Ainsley's fists. "But you're a little too late." He pointed to the field of scrubby grass where Megan and the others had squared off against the Silvan Sentry protecting the barbican.

Megan looked up at Ainsley and nodded. Letting out a war cry, she drew her sword and held it high overhead, ready to lead the charge. The warden shouted to the warriors in a foreign tongue and they all reached for their necklaces as one. Their hands closed around the large beads, and the sound of twenty orbs of glass smashing carried up to Ainsley. The warriors yanked off the necklaces and threw them on the ground, clenching their fists at their sides. Megan much preferred her own act of bravado, but she wasn't prepared for what happened next.

Beside her, the warden's hands paled, changing from a cocoa color to a dingy gray. His knuckles engorged into callused knots and the remainder of his hands swelled and developed the same hardened texture. His skin looked more like an elephant's now than a human's, but when Megan reached out and tapped the flesh, it felt as hard as rock.

"Fists of stone," she whispered.

With indestructible hands and bodies impermeable to arrows, the warriors of Obonia rushed across the grassland toward the fortress. Some of the Silvan Sentry already seemed aware of the warriors' special gifts and fled from their path. Those cocky soldiers left behind received a quick lesson in pain.

A wave of soldiers charged out to meet the warriors, swords and axes raised on what they assumed to be unarmed, unprotected men. The first man to reach them thrust his sword forward to plunge it into a warrior's heart. The warrior raised his left hand, and the tip of the soldier's sword imbedded itself between his fingers. The warrior wrapped his other hand around the sword's blade and bent it downwards, still gripping it in the fingers of his other hand.

The Silvan Sentry gasped and scurried back through the line of his own men with the warrior close on his heels. One of the soldiers on the parapet volleyed arrows at the warrior, but they all seemed to stop short of contacting any part of his body.

Scowling, the warrior took the bent sword and hurled it at the archer like a lethal boomerang. It missed the archer but managed to sever the arm of the man standing beside him before making its way back to the warrior who caught it in one hand. The archer took one look at the blood-spurting stump of his companion and threw down his bow and arrow, making a hasty retreat for the stairs. He didn't notice Ainsley barreling toward him.

"Let me help you get down." Ainsley crashed into the man with the full weight of his body, and the soldier tumbled off the parapet. Ainsley dusted his hands together. "Well, my work here is done. See you guys later."

He somersaulted backwards through the air and dipped down to join Megan, landing on the shoulders of an unsuspecting soldier and knocking him onto his stomach.

"Took you long enough," said Megan, bashing the hilt of her sword into the back of the man's head. "How many more cheesy one-liners were you planning to spew before you got down here?" She pointed behind Ainsley and he ducked so she could plunge her sword into the ribs of a man who'd been about to stab him in the back.

"Actually, I came down here *because* I ran out." Ainsley straightened and turned to a shower of arrows aimed at him and Megan. He spread his wings in front of her and let the remaining magical energy he'd stored repel the shots. "Come on. We have to get inside with Anala."

They sprinted toward the entrance of the barbican while the soldiers reloaded their bows. When Ainsley and Megan reached Anala and her guardians, the warden was smashing in the face of a Silvan Sentry while Anala was headbutting another. The soldier pushed her away and looked down in surprise as blood spurted from a circular wound in his chest.

"What—" The man gasped and crumbled to the ground.

Megan grabbed Anala's hand. "Come on."

The warden noticed them and forged ahead with Ainsley, knocking Silvan Sentry aside to clear the path.

"They're headed for the bailey!" shouted one of the soldiers from the parapet. "Lower the portcullis!"

Ainsley heard the screeching and clanking of a ratchet being turned and saw the portcullis give a shudder. He waved to Anala and Megan as the iron grate started to drop. "Hurry!" They ducked their heads and charged forward, slipping beneath the portcullis before it slammed into the ground.

"Wait for me!" cried Brighton, jumping through one of the holes in the grate.

"Why aren't you with Rella?" asked Megan.

"Those warriors have all but finished off Evren's men. I thought you could use some help," said Brighton. "Besides, I wanted to make sure you'd be all right."

"Awww." Megan smiled at him. "That's so—"

"Less lovey-dovey and more ass-kicking!" said Ainsley. The guards that had been on the parapet had descended the stairs to the outer bailey where he and the others were standing. Megan rushed at the soldiers to the right, swinging her sword rapidly in a figure eight that seemed to startle them into backing up. Brighton scurried up the legs of one of the men and bit him hard on the crotch. The man gave a feminine screech and his knees buckled inward as he hunched over on the ground.

Brighton gagged and spat on the ground. "Ugh. Remind me never to do that again."

One of the soldiers from the left side of the wall, the soldier Ainsley had first pelted with seashells, still had an arrow nocked and fired at Ainsley. The warden raised his arms and crossed his fists over one another, blocking the shot while Anala rammed the soldier with her head.

Another soldier grabbed Anala around the waist, but Ainsley punched the man in the small of his back and he released her, falling to the ground and writhing in pain. He grabbed at Ainsley's ankle, and Ainsley twisted awkwardly, trying to free himself.

Megan locked swords with a female soldier, and the two walked each other in a circle, trying to force the other to yield. Out of the corner of her eye, Megan saw someone move around her toward Ainsley, Anala, and the warden.

"Watch your back!" she cried, not taking her eyes off her opponent.

The soldier who was sneaking up on her friends raised his bow to shoot Ainsley, but Anala kicked back with her right leg. The force was that of a bucking bronco's, and it sent the man flying backwards into the portcullis. When his body struck, the portcullis emitted a dull clang.

Ainsley and Megan were down to the last few soldiers when the gates of the inner bailey opened. The action was enough to distract everyone from battle, even the Silvan Sentry, and they watched as Evren stepped through. His boots crunched over broken seashells, and his cloak stirred about his legs with a confident swish.

"Well, well." He stood before Ainsley and Megan, arms akimbo and legs apart. "If it isn't the cotillion crashers."

friend or foe

Evren gestured to his soldiers. "Return to your posts. These people won't give me any problems." He smiled at Ainsley and Megan. "Will you?"

"Not if you give us Onaj's horn," said Megan.

"Not if I give—" Evren chuckled. "Oh, you think I'll just hand it over to you?"

"If you want to live," said Ainsley.

Evren threw his head back and laughed until his shoulders shook. He grabbed onto Ainsley to steady himself. "Oh . . . thank you for that marvelous bit of mirth."

"It wasn't a joke." Ainsley swung his arm up and knocked Evren's hand off his shoulder. "Give us the horn or suffer the consequences."

Evren raised his hands and pretended to cower in fear. "Please don't tell your lady friends to attack me. I wouldn't want them to scratch me."

Megan narrowed her eyes. "Oh, it would be far worse than a scratching. I promise you that."

"Please." Evren snorted. "The only one among you with any power is him." He pointed to the warden. "If he wasn't on your side, you'd have nothing." Evren flung back his cape to reveal gold sparkling at his hip. In one fluid motion, he reached for it and held it aloft in both hands.

"Warden, Ainsley, close your eyes!" said Megan.

Ainsley ducked his head and jammed his eyes shut, but Megan's warning came too late for the warden. He'd looked up to see what Evren was doing and had become instantly entranced.

"You are my servant," said Evren. "And they," he pointed to Ainsley, Megan, and Anala, "are your enemies."

The warden turned on them and snarled, punching his fists together. Ainsley positioned himself between Anala and the warden. "Megan, get the horn!"

But Evren had already predicted her next actions and tucked away the horn when Megan launched herself at him. His fist struck her below the eye and stars spotted her vision as she wrestled Evren to the ground.

"Give it here!" She reached for his holster, and he twisted her arm behind her back, smashing his forehead against hers.

Megan screamed in pain and rage. She tried for a groin strike, but Evren raised a leg to block her, kneeing her in the stomach. "Stupid girl. I was a fighter before I was a nobleman," he said.

From several feet away, Brighton spoke up. "Funny. I was a thief before I was a ferret. Thanks for the golden doodad."

Megan and Evren both glanced from Evren's now-empty holster to Brighton who was busy pushing Onaj's horn across the ground toward Anala.

"Get back here with that!" snarled Evren. He tried to shove Megan from him and stand, but she dug her hands into his shirtfront so that he stumbled onto his knees.

"Anala, destroy the horn!" Megan managed to yell before Evren's fist smashed into her jaw.

The unicorn, who Ainsley had instructed to stand against the wall while he was pummeled, turned at the sound of her name. Her eyes lit up upon seeing her father's horn and she crept forward in reverence. With every footfall, the human appearance she had cast upon herself slipped to the ground in wisps of magic.

The boots on her feet gave way to golden hooves, her skirts to glossy white hair, continuing in this manner until she shook out her mane and raised high her own golden horn.

"Forgive me, Onaj," she whispered. Then, her back hoof came down hard on the severed horn. Sparks flew, and the horn skittered out from beneath her hoof, colliding with the wall.

But it remained intact.

"Shit," said Ainsley as the warden grabbed hold of his wings and began swinging him in circles.

Megan groaned, then yelped as Evren tossed her aside. "You fools can't destroy the horn," he said, running for it. Megan lunged at his ankles and tripped him. "Get off me, cur!" He kicked at her hands and stripped the skin from her knuckles.

Megan grimaced and used the straps of Evren's boots to pull herself up his legs. "Anala!"

The unicorn stamped her foreleg in frustration and trotted over to her father's horn, nudging it with her hoof. "It didn't work."

"Try something else! Fast!" Despite Megan's weight atop him, Evren was crawling toward the wall with remarkable speed.

"Touch it with your horn," suggested Brighton. "Maybe you can use your magic to destroy it."

Evren pointed to the warden. "Servant! Forget the flying boy and retrieve the unicorn's horn for me!"

Ainsley was actually grateful when Evren said this, for the warden had him upside down by the ankles and was preparing to pound Ainsley's skull into the ground. He dropped Ainsley and stepped over him, advancing on

Anala and Brighton. The latter was holding Onaj's horn vertical, with the point up, while Anala bowed her head and touched it with the point of her own horn.

The air in the bailey clouded with magic as Anala forced power from her core and out through her horn. She whinnied and snorted when the warden grabbed hold of her horn and tried to yank it off. The magic shooting through it surged up the warden's arms and his body seized as he spasmed uncontrollably.

"Get the *other* unicorn's horn, you imbecile!" cried Evren.

The warden released Anala, but he was still trembling too much to be able to pick up Onaj's horn. Instead, he kicked it toward Evren who wrapped his fingers around it and flipped onto his back, squashing Megan beneath him.

"Oh, no you don't!" Ainsley wrapped his hands around the horn as well and scrabbled with Evren for control. He didn't even think about the repercussions of his actions until he looked up at the glinting horn and Evren's wicked smile.

"You are my servant," said Evren. "And you want nothing more than to obey me."

"Ainsley!" Megan's voice was muffled. She shoved and kicked at Evren but he wouldn't budge off her. "Don't listen to him, Ainsley! Look away!"

And then she felt a rush of cool air as Evren rolled over, and she found herself staring into Ainsley's dull, lifeless eyes.

"Damn," she whispered.

"Things just keep getting better for us, don't they?" asked Brighton.

Evren straightened his clothes and dusted them off, all the while fixing Megan with an eerie grin. "To think, I was about to call my soldiers down here to kill you." He gestured to Ainsley who stepped forward obediently. "But I think I'll get more pleasure out of watching your friend do it." Evren settled himself on the steps leading up to the parapet and relaxed on one arm. "Ainsley, is it? Kill the girl and then that despicable thieving ferret."

For a moment, Ainsley didn't move, and Megan thought perhaps he was fighting the power of Onaj's horn. But when he turned to face her, she saw that all his wounds and bruises had vanished. He had been restored to optimal health while she sported a swollen jaw, a black eye, bruised ribs, and bloody knuckles.

"Oh, *this* is going to be fair," she muttered.

Evren feigned shock. "I don't think that's a very nice thing to say. Was it *fair* for you to charge into my domicile and attack my men?"

Megan didn't have a chance to respond. Ainsley beat his wings once and flew at her with fists raised. Megan ducked and backed toward the portcullis. Evren halted Ainsley with a word and retrieved Megan's sword that had been earlier thrown aside.

"Come now," said Evren, laying it at her feet. "If you're not going to fight, this isn't going to be fun." He returned to his position on the steps and called to Ainsley to recommence. Ainsley sauntered toward Megan, waiting for her to make one faulty motion and reach for the sword, but she remained with her back to the iron grate.

"Ainsley," she said, "he's lying to you. You're not—" She gasped and leapt to one side as Ainsley spun around and kicked the grate where she'd just been standing. "You're not his servant!" she finished. Ainsley snatched up Megan's sword and held it out to her.

"Fight me."

Megan braced her arms at her sides. "No, Ainsley."

He thrust out a hand to grab her throat, but she ducked and he ended up with a handful of hair. He gripped it tightly and dragged her away from the portcullis while Megan screamed, clutching at her scalp.

"Megan, you have to stand up to him, or he's going to kill you!" said Brighton. He scrambled up Ainsley's torso and bit him hard on the ear. Ainsley released Megan to swat at Brighton, and Megan scrambled to her feet and ran into the inner bailey.

"I wouldn't necessarily call that a wise decision!" Evren called after her. "Though it should produce entertaining results."

Megan locked the door of the inner bailey and looked around for something to brace it, but the foyer was empty for several feet before it split around two corners into separate hallways. Megan ran to the left.

She hated to leave Brighton and Anala outside with Ainsley, but she needed time to think. The *Tomdex* had said Onaj's horn would need a more powerful magic to destroy it, but she couldn't imagine what could be more powerful than the active magic of Onaj's own flesh and blood.

Megan rounded the corner and saw a massive oak table against one wall. Bending her knees, she hooked her hands on the underside of it and pulled it toward the door. The table was heavier than she expected, however, and she only managed to drag it a few feet before she heard pounding like a sledgehammer at the entrance to the inner bailey.

"Crap!" She turned on her heel and sprinted down the hall just as the door exploded from the wall.

"Why don't you stay and fight?" called Evren. "Things only get worse from here."

Megan soon realized he was right. The hallway joined with the one from the other side of the fortress and opened into a courtyard where a group of Silvan Sentry was gathered around Captain Kyviel. At the sound of Megan's approach, they all turned their heads, and she could see Bornias and Frieden among them. She skidded to a stop and started down the opposite hallway but almost collided with Evren.

"I'm sorry, Megan." Brighton appeared behind Evren, doubled over and panting. "I tried to stop them."

"Let's put on a show for all the soldiers, shall we?" Evren grabbed her arm and yanked her back toward the courtyard. He waved reassuringly to Captain Kyviel and the others. "We are lucky enough to bear witness to a true battle of the sexes. Everyone take your seats and enjoy yourselves."

He shoved Megan away from him and snapped his fingers at Ainsley. "Finish her, but . . . make the pain linger."

Ainsley fixed Megan with his blank eyes and sprinted toward her. The soldiers cheered as Ainsley swung at her and Megan blocked the shot with her arm. She was unused to face-to-face combat, however, and pain shot through her bones and into her shoulder.

"Sorry to do, this," she said, "but you leave me no . . . choice!" She aimed a kick at Ainsley's groin, but he stopped her foot and gripped it tightly. Megan saw the muscles in his arms flex, and then he jerked up on her foot, flipping her backwards to land in a painful heap on the hard stone. Applause and hoots of laughter filled Megan's ears as she stared at the feet of the soldiers from a cockeyed angle.

Brighton's face appeared beside her. "Next time, don't tell him when you're about to do something."

"You think?" Megan struggled to her hands and knees, and Brighton jumped onto her shoulder.

A tower stood in the center of the bailey and she limped toward it amidst the sound of catcalls. She glanced over at Bornias and Frieden, but they watched her with emotionless faces, her bruises and blood not drawing so much as a concerned frown.

The fact that they weren't hurrying to her rescue, that they didn't seem to care about the danger she was in, was more painful than any of the wounds she'd incurred, and Megan fought back tears as she climbed the ladder to the tower.

"No, no," said Evren the minute Ainsley began to follow her up the ladder. "Let's give her a head start. She isn't going anywhere up there."

These words were greeted with appreciative laughter, and Megan wished they were mindless drones instead of traitors to their king. If nothing else, they would at least be quiet. When she reached the top, she pulled the ladder up with an effort that made her muscles scream in agony.

"Um, Megan," said Brighton. "You realize Ainsley can fly."

"Oh. Right." She cursed and dropped the ladder so that it smashed into pieces on the courtyard floor. "Well, what do we do now?" Megan's lip trembled, and she felt the last bits of strength draining from her. "I don't think I can beat him."

Brighton nuzzled her cheek. "Then, we fight until we can't fight any more."

Megan bowed her head and gave it a small shake. "I don't want to fight my best friend."

"Would you rather lay down and surrender?" asked Brighton. "Would you rather Sir Inish's death meant nothing?"

His words stabbed at Megan's heart, and tears pricked her eyes. "Of course not."

"Then, this is how we end it. You can't save your friends from Evren. You can't make them see the truth."

Megan jerked her head up and felt goosebumps crawling over her skin. "What did you say?"

"I know it sounds harsh," Brighton squeezed his shoulder, "but—"

Resolve bubbling anew within her, Megan placed a finger to his lips and got to her feet. "When Ainsley gets up here, I want you to steal the bag from his pocket and give it to me." Without waiting for an answer, she peered over the edge of the tower and shouted down. "Okay. I'm ready to kick your ass now, Ainsley! And then . . . I'm coming for *you*." She pointed at Evren, and the soldiers hooted and cheered.

Evren wiped a speck of dust from his shoulder and sneered at Megan. "As you wish." He snapped his fingers at Ainsley again and pointed to the tower. Ainsley wasted no time in spreading his wings and pushing off from the ground.

"Hi!" said Megan when he drew level with her. "Shall we—" But Ainsley wrapped his fingers around her throat and squeezed before she could get the last words out. While she worked to pry his fingers from her jugular, Megan blinked at Brighton, and he climbed up Ainsley's leg and into his pocket.

Ainsley shifted around a bit and tried to fish Brighton out with his free hand. His preoccupation loosened his grip on Megan's throat, and she ducked her head to bite down hard on his finger. With an irritated frown, he jerked his hand back and slapped her across her already bruised jaw.

Though she knew Ainsley was under Evren's power, Megan was still shocked and a little annoyed that he would hit her. She stamped down hard on his foot and poked him in both eyes with her fingers. The attack seemed a bit slapstick to her, but it distracted Ainsley long enough for Brighton to re-emerge from his pocket.

A velvet bag dangled from his mouth, and Megan grabbed it, loosening the drawstring and dumping the stone of shared sight into her palm. She held the stone in front of Ainsley and wiggled it between her thumb and forefinger. "I think I have something that belongs to you."

Megan tossed it to him, and on impulse, he caught it. The instant Ainsley was the only person handling the stone, Megan reached out for one of his hands and placed it on her heart so that he was touching her skin and the pearl lodged within it. "See what I see, Ainsley," she whispered. "See the truth."

The Pearl of Truth

Images flashed in front of Ainsley's eyes, but they weren't his own. They were of the world as Megan saw it, softened images of her friends and loved ones: himself, Garner, Frieden, Bornias, and some white-haired boy, all in peril.

Ainsley struggled to be free of her, clawing at her arms, but the more contact he made with her, the more of her vision he could see. He tried to drop the stone, but his fingers clutched it ever tighter, as if knowing he hadn't borne witness to all he needed.

Harder, darker faces appeared in his vision, and they ended with Evren holding the golden horn. Ainsley saw images of himself just minutes earlier and witnessed Evren robbing him of his freedom with enchanting words that held nothing but lies. He remembered what he had been like before Evren's words, and he saw the truth. He was not a servant of Evren, Megan was not his enemy, and he had no desire to kill her.

But he couldn't let Evren know that.

Ainsley roared for effect and grabbed Megan by the shoulders, shoving her against the wall of the tower. The entire structure shook, and from the ground, he could hear cheers and various cries for him to end Megan's life. He held Megan by the throat and drew back a fist.

Megan winced and jammed her eyes shut, but instead of feeling knuckles slamming into her teeth, she felt the side of his fist graze her face. Ainsley punched the wooden wall beside her, and it splintered and buckled beneath his hand.

The crowd below released an ominous "Oooh." With their limited view of the happenings in the tower, it was obvious they'd assumed the worst for Megan. Megan had assumed the worst as well. She peeked through her eyelids and saw Ainsley looking right at her. Gone was the vacant stare, replaced with Ainsley's own defiant gleam.

"Hey," he whispered. "It's me again."

"I know." Megan grinned at him. "Good to have you back."

"Don't take this the wrong way, but we have to keep fighting." Ainsley spun her around and dangled her out the tower door.

The soldiers gasped, then chanted, "Drop her! Drop her!"

Megan made a great show of struggling with Ainsley and swung her fist at him. Just before she struck him, he lurched backwards and the two of them tumbled into the tower.

"So, now we know how to reverse the horn's effects," said Ainsley. He kicked the wall and Megan screamed, dragging herself by the elbows back into sight of the soldiers. They booed until Ainsley grabbed Megan by the ankles and hauled her back inside. He pretended to stomp on the small of her back and Megan howled, rolling behind a wall.

She let her wailing die down and said, "We know how to reverse it, but I can't go up to all these people and make them touch my chest." She pointed a finger at Brighton who had raised his hand. "Not a word."

Ainsley unhooked Megan's cape from around her neck and snagged it on a piece of rough wood, letting it flutter to the ground in shreds. "I don't see how we have a choice unless you can think of another way to reach everybody."

Megan thought for a moment while Ainsley threw himself against a wall. "Actually, I can, but I'll need you to get me down to Evren so I can steal Onaj's horn." She turned to Brighton. "I'm going to need your help again."

He puffed out his chest importantly. "Of course."

Ainsley nodded. "All right. You ready to go back down there?"

"Almost." Megan rumpled her hair and smeared blood from her knuckles onto her cheek. "Let's go."

Brighton crawled under the front of Ainsley's shirt, and Ainsley wrapped an arm around Megan's waist. "This might hurt a little."

Megan smiled at him. "After getting a fireball to the heart, stabbed through the ribs, and punched in the face . . . I think I can take a little more pain."

"Then, off we go." Ainsley tightened his grip on her and swooped down through the crowd to where Evren stood. Megan kicked and clawed at him until he grabbed her by the hair and tilted her head back so her neck was exposed to Evren.

"How thoughtful," said Evren. "You've brought her down to die in front of me. Well, you've got my undivided attention." He smiled and winked at Megan. "And you were quite the competitor."

Megan swallowed and glanced down her nose at him. "You seem to forget. The good guy *always wins*."

Ainsley shoved her into Evren, and she reached for the horn, yanking it from its holster. Evren grabbed for it but Brighton had dropped out of Ainsley's tunic and leapt onto Evren's arms, chomping down on his hand. Evren's scream was cut short when Ainsley punched him in the mouth, and Megan held the horn high overhead.

"I am your master!" she told the Silvan Sentry that were running at them, weapons raised. "You wish to protect me and destroy *him*." She pointed to Evren, and a handful of soldiers split from the group and sprinted after him.

"Stay back!" cried Evren. "It's her you want!"

But the soldiers kept coming, and Evren was forced to conjure an energy shield to protect himself. The remaining soldiers formed a protective ring around Megan and stood with their blades at the ready. She hadn't hoped to need them, but Bornias, Rayne, and Frieden were now glaring at her.

By calling an assault on their master, she knew she had become their enemy. Gritting her teeth, she shouted to her circle of defense. "The Silverskins and Governor Frieden want me dead. Keep them from attacking, but don't kill them!"

Evren countered with his own forces. "Bornias and Rayne, dispose of these traitors! Frieden, retrieve the horn!"

Steel and sparks flashed through the air as mage battled sentry. Bornias managed to hurl an orb of lightning at Megan before a Silvan Sentry tackled him to the ground, but Ainsley spread his wings in front of her. The electric energy knocked him off his feet, his wing was torn and charred, and he could smell singed flesh. "Megan, whatever you were going to do, you better do it quick!" he said, wincing as he folded his wing.

Megan placed the tip of Onaj's horn to the Pearl of Truth in her chest and drew upon the same thoughts she'd used to turn Ainsley. Instead of projecting into individual minds, however, the truths passed through the horn and manifested themselves as images for all to see. The effort brought beads of sweat to Megan's forehead, but the combat noises around her lessened considerably as everyone turned to watch.

"Servants!" shouted Evren. "This girl is trying to control your thoughts! Do not let her into your minds."

With those words, Bornias, Rayne, and Frieden were lost to Megan once more. Bornias chanted and the clothes of a Silvan Sentry ignited. Megan tried projecting the same thoughts again, but the sounds of fighting crescendoed, and she knew she had lost control of the crowd before Brighton even said anything.

"His power over them is too strong. You have to destroy the horn, Megan."

She shook her head. "I just have to try harder."

She revealed the lies Evren had told in the Pass of Light, how he'd used Onaj's horn to deceive the dignitaries in Pontsford and the people in the Port of Scribnitch. All the truths she knew about Evren swirled through the air until they thickened like a fog, making it difficult for anyone to see anything less than a few feet from themselves. They all stood still and quiet except Evren.

"Lies!" he cried. "She's trying to trick you!" This time, however, his protests brought no movement from his followers.

"I think it's working, Megan!" said Ainsley. "Keep going!"

Megan couldn't answer him. Her chest was beginning to hurt and she felt lightheaded from all that she'd revealed. If Evren managed to dispel the truth, she didn't think she had enough left in her to fight him again.

But then she heard a peculiar sound.

It was a splintering crackle like a pane of glass giving way to extreme pressure. Megan grimaced in horror as she imagined her pearl shattering into a thousand pieces, but as the crackling continued, she discovered its source and smiled.

Between her trembling fingers, Onaj's horn was breaking. Evil had changed it into a catalyst of deception, and the truth Megan forced through it was *almost* powerful enough to destroy it. She understood now, and she knew what it would take to finish the task.

Megan closed her eyes, and from her core, she expelled every truth she'd ever known, even those she'd kept secret from her closest friends. With each truth, Megan's heart beat a little faster until it felt as though it would tear a hole through her chest. The images came, thick and fast, and drained the very life from her body. She would have collapsed had the air not been dense enough to hold her upright.

Onaj's horn vibrated in her hands, and she felt her fingers begin to lose their grasp upon it. Megan knew it was too soon to let go, but she lacked the strength to tighten her grip. She cried out in despair and felt two pairs of hands upon her own, holding them steady and curling her fingers around the horn. The voices shouted again, and this time, Megan could make out three words.

"You did it."

She opened her eyes. The hardened texture of Onaj's horn changed to that of a brittle eggshell. With a last effort, Megan squeezed, and it imploded, crumbling into dust. Instead of falling to the ground, however, the dust spiraled upward, trickling into her nose and mouth. She tried to step back, to swat it away, but the dust persisted until every last particle had entered her body.

Megan sneezed several times. Her head felt stuffy and her skin grew feverishly warm. Light surrounded her, so radiant and white that it threatened to blind her. She shielded her eyes with a hand, but the luminous glow intensified, and Megan realized that the light was coming from *her*. It shone through every pore on her body and even from her mouth when she opened it to gasp.

Megan curled into a ball on the ground, awaiting the final retribution of Onaj's horn, whatever it might be. Her skin felt well past warm now, but the sweat that forced its way to her brow sizzled and dried in the intense light. The acrid smell of burning cloth curled up to her nostrils, and she watched the tunic and pants she wore smolder and shrink.

Megan's heart raced and her head pounded as it flooded with thoughts and images and voices, most of which were unfamiliar to her. Some of them were pleasant and comforting but others were almost too ghastly for her to stomach. She drew her legs even closer to her torso, screaming against the pain as her entire body became a beacon of light. The fortress around her, the sky above it, the entire *country*, became as night and was eclipsed by her brilliance.

Then, just as Megan thought she would combust, the magic of Onaj's horn ceased to fight her. It recognized where it was needed. The light pulled back into her body and siphoned upwards into her brain, cooling her skin.

Her mind began to sort through everything it perceived, and all of the thoughts and images and voices fell into place. Her head cleared, and her heartbeat slowed to normal. The truths she had brought forth vanished, along with the support that had kept her upright. Megan's knees buckled and hands reached to help her so that she tottered on wobbly legs.

Exhaustion had blurred her vision, but she knew she was out of harm's way. "Put me down, please. I need to rest."

The hands obliged, but they lowered her gently, cradling her in something soft that smelled of forest and family. Megan inhaled deeply and fingered the cloak wrapped about her. She didn't need perfect sight to know that its owner was a handsome goateed man with chestnut-colored hair and eyes the color of creamy jade.

Tears sprang to her eyes and spilled over, running into her hairline, leaving a cool trail on her skin. "Hi, Frieden." She buried her head against his chest and sobbed with relief and exhaustion and affection.

Frieden hugged her tight and stroked her hair. "You did it." His voice was proud but choked with emotion. "You saved us all."

Freedom

"Well, it took a while, but I think Rayne and Bornias gathered up all of the Silvan Sentry." Ainsley knelt on the ground beside Megan and Frieden. "They tried to run, but I guess they forgot the portcullis was still down."

Megan sat up, leaning on her elbows. "Where are they now?"

"Bornias created a pit in the outer bailey and dropped in all the soldiers that betrayed him with a few grimalkins." Ainsley rubbed a smudge of dirt from his nose unconcernedly. "They should be busy until the Silvan Council arrives."

"Is Evren down there as well?"

Ainsley shook his head. "He escaped somehow. Probably turned into a bird and flew away." He saw Megan frown, and he squeezed her arm. "Look, everyone's back to normal and you're still alive. That's good enough for me."

Megan knocked the wind out of him with a fierce hug. "I could not have succeeded without you."

"You're damn right," he said with a grin. Looking over Megan's shoulder, he could see a white-haired boy running toward them, the same boy Ainsley had seen in Megan's vision.

"Is she all right?" The boy skidded to his knees beside them. His clothes were ripped and he was bloody and covered with dirt. "Evren tried to get away so I chased him and bit him, and the bastard threw a pile of boulders at me."

Ainsley and Frieden stared at him.

"What?" The boy rubbed his arm uncomfortably. "He's still a bastard, isn't he?"

Megan smiled and pulled away from Ainsley. "Yes, but I believe their shock is for a different reason."

The boy nodded. "I'll admit I almost didn't think I'd make it out of there myself." He scooted closer to Megan. "But I had to make sure you'd be all right."

Ainsley watched the two converse and blinked hard. He leaned in close to the other boy who squirmed and inched back.

"Listen, mate," said the boy, "I know I've been inside your clothes but let's just keep it friends."

Ainsley goggled and poked him in the shoulder. "Brighton?"

"Who else would I be?" Brighton gave Megan a worried glance. "Did something happen to him while I was away?"

"Actually, something has happened to *you*," said Megan with a laugh. "Your Curse of Sargon has been lifted."

"Amazing." Frieden shook his head. "When Megan reversed the power of Onaj's horn with all those truths, she must have also reversed any lies attached them. That would include any *curses* cast with deception as their aim . . . like Brighton's."

"So, I'm . . . I'm human again?" Brighton raised his arms and scrutinized them. "But I look the same to me." His shoulders sagged a little. "Are you teasing? Because that wouldn't be a very funny—"

Megan grabbed him by the shirtfront and planted her lips on his. Brighton's eyes widened and then lazily slid shut as he wrapped an arm around Megan's waist and drew her nearer. When Megan broke the kiss, Brighton sighed in contentment. "That was *definitely* human."

Everyone laughed as he let out a whoop and ran about the room, attempting various acrobatics and leaping up to touch anything overhead that had been out of his grasp as a ferret. After he came dangerously close to strangling himself in the vines hanging under the tower, Megan rolled her eyes good-naturedly.

"I should go watch over him." She staggered to her feet, her strength not entirely renewed. "Otherwise he might not survive, much less be human, for much longer."

Ainsley and Frieden watched her go, and when she was out of earshot, Ainsley asked his surrogate uncle the one question he'd been wondering since Megan had destroyed Onaj's horn.

"She's different now, isn't she?"

There was no need for him to elaborate. Anyone who had known Megan prior to that moment could have sensed the change in her, but it was subtle enough that anyone who hadn't known her would never have suspected. Megan's eyes, though still warm and friendly, held an intelligence in them that made Ainsley wonder if she knew more than Frieden and Bornias and the master mage combined.

When she spoke, there was an eloquence to her words, even her jokes and sarcastic comments. She still laughed and smiled, but it was gentler, and her eyebrows had developed a permanent, but slight, furrow as if she were constantly troubled by something.

"Yes, she *is* different," said Frieden. "She's an oracle now."

"What?" Ainsley's shout of surprise was loud enough to halt Brighton, who had been dancing with Megan and spinning her in circles. Ainsley gave him a reassuring wave and cleared his throat, leaning toward Frieden. "She's an oracle as in . . . as in a wise, all-knowing power?"

Frieden nodded.

"How?"

"Megan destroyed Onaj's horn," said Frieden, "but the magical essence it held was too strong to simply evaporate into thin air. It had to find an outlet, a medium to allow it to be used again."

Ainsley's forehead, which had been wrinkled in confusion, smoothed itself. "Megan's Pearl of Truth," he said.

"Megan's Pearl of Truth," agreed Frieden. "The magic sought a source with just as much power, if not more, than Onaj's horn. The only logical choice was the same object that had destroyed it."

"So . . ." Ainsley chewed his lip, "if Megan already had a lot of power with the pearl . . ."

"That power has been enhanced a thousandfold. She can see the truth of deceptions hundreds of miles away that she has not even borne witness to. Her wisdom is beyond the ages, and she can now see things in others that do not have to be revealed with a lie."

Ainsley whistled under his breath and looked back at Megan who was giggling while Brighton tickled her. She looked so normal, so much like any other teenaged girl, that Ainsley found it difficult to believe. But he couldn't deny the changes he'd noticed in her. "Do you think she can see the future?"

"It's possible," said Frieden. "Many oracles can. The ability will reveal itself to her if she possesses it."

"Oh, man." Ainsley watched her a bit longer and rubbed his temples. "She already knows what she is, doesn't she?"

"Yes," said Frieden, "but I imagine she may not be ready to accept her duties yet. Life will be much different for her."

A lump began to form in Ainsley's throat, and he fought it down. "She can't come home now." He didn't even phrase it as a question. He already knew the answer. "Is there a way to reverse it? I mean, to stop her being an oracle?"

Frieden crossed his legs and rested his elbows upon them, stroking his goatee. "I believe this was her destiny, and I don't think we should be the ones to change her path."

"Why not? You let *her* alter your destiny." Ainsley pointed toward the archway of the courtyard.

Frieden turned his head in that direction and leapt to his feet as if a fire had been lit beneath him. "Anala!" He dusted off his clothes and smoothed down his hair with trembling fingers.

The unicorn, who had chosen to maintain her true form, gave a nervous shudder of her own and clopped forward, head bowed. "Hello, Frieden. I'm pleased to see you alive."

Frieden smoothed down his goatee several times in succession before Ainsley jerked his hand away. "What . . . what are you doing here?"

"She came to help us," said Ainsley. "We went to Purefalls Glade, and she agreed to come with us to stop Evren."

Megan appeared beside them, slightly out of breath. "Frieden, she came because she thought you might be in trouble."

Frieden's cheeks flushed, and his hand reached toward his goatee again. After Ainsley cleared his throat, however, Frieden's hand dropped back down. "You left the glade . . . to come save me?" He shifted his weight from foot to foot. "But I didn't even help *you* when you asked for it."

Anala pawed at the ground with her hoof. "I didn't deserve your help. I wasn't honest with you." She glanced up at Frieden. "But I did *always* care for you."

Frieden stepped forward and tentatively touched Anala's mane. "And I, you. Forgive me for leaving you to face the darkness alone."

Ainsley nudged Megan, who was watching the entire scene with watery eyes. "I think that's our cue to walk away. Let's check out the soldiers in the grimalkin pit."

She nodded and followed him, dragging her feet a bit to eavesdrop on the last bits of conversation she could. "I think someone is going to be a nascifriend again before too long," she said.

"Are you using your oracle powers to tell you that?" asked Ainsley.

"No. My common sense." Megan smirked at him, but he noticed she didn't act surprised at what he'd called her.

"So, you know you're an oracle, then," he said.

Megan nodded, her brows furrowing more than usual. She walked beside him in silence but stopped just before they reached the entrance to the outer bailey. "The whole concept terrifies me a little, to be honest. Out of all our strange experiences since we arrived in Arylon, I could never have foreseen something like *this*."

"Megan," Ainsley held her hands, "you have to live here now."

"I know."

Ainsley squeezed her fingers. "But, I'll come to visit whenever I can, and you'll have Rella and Brighton to keep you company while I'm away."

Megan smiled and shook her head. "Rella maybe, but not Brighton."

Ainsley released her hands. "*Please* don't tell me you're going back to Garner."

"No. Garner will be in the Folly, completing his nasci-friend training, and I am not really certain that he is the one for me."

"Then why not spend time with Brighton?"

Megan shrugged and opened the doors to the outer bailey. "He is human again after more than two years. He wants to go out and see the world, and I do not have time for that right now."

Ainsley cleared his throat. "Of course, you know that once he gets out in the world, there's a chance he won't come back."

"He will."

Ainsley narrowed his eyes at her. "Are you using common sense to make that assumption, or are you using your oracle powers?"

"Perhaps a little of both." Megan smiled. "But I will never be lonely. My parents are going to live with me, and as you said, you will always be coming to visit."

"Until someone figures out a way to destroy the Staff of Lexiam." Ainsley sighed and leaned against the wall. "Then it'll be goodbye forever."

"Impossible." Megan peered around the door, and then closed it against the noise outside. "The staff is more than just power, Ainsley. It serves as . . . a reminder of the balance that life needs. Air with fire, water with land, and good with evil. If any one overpowers the other, the world is thrown into chaos."

"Evren becomes a high and mighty ruler."

"Yes. And that is why it is impossible for the staff to ever be destroyed. It may sound strange, but the very knowledge that it exists keeps both good and evil in check. Both sides fear that it will be used against them, so both work to make sure it doesn't happen."

Ainsley stared at her and Megan frowned. "Don't you understand?"

"Oh, I understand. I just know *that* wasn't common sense."

Megan laughed and opened the door. Roars and shouts of fear drifted up from the pit, and Ainsley could see Rayne and Bornias talking with Master Oh and several members of the Silvan Council, none of whom seemed the least bit concerned about the men among the grimalkins. When Ainsley and Megan stepped into the outer bailey, Bornias looked up from where he was conversing with a Protector and began fidgeting and inching toward them.

"I see a worried old man that needs a hug," said Megan, "and you have someone waiting for you." She nudged Ainsley toward the portcullis where Rella waved at him from the other side of the iron grate.

A nasty gash split her cheek and a bloodied bandage had been draped around her arm, but the triumphant smile she wore lit up her face, and Ainsley thought she was more beautiful than ever.

He trotted toward the portcullis with a spring in his step that owed nothing to his wings. He and Megan had saved the world, and he would be returning home soon to tell his parents all about the adventure. And someday after his sister was born and old enough to travel, he would bring her to Arylon to meet the oracle, the unicorn, and maybe a black dragon.

But for now, he had a borrowed kiss to return.

The End